A SHORT HISTORY OF
ENGLISH ARCHITECTURE

A Short History of

English Architecture

by

HUGH BRAUN

F.R.I.B.A., F.S.A.

FABER AND FABER LTD

London · Boston

First published in 1950
by Faber and Faber Limited
3 *Queen Square London WC*1
as The Story of English Architecture
Reprinted 1956, 1960
First published in this edition 1978
Printed in Great Britain by
Whitstable Litho Limited, Whitstable
All rights reserved

ISBN 0 571 10714 1

CONDITIONS OF SALE

British Library Cataloguing in Publication Data

Braun, Hugh
    A short history of English architecture.
    1. Architecture – England – History
    I. Title
    720' .942   NA961

    ISBN 0–571–10714–1

CONTENTS

The figures in brackets appearing in the
text refer to the numbers of the illustrations

ILLUSTRATIONS[1]

BETWEEN PAGES 96 *and* 97

A. Chipping Campden Church in Gloucestershire
    (*Photo: Miss P. Furness*)
1. The choir of Norwich Cathedral
2. Salisbury Cathedral
3. The cloisters of Salisbury Cathedral
4. The keep of Rochester Castle (*Author's photo*)
5. The walls of Ludlow Castle in Shropshire
    (*Photo: Miss P. Furness*)
6. Under the central tower of St. Albans Cathedral
7. The nave of Durham Cathedral
8. The nave of Lincoln Cathedral
9. The gatehouse of Cooling Castle in Kent
10. Harlech Castle
11. Flying buttresses at Westminster Abbey (*Author's photo*)
12. The chapter house of York Minster (*Photo: Miss P. Furness*)
13. The chapel of King's College at Cambridge
14. Hullavington Church in Wiltshire
15. The great hall of Oakham Castle
16. Blakeney Church in Norfolk
17. The great hall of Hampton Court (*Photo: Royal Commission on Historical Monuments*)
18. Canterbury Cathedral
19. Shipley Church in Sussex
20. Basement of an ancient house at Guildford (*Photo: Miss M. Wood*)
21. South Wingfield manor house in Derbyshire

[1] Unless otherwise stated the copyright of these photos belongs to the National Building Record.

9

Illustrations

CHAPTER I

IN THE BEGINNING

Architecture is the art of designing good buildings. There have always been builders, a great many of whom were very simple people, building nothing more important than ordinary houses, some of them very poor and humble. Yet as they patiently followed their trade, many of these old craftsmen came to learn more and more about the art of architecture; so that in the end they were able to raise from the ground great palaces and cathedrals undreamed of by their ancestors.

But as the humble buildings came first, it is with these that we will open this book.

Our forefathers did not always live in houses. At first they had to live in trees: in lairs made from branches, high up out of the way of fierce animals. Later, when man discovered the use of fire, he was able to drive the animals from their caves in the rock and live in these himself, keeping a fire always burning in the cave-mouth so that the beasts could not return.

In those days our ancestors were hunters, living on the flesh of the animals they had killed. Later, we were able to tame animals and keep them for food; making clothes from their wool or hair instead of having to dress in skins. These tame animals had to be driven from pasture to pasture, often over long distances, so that it became necessary to provide some sort of shelter for the herdsmen when they had to go away from the cave. It was in this way that our ancestors first took to building their own houses.

Such homes, however, would have been only flimsy huts or shelters, quickly built, and abandoned as soon as the flocks had passed on to new pastures. It was the discovery of how to plough the land and grow corn for bread-making that altered the lives of our ancestors, by forcing them to live beside their fields. It was in this way that well-built houses first came into being; then villages and, in the end, public buildings such as temples or churches. Thus the discovery of metal for making ploughs brought with it the beginnings of architecture.

The first buildings were, of course, just shelters to protect people from the rain and snow, and the bitter winter winds. Wherever possible, it was arranged that a fire could be built inside to keep the family warm. In a house, the most important thing is the roof which keeps out the rain; the walls do not matter, for a roof can rise direct from the ground and does not need walls to support it. Walls are difficult things to build; they may need bricks or stones and someone who knows how to build these up. A roof is much easier; it only needs poles and something waterproof, such as thatch, to cover them.

In the west of England, where there is plenty of stone lying about, people learnt how to make a sort of beehive of stones, which was in fact a very rough 'dome'. In Cornwall and such stony parts of the country, you can still find the ruins of these old houses, with the roofs fallen in, hiding amongst the heather; they were probably built two thousand years or more ago.

If you can find a cliff, or a low wall of rock, against which you can lean poles, it is not a very difficult matter to build a shelter in this way, as the face of the rock makes half your house before you start. All you have then to do is to cover the poles with thatch, and your house is ready. The thatch can be heather or furze, laid upon the poles and weighted with turf; or it can be tied down with sticks of willow or some such springy wood. Early builders were very skilled in the use of willow wands, which they plaited in basket-work to make a sort of hurdle which was very useful for roofing houses. With reeds plaited into the framework, it was known as 'wattling', and was often daubed with mud to make a wind-proof screen.

The gypsies who still live in the green lanes of England, make huts by sticking two rows of willow wands into the ground and bending them towards each other, tying them together to make a sort of tunnel. These *tans*, as they call these willow huts, are covered with heather thatch or, in these days, often canvas or even tarpaulins. It was in thatched huts such as these that our ancestors lived many hundreds of years ago.

In those days, England was nearly all either moor or forest. In the east and south, the great forest was like a jungle, in which it was not pleasant to live except where the soil was chalky and the trees could not grow so thickly. So the first

In the Beginning

English homes grew up on the windswept western moors and on the downland hills and chalky plains of the softer south-eastern parts of England; while much of the country around remained a tangled jungle of forest in which only wild animals lived, and all was damp and sunless, and very muddy in the winter.

Neither our ancestors nor their flocks could live without water, so homes were often built near a stream. Beside this they would find willow poles and wands, and reeds for wattling, and mud for daubing, so that they could build their houses without having to go too far away for the materials. And so it was in these pleasant places on the banks of the streams of the south-east, where the forest was not too close, that our English architecture began.

In these parts of England, there are very few caves or even rock walls, so it was necessary to build all in the open, with only poles and thatch with which to make a waterproof house. The simplest way to build a hut is to have a circle of poles all leaning against each other in the middle and tied together there. This is just what our ancestors did, making wigwams of poles and thatch, in which the families huddled round a fire of twigs—kept small so as not to set the house on fire—that filled the place with smoke. There was a tiny door to crawl through, and no windows. Grass and all sorts of weeds would grow on the thatch, until it would hardly be possible to see the hut amongst the rubbish which was all about it. When the Normans came to England, the Anglo-Saxons were living in huts like these. It was centuries before ordinary folk were able to build proper houses; even as late as the seventeenth century many thousands of country people had nothing better than hovels for their dwellings.

The tent-shaped hut makes an uncomfortable home as there is no room to stand up near the edges, where the feet of the poles come down to the ground. As there was no means of raising the roof by building walls—which were an invention yet to be discovered—the hut builders gave themselves more height by digging out the floor, and placing the earth all round the feet of the poles. In the wilder parts of England, you can sometimes find a hollow in the ground, with a rim of earth all round it, marking where one of these old huts once stood.

It was in the stony country of the west that our ancestors first began to build walls. These were very rough heaps of stones, arranged in a circle so as to bury the feet of the poles and prevent them from slipping if the soil should be too rocky to stick the poles into it. The roofless walls of some of these fine huts may still be seen in Cornwall; in the Hebrides of Scotland large houses built in the same way still have families living in them.

Thus it is clear from the beginning that the two chief materials used in the old buildings of this country were wood and stone. In the western parts of England there was plenty of stone lying about, but not much wood. In the east and south, there was not much stone to be found, but plenty of wood: first for poles, and later—as our ancestors began to clear away the great forests—good strong timber for building fine wooden houses. So there have always been two styles in English architecture: one coming from the west, and one from the east. Sometimes one was the finer; then times changed, and for a while the other side of England would have better buildings.

But we are at the moment talking of Britain before the Romans, when our ancestors were living in humble huts, such as have been described above, scattered over the countryside— built as it were out of its very bushes, heather and reeds, so that houses and fields would seem almost to be a part of each other. Each hut was a family home; there would be no other buildings, for animals, even ponies, would be kept in the open and there would be neither stables nor byres. Grain was kept in the ground, so there were no barns.

As time went on, families began to draw together for company; in any case they were often sharing the same spring or living side by side along the banks of a stream. In this way, villages began to be founded. By and by, these villages began to quarrel with each other about rights to take water, or about the boundaries of fields and pastures. They might steal each other's animals and take part in various other kinds of domestic squabbles. Village leaders would rally their men and there would be fighting, groups of villages would join together against other groups, and in this way the country people would band themselves into tribes.

Fighting of this nature made our ancestors think about protecting their villages from attack. They made the simple discovery that if they dug a hole, people often fell into it in the dark, and that if they surrounded their village with a ditch,

unwelcome visitors might be likewise trapped if they should be
trying to creep into the place unseen. If the earth from the ditch
were placed along its inner rim, the enemy would then have to
climb up a slope twice as high as the one he had fallen down, if
he wanted to get into the village. A thorny hedge planted along
the top of the bank would make it still more unpleasant for him.
But even humble 'city walls' of this sort could only have been
built if the villagers could agree together as to who should do
the work. For these are 'public works', in which a number of
people have to join, under the leadership of the chief man of
the village. So from being just a family camp, or a cluster of
these, the village is becoming something more like a tribe, with
a ruler at its head who will direct its efforts in peace or war.

As villages formed themselves into tribes, each tribe often
made for itself a strongly fortified place into which the country
people could retreat with their flocks in the event of war. In
this way were formed the first towns of Britain. They were
usually built on high ground, on the summits of chalky hills
such as the South Downs, where the remains of their town walls
may still be seen in the great ditches and ramparts running
along the slopes. Each town probably contained a tribe, though
some towns probably banded together against other groups of
towns. A place in which a number of people are gathered together is generally a good place to sell things; these old hill-top
towns were thus probably market towns.

When houses first began to be built, each would hold a
family. As children married and started families of their own,
new houses would have been built, probably near to the first
house. The old father of the family would be the head man of
the whole settlement. But as villages grew still larger and families banded together, the leader of the village would become
more important. He might have a council of the heads of
families. As villages grew to towns, the houses of the leading
men and their families might well become better built than
those of ordinary folk; thus we see the beginning of what we
may call 'great houses'. But in the far-off days of which we are
speaking, the finest houses would still have been nothing more
than huts.

For many thousands of years—long after the day that saw
William the Conqueror landing on the shores of Sussex—our
ancestors lived in the very humblest of hovels. (It is only about

15

a thousand years since they first began to build their own stone churches, and even these were very tiny and roughly made.)

But three thousand years before the Normans came, our ancestors were building great stone temples in England. In those far-off days, the people living in the countries which lay at the eastern end of the Mediterranean had become very highly civilized: especially in Crete, Egypt, and Babylonia. In Egypt particularly, they were worshipping their gods in huge temples, with tall stone pillars joined at their tops by heavy stone beams: a style of architecture which later spread westwards to Greece, and, in the end, to the great city of Rome.

We know very little about the religion of our ancestors in the days before the Romans came. They had many gods, some of which they probably worshipped in the open air: on the tops of the high hills, or in clearings in the gloomy forests which covered so much of the countryside. About two thousand years before Christ, however, the tribe living on Salisbury Plain built themselves a temple of great stone blocks, some of them brought on rafts all the way from Wales. This great building, which we call Stonehenge, was something quite different from anything which had been seen in the country before. It was not built from pieces of stone found lying about, as was the case with the stone-walled houses of Cornwall we have already described. The stones of Stonehenge were all of great size, and it must have taken a great many men to move them about and raise them. The most important thing about the stones, however, is that each block was squared-up so as to make it look like a squared log of wood. The blocks were stuck into the ground as if they had been wooden posts, and were actually let into the stone beams which rested across their tops to prevent these from falling off; the 'joints' are like those a carpenter makes between his timbers. So we can see that Stonehenge was in fact a copy of a great building made of square wooden posts. Airmen looking down upon the fields of England have sometimes seen marks on the ground looking like vanished Stonehenges and when these places have been explored it has been found that the marks were really holes from which wooden posts had long ago rotted away. So, four thousand years ago, our ancestors were building temples of squared wooden logs stuck into the ground and with beams laid across their tops. In those days, the priests made everyone join in the building of great temples,

16

In the Beginning

even though the homes of the people were just humble huts made of poles.

We do not know very much about this early architecture of wooden posts and beams, but it must have been a very powerful tribe that raised the great stones on Salisbury Plain. It was not until more than a thousand years later that the people of Greece, who also built temples of posts and beams, began to build stone copies of these. The builders were far more skilled than those of Stonehenge; for, during the thousand years, bronze tools had come to be used for cutting the stone and ornamenting it.

So what had been simply stone copies of square wooden posts became round stone columns, with a large stone block, called a 'capital', to take the weight of the stone beams or 'lintels'. The columns of the early Greek temples were very plain and sturdy and the capitals have an underneath portion which is something like a cushion; these are the 'Doric' capitals.

There is an old story that a sculptor living in the Greek town of Corinth, whose little daughter had died, placed upon her grave a basket of her toys, with a piece of stone slab to act as a lid. Visiting the grave one day, he saw that the ferns he had planted on it had grown up, and were curling round the basket of toys in such a pretty way that he set to work to copy the effect. In this way he invented a new kind of capital, which came to be called the 'Corinthian' capital, and set a new fashion in Greek architecture known as the Corinthian style (47).

When you are looking at pictures of Greek temples, you should take careful note of the rows of columns which make what is called 'porticoes' round the building. Note, too, that the roofs of the temples are not very sharply pointed. If we had built roofs like this in England, the snow would have piled up upon them and perhaps made them fall in. There is hardly any snow in sunny Greece, but in England our ancestors had to make their roofs very steep so that the snow would not lie upon them. Instead of the overhanging 'eaves' of English buildings, which throw off the rain and keep the walls dry, the Greek temples have only a stone moulding called a 'cornice'. Notice how the cornice runs up the ends of the roof in a triangle (this triangle, which is called a 'pediment', we shall meet again later in this book). Ancient Greek architecture, which was later copied by the Romans, belongs to what we call the 'Classical'

17

style, which starts to come into England during the reign of Elizabeth.

Let us try to imagine what English architecture looked like when the Romans came. The great temples of the days of Stonehenge were forgotten ruins by that time; the finest buildings were very small square temples built of posts stuck into the ground, and surrounded by a simple wooden shelter, or 'portico', with its roof propped up by a few posts. There were strong towns on the hill-tops, surrounded by very deep ditches, behind which towered huge ramparts of earth crowned by stockades of wooden posts placed close together. In the west, where the soil was too rocky for digging, there were a few towns protected by rough walls made out of pieces of stone piled upon each other. Behind these walls of earth, stones, and timber were humble huts: tent-shaped like a Red Indian's wigwam, and thatched with heather and reed, probably covered with grass and weeds and surrounded by rubbish of all sorts. In some of the most important cities in the south-eastern parts of England, where the seas which separated them from the more civilized mainland of Europe were not so wide, the Britons may have been building a few fine houses of wooden posts stuck into the ground in the style of their small temples. But most people, in town and country, were living in simple huts. Only the hills, moors, and plains had farmers living on them; much of the countryside was still dense forest.

It took many years for the Romans to make much change in the appearance of Britain. They did not come as a new race, looking for a new land to settle down in, as the Anglo-Saxons did after them; they only wanted to see what they could get out of the country, to take away to Europe.

Their soldiers conquered the land and brought law and order to the tribes. In some places the Romans laid out large camp sites for their troops, surrounding them with earthwork defences like those of the old hill-towns, but all tidily planned with the tents set out in rows with lanes between them, and the general's headquarters in the middle. The whole camp was roughly square, with a gateway in each of the four sides, except where the site was on top of a cliff or beside a stream or marsh. As the climate was too wild for tents, these were often replaced by proper huts, so that the camp became a town of wooden buildings like a mining camp in America, but all very strictly laid out with the roads crossing each other in squares, and with earthen ramparts and stockades surrounding everything.

After the Romans had been here for many years, these old camp sites became proper towns, each with a market-place or 'forum' in the centre. Some of the Britons came down from their hill-tops to live in the new Roman towns, where they began to build shops and start trading.

Although at this time the buildings of Rome and the great cities which the Romans were founding round the shores of the Mediterranean were very large and magnificent, there were none of these in this country. There were no masons to work the stone necessary for building great 'Classical' temples, palaces, and public buildings; probably few masons would have wanted to come over and live in Britain with its rain and fogs, its great oak forests, and its wild Celtic people. Most of the Roman buildings were therefroe made in timber framed-up by carpenters: very much in the style of the half-timber houses we see in our villages to-day. But the Roman houses probably only had one floor, like a bungalow. As well as houses in towns, the Romans (some of them probably retired soldiers) bought land and built themselves farmhouses or 'villas'. These houses were much finer than anything the Britons had built, and included stables for horses and byres for cattle as well as barns for storing grain. Some of them had several rooms; some had a portico, with a roof supported by wooden posts and beams, passing along the side of the building, so that the owner could pass from one room to another without getting wet. As a better protection for his animals, the Roman farmer in England often arranged his house and other buildings around a yard, as farmers do to-day.

The rough 'rubble' walls which the peoples of the west of England had been using for their town walls were made of stones heaped up without anything added to hold them together. The Romans, however, used what is called 'mortar'. All proper stone walls have their stones 'laid' in mortar, which is usually made by burning limestone so as to get lime, and then mixing this with sand or very small chippings of stone; you may have seen bricklayers laying their bricks in mortar made in this way. The Romans knew how to burn limestone for making mortar, but they could not always get the right stone, and so they often had to lay their stones in mud instead. Right through

19

the Middle Ages we went on building cheap stone houses with mud mortar.

The Romans liked to build low stone walls underneath the bottoms of their framed-up timber walls, to keep these from rotting. Where they could not get stone, they burnt the clay of the fields to make bricks, and used those instead.

The retired Roman soldier who settled in this country must often have sighed for the sunny Italy he had left. He must have hated the English winters. Whenever possible he arranged for his farmhouse a scheme of central heating by making a brick floor supported on small brick pillars; underneath the floor he led hot air from a furnace also built of brick. So altogether you will see that the Romans in Britain made very good use of their burnt-clay bricks (which, by the way, were large square slabs about half the thickness of a modern brick) and so were almost able to make up for the lack of masons to work stone for them. Another use which the Romans made of burnt clay was in the roofs of their buildings. Instead of thatch, which was apt to catch fire, they covered their roof timbers, or 'rafters', with thin overlapping tiles, each of which had a raised rim along the sides which touched; the crack between these two rims was covered by tiles shaped like half a drainpipe and laid upside down to keep the rain out of the joint.

Long after the Romans had left this country—even after the coming of the Normans—English builders were still foraging amongst the ruins of the old towns for the bricks which the Romans had made. Sometimes it was not possible to collect enough stone and find enough masons for the building of a great church; for this reason the whole of St. Albans cathedral is built of Roman bricks.

Although for perhaps three hundred years Roman Britain enjoyed a prosperous existence, with good crops providing most people with enough to eat, and a flourishing trade with the rest of the Roman world, our little colony must always have been rather a backward part of that world. The whole country was never quite conquered. Away in the north, beyond Hadrian's Wall, there were always the wild people of Scotland; and pirates from Germany, which the Romans had never tamed, were always raiding the coasts. So the time came when the Roman towns had to surround themselves with great walls of brickwork: very thick walls, along which the sentries could patrol, and with towers here and there upon which they could stand the engines of war which threw spears and large stones at any enemy who should attempt to assault them. Most of us have probably at some time seen the old walls of a Roman town; either forming part of a city wall of the Middle Ages, or standing abandoned in the middle of fields, with no trace left to-day of the wooden houses which once stood within them.

Throughout the Roman stay in Britain, the people gradually changed their ways. Their old tribes disappeared, as the Roman laws took the place of those which the Celtic leaders had made for their people. The old hill-towns were abandoned and left to the sheep of the downlands, while the new towns in the valleys became more and more popular. Except for the fine wooden villas with their red-tiled roofs which the Roman farmers had built (not too far away from their market towns) the countryside did not change very much, but some of the hut-villages of the Britons were probably now being founded beside the great roads which the Romans had driven through the forests in order to join together the new towns they had made.

But it was into Roman Britain—into this still half-civilized countryside with its humble huts and its crowded cities separated by miles of forests—that something crept which was to play a great part in the life of the country and its architecture. With thes oldiers from Rome were some who followed the new religion of Christianity. Very slowly the Christian teaching spread among the Britons—so far only one church of Roman days has been found in this country—but it had come to stay, and even the savage invasions of pirates from the eastward, who drove away the Romans and brought their cities to ruins, did not succeed in driving Christianity away. For many years, however, the British Christians had to hide in the wild country of the west, where the Anglo-Saxons could not reach them.

CHAPTER II

THE ANGLO-SAXONS

We still know very little about the Anglo-Saxons, and how they conquered this country. They came at a time when the Romans were going back to their own country and the Roman law and order was leaving England. After they had gone, Britain passed into the 'Dark Ages', a period of fighting and ruin about which we still know very little.

We know that the Anglo-Saxon pirates came raiding across the sea from Germany and the Low Countries, and that their raids grew ever stronger and more frequent. It seems probable that gradually they brought complete disaster upon our land, which had for so many years enjoyed, under the Romans, peace and prosperity. As they roamed over the countryside, they entered and burned most of the wooden buildings and towns, driving the people who lived there into the fields and forests. Some of the Britons probably came back later to work for the invaders, but many must have fled westwards into the wilder country on the borders of Cornwall and Wales, to start new lives there—out of reach, they hoped, of the pirates who were still coming, in ever-increasing numbers, across the eastern seas.

There were two main races of invaders: the Angles and the Saxons. The Angles came across the North Sea and settled in Yorkshire, Lincolnshire, Norfolk and Suffolk; from these districts they pushed westwards into the heart of the country and founded the great Kingdom of Mercia. The Saxons sailed down the Channel and settled in what are now Essex, Sussex, Hampshire and Dorset. Those from the last two counties founded the important Kingdom of Wessex. Thus England became two areas, with the Angles in the east and midlands, and the Saxons in the south and towards the west.

In the west of England itself, the people who were left over from the days when the Romans had ruled still lived undisturbed. Many of these people were probably Christians; there was an important Christian settlement at Glastonbury in Somerset. On Holy Island, in distant Northumbria, there was another Christian outpost.

The pagan Anglo-Saxons began to settle over the countryside and lay out their new farms; they were all farming people, and had never lived in towns as the Britons had been doing during the Roman period. They came into the country as large families; each of these took over a piece of countryside and began to clear it in order to form fields and pastures. These energetic farmers began what had not been tried so far: they started at last to cut down the great forests. In doing this, they were not only able to clear land for their farms, but were also able to provide themselves with timber for building their houses.

Although the Anglo-Saxons lived in huts like those of any other primitive people, their family farms or villages had each a large building of a kind which was new in this country. It was a sort of barn, in which the family all lived, together with some of their more valuable farm animals, chief of these being the great oxen which drew the farmer's plough. This building, which was called a 'hall', was not round in shape, like the ordinary hut of those days, but had a roof like that of a house of to-day, with two slopes meeting at the top to form the sharp edge which is called the 'ridge'. From either side of this ridge the rafters sloped down towards the ground. None of these buildings are left to-day and it is not certain just what they looked like, but it is possible that they had no walls and only a huge roof which rose straight from the ground. A building as large as this would probably have had its roof supported by wooden posts inside. In some cases there may have been a row of these propping up the ridge; but probably most halls had two rows, each supporting the middle of the roof on either side.

Let us try to imagine what the inside of one of these building may have looked like. Going in through a small doorway at one end, we should have found ourselves in a dark place rather like a large tent, but with the two rows of square wooden posts passing down either side. Between these posts we might see the oxen standing in their stalls; walking between them up the middle of the hall, we should come, just before we arrived at the far end, to a fire burning (if it should be winter time) on a hearth in the middle of the floor. At the very end of the hall

23

would be rough beds for the Anglo-Saxon farmer and his family. It was barn-like halls of this sort that the Anglo-Saxon farmers were setting up in many of the villages which they were beginning to found throughout their new kingdoms.

As the forests of Britain began to melt away before the axes of the new settlers, the England we know was at last beginning to appear. In the Anglo-Saxon village, one of its most important men was the village carpenter, who was called, in those days, a 'wright'. It was he who used the fallen trees of the forests to make everything the villagers needed, such as sledges, boats, and even the very houses themselves.

As the new villages settled down to a more comfortable existence, the owners of the big 'hall' farmhouses began to turn out the animals from these buildings and provide simpler sheds for them to live in. In this way the hall became a house only, and not a byre or barn as well. This made the hall itself much smaller than it had been before; but, as there were now no animals, it must have become tidier, cleaner, and indeed a far more comfortable place in which the head man of the village and his family could live.

The hall had now become a sort of large square hut, with its roof propped up by four strong square posts; in the very middle of these was the fire burning upon the earthen floor. A building like this probably made quite a comfortable home; not so very different from the humble round hut of poles, but providing far more space in which a large family could sleep, and take their meals in winter round a cheerful fire.

When people first began to build with wooden posts, they just stuck them into the ground, as we do the posts of a garden fence to-day. But posts treated like this are apt to rot in time, so the Anglo-Saxons, who were very expert carpenters, laid large beams on the surface of the ground and planted the feet of their posts upon these. At first the roofs, which were propped up by these posts, probably also rested on beams laid upon the ground. Later, however, when the carpenters discovered how to make actual wooden walls, they were able to set these also upon beams and rest the bottom ends of the roof-rafters upon the tops of the walls they had made.

In order to make a square beam or post from a tree-trunk, the carpenters had to slice off the four sides. Each slice formed a plank which could be used for the wall of a building; the planks were stuck upright, round side outward, between the beams at the foot and at the top. The church of Greensted in Essex is still left to show us what such walls looked like.

The roofs, of course, were very steeply pointed, in order that no snow should remain upon them. Sometimes they were covered with thatch; often, however, the carpenters, who were expert in making all kinds of things out of wood, covered their roofs with wooden tiles, called 'shingles', split from pieces of the tree-trunks which were of no use for making big beams. The roofs always overhung the walls, so that the rain should not drip down and find its way into the cracks between the planks. Later on, in some very fine houses, the roofs were brought out so far that they were able to form a portico: a long shelter, supported by small posts, running all round the building.

The doorway to a hall (once the oxen had been moved out into their own shed) would be as small as possible; for everyone wanted to be as comfortable as he could be inside the building, and no one wanted holes through which the wind could enter. High up in the roof there would have been a couple or more small holes through which the smoke from the fire could escape. These holes, which at the same time served as windows, probably provided the only light to the inside of the hall when the door was closed. As a matter of fact, the door was nearly always left open—in winter, when the fire was burning, it had to be, in order to help the smoke to escape upwards into the roof and out through the holes provided. The Anglo-Saxons had no use for windows; they could not read, and provided the inside of the hall was not absolutely pitch dark they were quite happy with very little light. Holes of any sort only let in the wind; that is why the Anglo-Saxons called them 'wind-eyes'.

By the end of the sixth century after the birth of Christ, the Anglo-Saxons had covered the English countryside with their well-run farming villages, each with its hall. They had also settled in the ruins of some of the old Roman towns and were busily starting to trade across the seas to the Continent of Europe. They had set up seven kingdoms in the country, some of them Anglian and some Saxon. But they were still pagans.

In those days, the headquarters of the Christian Church was Rome. The churches in Rome itself were very simple buildings; for, although they were very large compared with the houses of those days, and were built of stone, their roofs were supported in very much the same way as those of the early barn-like halls of the Anglo-Saxons. Instead of the wooden posts, however, there were two rows of stone columns, set closely together like those of a Greek temple. There were good windows with glass in them; and so that the middle part of the church should not be too dark its roof was raised higher than the roofs of the 'aisles' on either side by building stone walls, with windows in them, upon the two rows of columns which passed down the building. The part rising above the side roofs and carrying the main roof is called the 'clerestory'; it always has windows in it.

In 597, a Roman monk, St. Augustine, settled in Kent and began to teach Christianity to the Anglo-Saxons. He was able to get them to build the first churches that England had seen since the Romans had gone away nearly two hundred years before. He had brought monks with him who could show the local people how to build, not with timber posts as was their own custom, but in a more lasting way. He built his churches in the ruins of the Roman towns of Kent and Essex and all the bricks which his workmen needed were collected from the ruined Roman houses.

St. Augustine's churches were very humble buildings, smaller than many an ordinary cow-byre of to-day, but they were much finer than anything the Anglo-Saxons had ever seen. They had brick walls, with 'gables' at each end of the building, and an ordinary roof with a 'ridge' and two 'eaves', just like any building of to-day. In order that they should have at least one of the special kinds of improvements that the Anglo-Saxons used in their very finest buildings, St. Augustine surrounded his churches with wooden porticoes or shelters. The brick walls did not need the protection of porticoes, but they made the church look more important.

At this time every Roman church had at one end a bulge, rather like a very large bow-window without the window, in which they placed the altar; this bulge is known as the 'apse' (1). Augustine's churches all had a small building joined on to the east end of the main body of the church and ending in a bulge or apse like the churches of Rome. In England all churches still have these two chief parts: the main body of the church, known as the 'nave', in which the people gather together to worship, and the smaller part at the east end, known as the 'chancel', which contains the altar.

After St. Augustine, several Anglo-Saxon kings and bishops built smaller churches designed on the same lines as those he had founded. One of the most perfect of these to-day is that at Bradwell in Essex, which was built in the year 654. The tiny church has lost its apse and wooden porticoes, but its little nave, built of Roman brick from the ruins of the Roman port in which it was founded, is much the same as when our ancestors worshipped in it nearly thirteen hundred years ago.

The Christianity which St. Augustine first brought into Anglo-Saxon England did not spread over the country all at once. A hundred years after his day, other famous missionaries took up the story where he had left it. From Holy Island, St. Wilfred began to build a few churches in the north of the country; while from Glastonbury St. Aldhelm began to found some as well.

About this time, a great empire, called the Holy Roman Empire, was rising on the Continent of Europe. Its emperors ruled from Aachen on the River Rhine. The old Roman empire was by this time very much decayed; the great city itself, headquarters of the Roman Catholic Church, had lost all its ancient power to the new empire in the west.

Away to the east was the mightiest empire of all: that of the Greek emperors of Constantinople, the great Christian city which stood where Europe and Asia met. While the Roman churches were humble and simple in their arrangement, those of Constantinople were very magnificent and elaborate, and were in fact setting the fashion in church building throughout the Christian world.

It would take too long to tell about the wonderful architecture of the 'Byzantines' (as the people of Constantinople were called, after the old name of the city). They lived so near the east, where people roofed their buildings with great stone domes, that they, too, used this form of roof. As you cannot build a dome upon a long building like a Roman church, the Byzantines built their churches round or square or perhaps eight-sided, with the dome rising above all. Round this high middle part were lower portions like the 'aisles' of the Roman churches; but the Byzantine aisles went all round the church. As there was a heavy stone dome to carry, instead of the timber

27

roof of the Roman church, the Byzantines dared not use slender columns, which would never have borne the weight; they used, instead, huge masses of stonework called 'piers' between which very large arches supported the dome above.

These churches of eastern Europe were not long barn-like buildings like the Roman churches, but were more squarish and had high middle parts finished with round domes. In western Europe, where no one knew anything about building domes, the church was covered with an ordinary wooden roof just like that of any other tower. Churches like this, with a tower in the middle, were becoming popular all over the countryside at the time when Christianity was beginning to take a hold in the parts of the Continent near to this country. But there was one very great difference between the churches of Constantinople and those of England. Whereas the skilful Greek engineers always built in stone, the Anglo-Saxon 'wright' only knew how to build in timber.

Although Anglo-Saxon England never actually formed part of the Holy Roman Empire, we were only separated from it by the North Sea. Charlemagne, the emperor who lived about the year 800, was friendly with Offa the Great, the Anglian King of the Mercians and the chief ruler in this country. (It is interesting to note that Charlemagne also exchanged letters with Haroun ar Raschid, the famous Caliph of Baghdad who was ruling his great empire at the same time.)

Unfortunately we have utterly lost, as well as the old Saxon halls, all the early Saxon wooden churches. For, soon after the days of Charlemagne and Offa the Great, England began to suffer from the terrible raids of the pirate Norsemen, who swept through the country time and time again, as the Anglo-Saxons had in their day three hundred years earlier. The pagan pirates burned everything burnable, especially the poor wooden churches of the Anglo-Saxons. It was not until a Saxon king of Wessex, Alfred the Great, came at last to save the country, that England was able to settle down once more to a period of peace and prosperity.

There are still some wooden churches remaining in Essex, and these are probably very much like those which were being built throughout Anglo-Saxon England during its great days: a hundred years before the Normans came. They are very simple buildings, only about twenty feet or so square. Their high wooden roofs are propped up upon four enormous square posts standing on two large beams or 'sleepers' laid upon the ground to carry them. The tops of these four posts are joined by other beams; on top of these beams, four smaller posts carry the upper part of the centre of the church, which is finally covered with a roof in the shape of a pyramid.

Outside the four great posts, and three or four feet from them, are the wooden walls of the building, framed-up as has been explained earlier on. These walls are quite high, perhaps twice the height of a man, and very much more than is actually necessary; certainly far more than would have been the case if the building had been a house or hall instead of a church.

These churches are in fact all very high buildings, much higher indeed than either their length or width. For when a man is building a home he only builds what is necessary; but when he is building a temple or a church in which to worship his God, he builds not merely what is necessary but in order to show the very best that he can do. So in churches the builders always tried to build as high as they could just to show their skill. You will notice this very much more when we come to the great cathedrals of the Middle Ages.

We have so far spoken only of the 'nave' or main part of the church, but these wooden churches had of course a small wooden chancel sticking out on the east side to hold the altar. While talking of churches it is perhaps interesting to mention that, as the altar of a church is always at its east end, if you are standing inside a church facing the altar, the north side of the building is on your left hand and the south side on your right.

We can still see some Anglo-Saxon wooden churches which were built about the time of the Norman Conquest. They are nearly all in the south-eastern counties of England, where the forests still provided plenty of timber for them. As you go into these churches, you will notice the two great ground-beams or 'sleepers' which carry the four thick posts with the beams which join their tops. Between the posts, and stiffening-up the whole framework, there are usually sturdy wooden arches passing across the building. The two timbers, of which each arch is formed, sweep gracefully upwards to meet in the centre, underneath the beam which crosses above. As you look upwards into the tangle of beams which stiffen the upper part of these tower-like timber churches, you can see the many patterns invented by the Anglo-Saxon 'wrights' for this purpose. The timberwork was fastened together, not with nails, but with wooden pegs. Whole churches could be framed up by the village carpenter in the yard where he worked, the pegs knocked out again and the building taken down and moved to wherever it was wanted. It could be moved in fact any number of times, simply by knocking out the pegs.

We have been speaking of Anglo-Saxon England, the country of the great forests. But away to the west, where there was no timber, they had been building small stone churches ever since the days of the Romans. The design of these churches was the same as was followed in the Christian lands of Ireland, Cornwall, Wales, and all those districts which had not been touched by the Anglo-Saxons. Each church had a small nave, narrow and tall, with the usual chancel at its east end. These tiny churches were in the Roman style and not the Byzantine; for it was Roman monks who kept Christianity alive in the west. Both St. Wilfred and St. Aldhelm had built stone churches when they had been missionaries on the borders between Anglo-Saxon and Christian England. Two or three of these churches remain in Northumberland, and the little church built by St. Aldhelm at Bradford-on-Avon in Wiltshire may fortunately still be seen there. When we look to-day at this beautiful little building, it is very difficult to realize that it is well over twelve hundred years old.

It is probable that St. Aldhelm brought over masons from Italy to build his churches. For in Anglo-Saxon England everything was made of timber. Only in a few parts of the country was there enough stone lying about ready for use, and no one yet knew anything about getting stone out of quarries and cutting it into proper shapes for building into walls. In some parts of Anglo-Saxon England, however, there was a certain amount of loose stone—'rubble' it is called—ready to hand, especially in Northamptonshire and parts of the Saxon kingdom of Wessex.

The first experiments made by the Anglo-Saxons in building stone churches probably came about when they began to take away the old boarded walls and replace them with walls built of rubble stone. By this means it was actually possible to build right up to the level of the cross beams passing over the tops of the four great posts. If the walls could be made to carry the ends of these beams, the posts could then be taken away; this made the inside of the church far more roomy. The church is then a stone tower with a steep wooden roof; this possibly in two stories, like the middle part of the ancient church of Breamore in Hampshire.

Early Anglo-Saxon walls are nearly always very clumsily built, with the stones stuck anyhow into their mortar of lime mixed with sand. In places where the stone lay about in thin slabs instead of just shapeless lumps, it was possible to get a much stronger wall by laying the stones sloping and leaning against each other. By making each row, or 'course', of stones run in opposite directions, they made a pattern on the walls rather like a fish-bone. So walls built like this are called 'herring-bone' walls.

The great difficulty in building any kind of stone wall is the making of the corners; for, unless you are very skilful, the stones at the angles of a building will drop off. You cannot possibly make corners in herring-bone work for instance, nor in any kind of rubble stone work. Flints, which are the only building stone you can find in Norfolk and Suffolk, are so slippery that many of the old church towers there have to be built round so as to have no corners at all. To have a really good corner on a stone wall you must have large stones, cut squarely, and well set upon the wall and held into it. The Anglo-Saxons had no workmen who could dig for, and square up, their own building stones for this purpose, so they had to explore the ruins of Roman buildings and use old stones from these for their corners. Sometimes they were able to use Roman bricks; they soon learnt how to build their corners quite skilfully with these.

They had a strange way of using square stones on the corners of their buildings. They were so used to working with wooden posts that they set their stones up on end in the same way. They found, however, that if they put too many stones on end without putting one flat to tie the corner back into the wall, their stones would sooner or later topple down and their work would be undone. So they laid their stones, first on end, and then flat; this trick of putting long stones up on end, held in place by shorter stones laid properly every so often, is called 'long and short' work.

We have talked about the Anglo-Saxon windows which were

usually merely small holes cut through the boards which formed part of the wall of a building. When the Anglo-Saxons were building a stone wall and wanted to leave a window, they very often built into the thickness of the wall a piece of board with a hole in it. As their walls were rather thick they let the window throw a little more light by sloping back the stonework on either side of the board, so as to widen the window opening on each side of the wall. Sometimes they cut the hole in the board so big that it filled up almost the whole of the opening in the stonework. As this was apt to be rather too large for comfort, they then sometimes stretched some kind of cloth across the hole in the board to keep out the wind, soaking the cloth in oil so as to let in a little more light. When they began to get really clever at cutting stones to the shapes they wanted and build them into the wall, they could then make a stone frame on the outer side of the wall and fit in their window board behind this. They then sloped back the thickness of the wall inside the building so as to get as much light as possible.

Doorways to Anglo-Saxon churches are always very small; never any larger than they need be. Inside the building there always has to be a doorway leading from the nave to the chancel. An inside doorway like this could be as large as you could make it; for there is no need to worry about the draught. So these Anglo-Saxon 'chancel arches' are sometimes quite broad openings, arched at the top and often ornamented with strips of stone passing round them. Once the Anglo-Saxons had learned how to build rough stone walls they were not long in discovering how to cover the openings they had to leave through these with an arch instead of a stone beam or 'lintel'. All you need to make an arch is a round wooden frame to build it on; once the mortar in which the arch-stones are set is dried out, you can take away the frame and the arch will stand.

The great man of the Golden Age of Anglo-Saxon England was the Archbishop of Canterbury, St. Dunstan, who lived a hundred years before the Norman Conquest. It was he who brought over to England the monks who were to found those great abbeys which were to spread throughout England in the centuries to come. We shall see in the next chapter what sort of churches these monks built; and how, not only were they far finer than the humble little buildings which the village carpenters were raising, but also how the builders were gradually

altering what had come to be the Anglo-Saxon idea of a church
—that is to say a tall tower-like building—into a long rambling
church like the great cathedral of the Middle Ages. But even
these great cathedrals still keep a memory of the little old
Anglo-Saxon wooden tower-churches in the high tower which
rises out of the very centre of the building (18).

CHAPTER III

THE BUILDINGS OF THE MONKS

The old monks who first began to spend their lives in the service of religion lived alone in small huts or 'cells'. In England monks have nearly always lived together, near to a fine church which they have built, and in which they attend several services every day. In the days of the Anglo-Saxons, the life of the monks was laid down by a 'rule' which was thought out for them by St. Benedict; the monks who followed this rule are said to belong to the 'Benedictine Order'.

Monasteries, that is to say the houses in which the monks live, have existed in England from quite early times. Even before the days of the Anglo-Saxons, there were monks living in various parts of the country in little settlements of huts surrounding a small church. As monks were supposed to have left the life of the everyday world, they were usually reminded of this fact by having their monasteries enclosed within a wall. This is the real meaning of the word 'cloister'; the 'cloistered' monk was one who lived a life enclosed behind a wall.

When Christianity first began to spread through England, the Roman missionaries who brought the new religion appointed monks to look after the Christians in various districts of the country, each of which was usually the area belonging to a tribe, or a kingdom. These monks were the first bishops. The districts that they looked after were called 'sees'; this word, meaning a 'seat', was used because the bishop was supposed to have a particular church which always contained his chair or throne. The Latin word for 'chair' gives us the name of the church itself—'cathedral'. The first cathedrals were no different from any other churches except that naturally one of the finer churches would be chosen to house the bishop's throne.

Sometimes the bishops set up their sees in churches belonging to monasteries. We saw in the last chapter how the Anglo-Saxon parish churches had a 'nave', in which the people sat,

34

The Buildings of the Monks

and a 'chancel', in which was placed the altar. In the monks' churches, the monks themselves formed the congregation, so that the nave became their 'choir', in which they sang their services. Monks were not priests, so each church had to have a priest to conduct the services before the altar in the chancel. From the Latin name for priests these chancels of the monks' churches came to be called 'presbyteries'. As time went on, the monasteries became very wealthy and powerful, because people were always leaving them money. The monks' churches began to grow larger, so that ordinary people could join in the services; this was done by building on a 'nave' to hold all the local people. So the great churches of the monks came to be designed in three parts. If you go into a cathedral—especially one which used to be a monks' church before Henry VIII turned them all out—you can easily see these three parts. As you go in by the west door at the end of the building, the nave (8) stretches away before you. As you walk up this, you will probably come to a 'screen' which divides the nave from the 'choir'; the monks' part of the church in which you will probably still be able to see their fine seats or 'stalls' (1). At the east end of the choir is the open space called the 'presbytery', which ends in the great altar; the presbytery often has fine tombs lined along it under the arches.

The largest monasteries were ruled by a monk who was elected 'abbot'; such monasteries were called 'abbeys'. The abbot's second-in-command was known as the 'prior'; smaller monasteries, which had no abbot at their head, were called 'priories' and were ruled by a prior.

The first great monasteries of the kind that we see in ruins all over England to-day were founded about a hundred years before the Norman Conquest through the efforts of a great Archbishop of Canterbury called St. Dunstan. These old monasteries were all built in connection with some great church, specially built by the monks to form the finest buildings for miles around. For six hundred years, the churches of the monks remained the most magnificent buildings in England.

Let us consider what these great buildings looked like at about the time when the Normans were invading the country. Each church was built round a central tower, on each side of which were four arms, making the church cross-shaped or 'cruciform'. The arm on the east side of the tower was the pres-

35

bytery; at the extreme end of this was one of those bulges called 'apses', which we talked about in the last chapter, to hold the altar.

As the abbeys grew more and more wealthy, the monks began to find that their old presbyteries were too cramped for them; so that they had to pull them down and make them longer. In this way, nearly all the old apses disappeared.

On either side of the central tower was a projecting chapel known as a 'transept'; this contained small altars for less important services on Saints' Days, and for ceremonies such as weddings or for saying prayers for the dead. On the west side of the central tower—that is to say opposite the side where the altar was—the monks built their nave; this was often a very long building which could hold a great number of people.

A huge church like this could not be built all at once; the monks had to build it up, piece by piece, as they were able to get money, and find workmen and stone and other materials. To them a very important part of the church was its central tower, because their choir was underneath it. Also very important was the presbytery with the altar in it; so this part too had to be built at the beginning. The central tower had to have four arches into it leading into the four arms. Arches will collapse unless they are propped up by pieces of wall on either side; so it was necessary for the monks to build at least part of every one of the four arms, to support the central tower. So, together with the presbytery, they usually built the two transepts; they also had to build at least part of the nave in order to prop up the central tower all the way round.

We are talking of the very finest churches, which had to be built piece by piece. As it was intended that the building should hold a large number of people, the monks found that the small bit of nave they had built was not worth while having for this purpose; so they generally put their own choir seats into it, and so left the central 'crossing', under the tower, quite free and open. This gave a much finer effect, so they kept the arrangement even after the nave had been built. The builders of the great churches of the Middle Ages tried to raise the roofs of their churches as high as possible, so as to make each building stand high up above its surroundings. So they made the walls of their churches very tall; then the steep roofs made the church look taller than ever. In order to give as much room as possible

The Buildings of the Monks

inside the church, the monks followed the same plan as in the old churches of Rome, and supported their high walls upon rows of pillars, so that 'aisles' could be built out on either side. The Romans carried their walls on stone beams passing from pillar to pillar; the monks used arches instead. A row of arches is called an 'arcade'; it is these arcades of the monks' churches, especially in their naves, which make the insides of the great buildings look so fine (7).

In order to get still more accommodation for worshippers, the monks made their aisles two stories high, with arcades to each story looking into the centre of the church. These upper floors or 'galleries' over the aisles of great churches are called to-day 'triforium' (actually it is a mistake to use this word but nearly everybody does so to-day). The central part of each arm of the church had to rise high above the roofs of the galleries over the aisles, in order that windows might be placed there to light it. This row of windows (which we saw in the old churches of Rome) is called the 'clerestory'. So inside a great church you may see three stories: the main arcade, the 'triforium' arcade, and the clerestory (8).

It was not until after the Norman Conquest that the eastern parts—the presbyteries—of the churches began to have aisles like those of the nave. Nearly all these fine presbyteries disappeared when the monks had later to make them longer; only those which happened to have been built long enough at the time remain to us to-day. As these old buildings all ended in 'apses', the aisles of the presbytery were often made to go right round behind this, so that the monks could walk all round the altar in procession. The picture (1) of the inside of the presbytery of Norwich cathedral shows how the wall of the apse had to be carried on arches, like the rest of the main walls of the church.

High above each of the four arms of the church rose its tall pointed roof; all four roofs met up against the four walls of the central tower, which was brought just high enough for it to be possible to place windows in its walls, to light the floor of the crossing far below. These central towers of the great churches of the time of the Norman Conquest were called for this reason 'lantern towers'; they were roofed with tall wooden spires, often covered with shingles. These *central* towers, which are really the remains of the first tower-like churches the Anglo-Saxons built, were never meant to carry bells. At St. Albans cathedral the belfry story was added after the tower was built. The 'lantern tower' had only a single row of large windows in it; a hundred years after it was built, the monks took off the wooden spire-like roof and built another story, on top of the 'lantern', to hold their bells.

The proper place for a bell-tower was at the end of the nave, into which it could call the country people to their services. At first, the monks began to build their bell-towers here; the very beautiful example at Ely cathedral is one which had another story added to it two hundred years later. But as time went on, the builders began to prefer to have two towers at the west end of the nave, with the great entrance doorway between these: this fashion went on right to the end of the Middle Ages (18).

We have now seen something of the most important building in the monastery of the Middle Ages: its great church. The monks who worshipped in the choirs of the abbey churches slept in a long two-storied house, the upper floor of which was one long room like a school dormitory. 'Dormitory' was, in fact, the actual word used by the monks to describe the room in which their rough beds were ranged side by side along each of the long walls. You will remember we said that the great churches had on either side of the central tower a projecting wing called a 'transept'. The monks' house was joined on to one of these transepts, from the end of which it stuck out, at right-angles to the main length of the church. It was usually added to the transept on the south side of the church, so that the great mass of this building would protect the monks' house from the north winds instead of taking away all the warmth of the sun from it, as would have been the case had it been on the other side. The monks reached their dormitory by a wide stone staircase which passed up the outside of its long west wall to a door at the top. From the foot of this staircase, a path led along the foot of the wall to a doorway in the angle between the nave and the transept.

Not only during the daytime did the monks have to go to church to sing their services; they had to go in the night as well. That is why the monks' house was always joined on to the church so that a staircase, called the 'night stair', could be made in the thickness of the walls; down it the monks could pass from their dormitory into the church without having to go

The Buildings of the Monks

into the open air. The inside of the dormitory was just a long room with a few small windows in it. At first the monks' rough beds were just ranged along the walls; later, however, they began to build wooden partitions round their beds to keep the draught off and make them more private. At the end of the ground floor of the monks' house farthest from the church was their common room.

At this end of the house was a long narrow building. On the first floor of this building was a row of closets for the use of the monks; these closets were really not so very much unlike our own water-closets of to-day, for a nearby stream was made to run through the ground floor of the building to help with the drainage. It is the long tunnel-like drains from these 'reredorters', which people to-day sometimes imagine are 'underground passages'.

In the last chapter we have spoken of the hall of the Anglo-Saxon family, in which it lived and took its meals. In the days of the great monasteries, people had learned to make themselves more comfortable; really good houses were always designed in two stories, so that people could sleep on the upper floor away from the ground. The hall, however, still remained the chief place for taking meals; indeed we shall see, later on in this book, how it became more and more important a room as time went on. A hundred years after the Norman Conquest, every important house had a 'great hall', in which the master of the house and his family, and also his servants, could take their meals. The monks, too, had great halls attached to their monasteries, in which they all met together at meal times. The great halls of the monks, which were called 'refectories', were always built opposite to the nave of the church, on the same side as the monks' house joining on to the end of the transept. The 'upper' end of the refectory usually almost touched the end of the monks' house farthest from the church; but the two buildings did not actually join up, because one was a two-storied house and the other a great high hall. At the lower end of the refectory was a doorway, opposite to the church, which the monks used when they went in to meals; near this was another doorway which led to the great kitchen where their food was cooked.

If you will now think over what has been explained of the arrangement of the three chief buildings of a monastery, you will see that the nave of the great church, the monks' house, and the refectory, were set out to form three sides of a square; so that, if you closed up the side opposite the monks' house (that is to say, the western side) with a wall, you would get a square yard. It was this yard which, during the Middle Ages, came to be known as the 'cloister'; in it, the monks spent the greater part of their lives. There was no need for them ever to leave it; for around it lay all the buildings of the monastery in which they lived.

The doorways leading from the various buildings into the cloister yard would be joined up by a path passing all round it. Anybody walking along this path when it was raining would get all the drips from the roof on his head; so it was usual to cover the path over with a roof, supported on wooden posts and beams like one of the old Anglo-Saxon porticoes. As the monasteries became more and more wealthy, and took to making their houses more and more beautiful, they replaced the wooden posts and roofs with stone arcades and stone roofs, of a kind which we shall talk about later. Many of our great abbey churches and cathedrals have lovely cloisters (3). We can walk all round the four sides, between the walls of the buildings and the graceful arches through which we can see the green turf of the cloister yard.

Every day, the monks met to discuss the business of the monastery. The meeting was called a 'chapter', because it opened with the reading of a chapter from some religious book. A special room was always provided for the meetings of the chapter; it was called the 'chapter house'. After the church itself, this was always the most beautiful building architecturally. It was placed next to the church, and sometimes formed part of the ground floor of the monks' house; but, as this was not very high (owing to the fact that the monks' dormitory was on the floor above), it was difficult to make a really fine chapter house in this position. So the monks usually made this part of the ground floor of the monks' house into a kind of entrance hall, building the chapter house itself on the east side of the monks' house; here there was nothing to prevent it being as large and tall as they wished. There are very many beautiful chapter houses belonging to our great cathedrals and abbeys (12).

If you are following the arrangement of the buildings of a monastery as they are being explained to you, you will see that

The Buildings of the Monks

the chapter house is not very far away from the presbytery, or eastern arm of the great church in which the altar was placed. It was round this eastern arm and its altar—the most holy part of the whole monastery—that the graveyard lay. On the side of the presbytery nearest to the monks' house was their cemetery; on its opposite side lay the graveyard of the country people. A passage led from the cloister, passing between the church and the chapter house, to the monks' graveyard; through this passage, the monks who died would be carried on their last journey.

Standing by itself near the monks' graveyard was a building which was their hospital; it was called the 'infirmary'. It was a large hall, often divided up by rows of pillars and arches, like a church. The beds of the sick persons were arranged down the side walls, just as in a hospital to-day. At the east end of the infirmary hall was a small chapel where services could be held.

We have now mentioned all the most important buildings which made up a monastery of the Middle Ages. You will remember that, when we described the cloister yard, we found that three sides only of it were lined with buildings. Generally, however, the fourth—or west—side was closed in by a long building which was chiefly used for the storage of food and various things belonging to the monastery. Where this building joined on to the nave of the great church a passage was left, leading from the cloister to the outer world. This passage was the entrance to the cloister; people who had business with any of the monks—for instance in connection with buying food— met and talked together in this passage, which, from the French word for 'talk', was known as the 'parlour'.

As monasteries got wealthier and more comfortable, their abbots began to give up sleeping in the monks' dormitories, and to make private chambers for themselves in the range of buildings on the west side of the cloister. The abbot's chamber was generally at the end nearest the church; here he could both see what was going on around the parlour beneath, and also perhaps have a window into the church so that he could take part in the services without having to trouble himself to leave his chamber.

As these monasteries, most of which you will remember followed the 'rule' of St. Benedict, grew still more wealthy and comfort-loving, there were complaints that this sort of thing was not what they had been founded for. Not very long after the Norman Conquest, a French monk named St. Bernard invented a new rule. St. Bernard's own monastery was called 'Citeaux' and his rule is known as the 'Cistercian'. Most of the Benedictine monasteries had either been founded in towns or else, owing to their wealth and the trade which grew up around them, they began to find themselves the centres of new towns. St. Bernard thought that monks should live in the country, far away from all the temptations of town life.

His problem was this: how were his monks to support themselves in the wild places that they chose for founding their monasteries? But the Cistercian monks took up sheep farming; looking after their flocks, making their monkish clothes from the wool and selling what was left over to provide them with the money to buy food and other needs. The difficulty about this was that the monks, spending the livelong day in the open air with their flocks, could never find time to attend the services in their church; this meant that they had to find someone to look after the sheep for them. So every Cistercian monastery had a number of country people called 'lay brothers', who were not real monks, but lived in the monastery and helped with the farming. These lay brothers lived in a long house, just like that of the monks themselves and lying opposite to it along the west side of the cloister. The Cistercian monks arranged their refectories differently from those of the other kinds of monks; building the great halls end-on to the cloister and lying between the two houses—those of the monks and the lay brothers—so that the three buildings all stood side by side.

Most of the large Benedictine monasteries, which were founded in towns, have now disappeared, except where a great church has been saved to provide a cathedral for a bishop. All the other buildings were long ago pulled down, so that the stone could be used by the townspeople to build their houses. But in the peaceful countryside of England, particularly among the Yorkshire moors and dales, we may still see the ruins of huge Cistercian monasteries, built so far away from the towns that it was never worth while troubling to pull them down and cart the stones away.

Let us imagine ourselves paying a visit to a large Benedictine monastery of the Middle Ages. We have arrived at the market square, on one side of which is the beautiful west front of the great church, with its two tall towers and its fine large door-

The Buildings of the Monks

way between them. As we stand facing this a high wall rises on our right hand. In it is a large tower beneath which is a wide archway. This is the 'great gate' of the monastery. On either side of this gateway are small buildings: shops and offices, including one—the almonry—from which gifts of money and scraps of food are handed out to poor people. Some of the shops sell little statues of saints, and bottles of medicine. If we take a look inside the great gate and glance across to the left, we shall see the long building in which are the monks' storerooms. Looking round to the extreme left, where the high wall of the monastery meets the corner of the church, we shall see the archway of the 'parlour' which leads into the cloister itself.

As we go into the great church, we pass up between the tall pillars of the nave, to the altar which stands at its far end, with a carved screen of stone behind it. On either side of this altar are the little doors leading into the choir of the monks. If we go through either of these doors we shall find ourselves in a dark space; beyond this is another screen, with a door in the centre through which we can see the whole of the monks' choir and their great altar far away at the east end of the presbytery. Between the second screen, through the doorway in which we are looking, and the central crossing where the light from the tower streams down to the point where the transepts meet, are the wooden 'stalls' in which the monks sit. If we pass on between these stalls, we can stand right under the central tower itself, and look up to the windows, high above us, from which the light is coming. On our left hand and on our right stretch the transepts. That on our left hand, that is to say the north side, will have large windows in it; on the other, there will be none, for the monks' house is on this side.

Let us now suppose that we are standing with the monks in their stalls at the end of an important service, the last part of which is to be a procession round the buildings of the monastery. With our fellow monks we form into line, two and two, in the centre of the choir between the stalls and move off eastward towards the great altar. The procession bears to the left into the north transept, pausing at the altars there, and then turns off eastwards, into aisles surrounding the eastern arm of the church until it has gone all round this and entered the south transept. As soon as we leave this, we turn to the left, through a doorway, and suddenly come out into the cloister. As we go on, straight forward, along the eastern alley of the cloister, we first see on our left hand the passage which leads to the graveyard of the monks. Next we pass, also on our left side, a doorway having on either side of it a fine window. If we should leave the procession and slip through this doorway, we should find ourselves in the entrance hall of the chapter house lying beyond. But we must keep on, along the eastern alley of the cloister, until we come to the foot of the great stone staircase leading up to our dormitory. Here, however, the procession turns to the right along the south alley of the cloister.

Looking through the arches, and across the green turf of the cloister yard, we can now see, rising up beyond, the great mass of the nave of the church. Just as we get to the end of the alley, we see on our left side the fine doorway leading to the great hall or 'refectory'. Beside this door there is a large alcove, perhaps beautifully ornamented, with a shelf running all along it with earthenware basins arranged in rows; this is where we should be washing our hands if we had been going in to a meal in the refectory. But the procession passes on, turning once more to the right, and along the western alley of the cloister, which has several small doors in it leading into the storerooms which lie alongside.

In front of us, at the very end of the cloister, we can see the fine doorway which leads back into the nave of the church. Just as we reach this, on our left side, we pass the passage leading to the outer world. But our procession goes on through the door and into the nave of the church. When we get into the middle of this we turn to the right and walk up the nave towards the people's altar: forming up, facing each other in two rows, before it. Once the abbot has made certain that we are all present, we turn eastward once again, go through the two little doors which lead into the dark space, where we join up once more to enter the choir.

We have now learned something about the great monasteries which were built throughout England during the Middle Ages. Most of them were founded soon after the Norman Conquest. A great deal of money was spent on them; an enormous amount of labour must have gone into the raising of these interesting buildings. They soon became very popular and the number of monks increased. People left a lot of money to beautify the great churches. The abbots began to realize that it was a good thing to bring in money to the monasteries; for they could not only improve the appearance of their buildings, but also make themselves much more comfortable. So they were for ever thinking of ways by which to advertise their monasteries throughout the countryside. From very early days they took pains to build great naves to their churches, in order to get as many of the country people into them as possible.

If a very holy man died and possibly was later made a saint, he was made much of by the abbots. An abbot would try to arrange for a saint to be buried in his great church, in order that people would come from far to visit the tomb and bring offerings to the monastery. We have seen how the monks were buried in the graveyard which lay beside their house. The abbots were buried beneath the floor of the chapter house. The great men of the district were buried beneath the presbytery of the great church; so it was a good thing to enlarge the presbytery, in order that more people could be buried in it, leaving money to the monastery to pay for prayers to be said for their souls. If an abbot was so lucky as to have a saint buried in his church, he might enlarge its presbytery to a great length, in order to provide a special chapel, large and very beautiful, at the extreme east end of his church, behind the High Altar. As we walk round our great churches to-day, we can see from their architecture how, all through the Middle Ages, their eastern arms were for ever being built longer and longer.

In the old days people liked to be buried in churches. In Rome saints were often buried beneath the altar, sometimes in an underground room, called a 'crypt', which was used as a small chapel for people who wished to come and pray at the tomb. In the great churches built in this country after the Norman Conquest, the whole presbytery was sometimes built with a basement beneath it; important people were buried under its floor, and the pillared crypt could be used as a large chapel in which prayers could be said for them.

We all know how the end came at last to all these beautiful buildings of the monks. So many people had left their lands to the abbeys that these had come to own a great deal of England, which was not a good thing for the country. The religious ideas upon which the monasteries had first been founded had long been forgotten; so that the monks, who were supposed to lead simple lives, worshipping God, were often idle, lazy and far too interested in their own comfort. The great abbeys, which had been enlarged in the days when they were very popular, in order to take the numbers of monks who were coming into them, were now half empty; people were not so interested in religion at the end of the Middle Ages as they had been at the beginning. The huge monasteries were becoming neglected, and people thought that they simply meant that a great deal of English land had fallen into the hands of idle people. In 1539 Henry VIII decided to sweep them all away. He seized all the treasures of the monasteries, turned out all the monks and gave them small pensions. Their lands he gave to various people whom he wished to favour.

Apart from the actual treasures of the monastery, the most valuable part of the buildings was the lead which covered their roofs. Workmen climbed all over these roofs, stripped off the lead and threw great rolls of it down on to the ground. Inside the choirs of the great churches, the beautiful carved seats of the monks were broken up and made into huge bonfires, over which the lead was melted in cauldrons, run into moulds, and then carried away to be sold for the benefit of the government. And so the monasteries soon became roofless ruins, blackened by the smoke of their burning woodwork.

The people to whom the king had given the lands of the monks were needing houses to live in, for the monasteries themselves were no use for this purpose. To build houses they needed stone. Any amount of this was ready to hand in the ruins of the monks' buildings; the problem was how to get at it quickly. So miners burrowed under the foundations of the huge pillars which supported the central towers of the great churches, propping up the walling above with timber beams as they did so. When they had gone far enough, they lit a fire amongst these beams and burned them; so that the great towers fell, bringing all about them to ruin. It was then merely a matter of collecting and cleaning the stones from mounds of rubbish which once had been the beautiful buildings of the monks of the Middle Ages.

CHAPTER IV

THE COMING OF THE CASTLES

In the first chapter we talked of the way in which our ancestors protected their hill-top towns from the attacks of an enemy by digging deep ditches, throwing up the earth to form a rim inside the ditch, and planting sturdy stockades of timber posts along the top of this earthen rampart. We have also seen how the Roman soldiers protected their camps in the same way; in this case, however, the earthwork was much more quickly and easily made, and the ditches not nearly so deep, as were the town ditches of the Britons. When the Roman camps became towns, however, the ditches were often deepened, in order that the defences might be made stronger against more serious attacks. Later on, the Romans built strong walls of brick, with towers here and there for carrying engines of war, along the inner edges of their ditches, often using the earth from the rampart to make a slope at the back of the wall up which their soldiers could scramble quickly to its top.

During the terrible days when the Danes were sweeping to and fro across England, burning and killing, the Anglo-Saxons —who had never lived in the hill-top towns of the Britons and had made very little use of the walled Roman towns—were mostly all living in quite unprotected farms, scattered over the countryside. But when Alfred the Great at last managed to stop the worst of the raids, his children, Edward and Ethelfleda, built a few camps—called 'boroughs'—in the heart of England; they surrounded these boroughs with earthwork in the old style, so that the country people could gather together behind defences of some sort when there was a bad raid going on. But as soon as everything had settled down again, everyone soon forgot all about the defences. The Anglo-Saxons never seem to have been able to take a proper interest in public works of any sort.

But on the continent of Europe at this time, the great fami-

47

The Coming of the Castles

lies were always fighting each other, and had taken to surrounding their houses with defences. They were actually digging ditches around their farms and raising earthen ramparts, either with thorn hedges along the tops, or even wooden stockades. The difficulty they had with a small earth fort of this sort was that the rampart within the ditch took up such a lot of room. If they set out too small a circle, dug the ditch round it and piled the earth in a rim inside it, they found they had too little space left in the middle. So what these country squires did was to spread the earth which they took from their ditches all over the space within so as to form a broad low mound. Upon these low mounds, which they called '*mottes*', they built their houses; round the edges of the mounds they planted their stockades or hedges.

The Latin word for a fortress is '*castrum*'. A small fort is called '*castellum*' and from this word, by leaving out its Latin ending '*um*' you get the word 'castle'. That is why the small earthen forts, privately owned and not part of the defences of a town, came to be called castles.

When William the Conqueror brought his companions over to England to seize the farms of the Anglo-Saxons, the first thing that the invaders did, when they took over their new lands, was to build earthwork castles to protect their homes from the possible anger of the Anglo-Saxon peasants.

It was not always necessary to go to much trouble in making a castle of this sort. In the west of England, for example, it might be possible to find a place so strongly defended by rocky precipices that there was no need for anything to be added to them. Or there might be a cape sticking out into the sea, across the neck of which a short line of ditch will complete a castle. If you should settle down upon the banks of a marshy stream which no one can possibly get across, half your castle is made already; all that has then to be done is to set out a half-circle of ditch and bank for protection on the side away from the stream. The same thing might happen in the case of a castle on the edge of a cliff; if there was a place where there was some deep ravine cutting into the cliff edge, possibly only a quarter-circle of ditch would complete the castle.

But in most places in England there were no such natural defences to be found. So the Normans often had to make the whole castle without any help; surrounding the place with a

48

The Coming of the Castles

ditch, and either raising a rampart of earth on its near edge or spreading the soil to make a low mound. With small castles, it was almost always necessary to make mounds, but with large castles—such as, for example, those that William the Conqueror's men built from which to police the countryside—the high rampart was not only a better defence but did not take up enough room to matter. The ordinary man's castle was usually set out in a circle. William the Conqueror and his chief men, however, followed the example of the Romans and made their castles nearly square, with the corners rounded off so that the palisades could sweep easily round them and leave no corners to be cut off by besiegers.

There had to be, of course, a gap in the stockade for going in and out; at this point there had to be a bridge across the ditch. These bridges were all framed-up in timber, supported upon wooden trestles rising from the sides of the ditch, and with a flooring of planks; very often it was arranged that part of the flooring next the gate in the stockade could be taken away when the castle was being besieged.

The house inside the castle we shall talk about in another chapter, as it was no different from any other house; the defences around it, which made it into a castle, were quite separate and had no connection with it. It has been explained before that most of the English castles at the time of the Norman Conquest were simply important farmhouses protected against possible attack. The large castles of William the Conqueror, however, were more like Roman camps; there were huts in them to house the soldiers, and possibly, as time went on, a wooden hall in which these could take their meals.

One of the great dangers the castle builders of all ages have had to face is how to keep the besiegers from getting up so close to the defences that they themselves are in fact protected by these from the efforts of the garrison to drive them away. So we find that all stockades or walls have a strip of ground in front of them which is known as the 'dead ground' and it is most important to have some sort of high place from which the garrison can overlook this strip.

If we go back to what we were saying about the mound-castles, you will remember that they were started by marking out a circle in the sand and digging a small ditch all the way round this; then piling up the sand in the middle of the ring so as to form the mound. By deepening the ditch just a little, and adding the earth taken out of it to the top of the mound, it is possible to make this quite high, with perhaps just a very little flat space left on the top. That is what the Normans did with some of their castle mounds; they found that with a very little amount of extra work they could raise a tall hill of earth, with just a small flat space on the top of it. A hill like this made a very strong place to go to if the castle was being attacked; as the enemy had to scramble down into the ditch, and then clamber up a very long slope, while all the time the defenders worried him by shooting at him and rolling things down upon him. Of course a mound like this was no use for building a house, as there was no space on the top; but it was a very useful thing to have one of these tall mounds as a part of a castle to which you could retreat if the main portion should be captured by the enemy. As this main portion of the castle was known as the 'bailey' and the Normans called a mound a 'motte', castles which have both of these are known as 'motte-and-bailey' castles.

The ordinary private castle-builder could only collect labourers for building a high 'motte' if he were a very big land-owner like one of the great Norman barons. William the Conqueror, however, when he built his large castles all over England—especially beside the Anglo-Saxon towns for the purpose of keeping law and order in the country—built in each one a large high motte to overlook the whole.

In the England of those days there were very few tall buildings. Only the central towers of the monks' great churches rose above the fields. But here and there the mound of a Norman castle could also be seen. And where to-day the abbey tower has long ago tumbled down into ruins, the castle mound may still stand as high as when it was built. And we have not forgotten why the Normans heaped up their mottes; for children playing on the seashore still pile up their mounds of sand, climb to the top, and call out 'I'm the king of the castle'.

Scattered about the country in lonely places, you may sometimes find very tiny motte-and-bailey castles. These were probably built during some war or rebellion; either by some robber baron who wanted to raid the countryside, or by the king or some other important personage as a camp from which he could attack a nearby castle. When you find these lonely mounds and

The Coming of the Castles

ditches you must try to imagine what they looked like when they had their rings of stockades and their wooden bridges crossing the deep ditches.

In the years after the battle of Hastings the Normans built hundreds of castles all over England: some to live in, and others either for keeping order or for raiding from. On the one hand we have these castles of earth and timber, and on the other we have the great abbey churches of the monks: these were what the Normans brought to Anglo-Saxon England.

In many places the houses inside the defences of the castles were just wooden halls. Some of the castles, however, had inside them great stone houses, of which the finest, that in which William the Conqueror himself lived, is the White Tower of London. Except for a few houses which had several stories they were mostly two stories in height like the ordinary house of to-day. In those days, however, the most important people never lived on the ground floor of a house, where it was very dirty—owing to the fact that the floor was the earth itself—and because you could only have had very tiny windows or somebody might have got in. For the same reason the fine stone houses of the Normans had no doors to the ground floor. The entrance was always on the upper floor, and was reached by a broad flight of stone steps rising up from the ground outside.

In the case of these castle houses, which were called 'keeps', the main floor had two rooms. The entrance was in the larger of these, near one end; this room was in fact the 'hall', and the owner of the castle had his meals at the end of it farthest from the entrance doorway. In the Middle Ages, a room always had a 'lower' and 'upper' end; the 'lower' end being where the entrance doorway was, and the most comfortable part of the room, away from the draughts, being the 'upper' end. At the very end of the hall inside the castle keep was a doorway, passing through the wall dividing the hall from another room, rather smaller, which was the 'chamber' in which the owner of the castle and his family slept. We shall have more to say in another chapter about the arrangements within a house of the Middle Ages.

These strong stone houses inside the castles, which we have called keeps, had very thick walls—ten feet or more through—on the outside; so as to make it difficult for an enemy who might capture the bailey, in which the keep stood, from getting into the building. The keep had only very tiny windows in its ground story, the whole of which was taken up by the goods of the owner of the castle. Everything he possessed might be in these dark basements; for there were no banks in those days, and you had to look after everything you had yourself. Of course there would be a certain amount of food always kept in the basement of the keep in case the owner and his family should be besieged in it.

The weakest point of any kind of building is its entrance; often, therefore, the doorway on the first floor of the castle keep was protected by a small tower, making a sort of porch, from the side of which a flight of steps passed down the main wall of the keep to the ground. The basement of this little tower or 'fore-building' was generally the castle prison. The only way into this was through a trap-door in the floor of the porch above; so that nobody could get out of it unless somebody lowered him a rope or ladder.

Another very weak point in the castle defences was the entrance through the palisades surrounding the bailey, for the enemy might set the wooden stockades and gate on fire. So many of the Norman castle-builders had small towers built at the entrance, with a tunnel underneath through which the enemy would have to fight his way if he wanted to get in. These towers built over the entrance passage of a castle are called 'gatehouses'; there is a very old one at Exeter castle.

The Norman keeps which we have been talking about were not really towers; they were simply very strong two-storied houses. But at the time when the Normans were settling down in England, they were discovering how to build tall stone towers to their churches. It became fashionable for the castle of a powerful Norman baron to have, if possible, a tall stone tower in it; this would look very fine and from its top the defenders could look all over the countryside to see who was approaching. After about the end of the reign of William the Conqueror, therefore, the Normans began to give up building their huge stone houses and to raise instead tall 'tower-keeps' in their castles. They did this by putting the 'chamber', in which the owner and his family lived, on top, instead of alongside, the 'hall' in which everyone took their meals. Of course they squared-up the plan so as to make the tower roughly the same on all four sides. These tower-keeps also had very thick

The Coming of the Castles

outer walls, and were generally three stories high: a basement for storage, a first floor with the entrance doorway to the hall, and a second floor on which the family lived. One of the finest of these tower-keeps is that at Rochester in Kent (4).

In the art of fighting wars, whenever one side has a good idea the other side has to set to work to think of something too. When the Normans started to build their great stone towers, other Normans had to think of some way of getting into them. As it was too difficult a job to fight your way into a building like this, the only thing to do was to try to destroy it. There were, of course, no cannons with which you could batter it down. But the Normans had another idea: they set to work and 'undermined' it. The scheme was to start driving a tunnel under the ground, from a safe distance away, until you were underneath the wall of the tower. As the miners went forward they propped up the roof of the tunnel with wooden posts and beams. When at last they had got to the point where they were underneath the wall of the tower, they could then leave their 'mine'— as it was called—after they had lit a fire amongst the wooden posts; for as the posts burned through, the tower above would fall. The best part of the tower to undermine was one of its corners; the stronger and heavier the corner, the more easily would it fall down if you undermined it.

As soon as the Normans realized that the enemy might undermine the corners of their stone towers, they gave up building them with corners and made them round. Although round towers were very awkward to build and very uncomfortable to live in, they at least could not easily be undermined. It was Henry II and his Anglo-Saxon engineer, Alnoth, who thought of this idea and who first built round tower keeps.

The Norman castle-builders now had fine strong houses to live in, or to retreat to if the castle bailey were captured by the enemy. The defences of this bailey, however, were still only wooden stockades which the enemy usually tried to burn by hurtling masses of blazing stuff at them from his siege engines. So the Normans had to set to work to build walls of stone in place of the wooden stockades. It was about the reign of Henry I that these stone 'ring-walls' first began to be built round the castle baileys; although strongly built they were not very high —perhaps less than twice the height of a man. Another part of the castle which had its wooden stockades changed to low stone walls was the top of the 'motte'. A tall earthen mound with a stone wall on the top is called a 'shell keep'. The famous Round Tower of Windsor is the shell keep; in the reign of Queen Victoria it was made twice as high as it had been when a Norman king first built it.

When the Norman barons became more and more wealthy and powerful, and began to collect small armies of men about them, they had to enlarge their castles by adding another bailey. These extra baileys are called 'outer wards'; they were usually added on the opposite side of the great motte to the first bailey so that the motte could overlook the whole castle.

We are now beginning to see how the Norman castle grew up, from being a very humble affair of earth and timber, to become a stone castle more like the sort of thing we are used to seeing to-day, with its strong walls rising behind the deep ditches, and the great tower or 'keep' overlooking all. Inside the castle walls there would have been all sorts of buildings, provided from time to time: a comfortable hall of wood or stone, a chapel, stables for the horses, huts for the garrison. When there was a siege, everyone felt safe behind the castle walls which the siege engines of the days of the Norman conquest of England could batter with their heavy stones without having much effect.

But in the middle of the reign of Henry II the Norman castle builders received a bad shock. Up to this time the only engine the besiegers had been able to use was one which had been known since the days of the Romans. It could throw heavy stones, and masses of blazing stuff, but it could not throw them very far, and—what was more important—could not throw them very high in the air. But one day a terrible new engine was brought over by Henry II from France, for the purpose of besieging the castle of one of his rebellious barons. It was a huge affair: a long heavy beam balanced at the top of a very strong wooden trestle. One end of this beam was heavily weighted; the other end was held down with ropes to the ground, and whatever the besiegers wished to throw was fastened to it. When the ropes holding the end down were let go, the weight at the other end of the beam suddenly dropped, and the whole huge beam swung round and threw whatever it had been loaded with high in the air at a terrific speed.

With engines like this against them, the people inside the

castles were no longer safe. Great stones would come hurtling over the low walls, hit a stone building, and burst in a shower of splinters—terrifying the garrison. There was only one thing to be done; the castle walls would have to be made very much higher. So it is that they appear as we know them to-day, rising high into the air so that no stones could be slung over their tops. Along the tops of these high walls, which are called 'curtains', sentries could walk up and down; protected by a 'battlemented' parapet, they could shoot through this at the besiegers.

But a new difficulty had now arisen. The walls were so high that the defenders could not see what was going on below; unless they leaned out, in which case they were promptly shot at by the besiegers. This was a serious matter, because it made it so easy for the enemy to get right up to the foot of the walls and start to undermine them. At first the defenders built out a kind of wooden balcony from the top of the wall, with a wooden screen in front of it. They could look through the cracks in the floor and see what was going on; but the besiegers could smash these wooden balconies to pieces with their great stones, so this was not a very good idea. At last the castle-builders decided to build their parapets, not right on top of the wall, but on the ends of strong stone brackets sticking out from it, as may be seen in the picture (9) of Cooling Castle in Kent. They could then look down between the brackets at the bottom of the wall, while the enemy could not see them because they were still behind the parapet.

There was yet another way of arranging for the defenders to keep the whole of their high walls in view, and watch if the enemy were trying to interfere with them. This was by building towers, sticking out from the wall here and there; from the sides of these towers, they could see everything that was going on at the foot of the curtain walls between (5). When these castles were first built, they did not have proper windows in the outer walls in case the enemy should shoot arrows through these; they only had narrow slits, called 'loops'. Some people suppose that the defenders shot arrows through these loops at the besiegers. It would, however, have been impossible to do this; the only shooting the defenders did was through the parapet at the top of a wall or tower. These loops were made simply so that the garrison could see what was going on and not be seen themselves. It was very awkward trying to watch through a narrow slit like this, as you could only see somebody if he were right in front, or moving away or towards you; so it was found to be better to have a cross-slit as well, so that you could also see people passing in front of the window from side to side.

When they began to build towers sticking out from the face of the castle wall, they found it a good idea to have the entrance to the castle between a pair of these 'wall-towers'. The old gatehouse tower was still there, but it now had a tower at each side as well, making it far more awkward for the enemy to get in, as he could be shot at from the sides of these two towers. This kind of very strong gatehouse began to be built during the reign of Henry III, from which time most castles had entrances of this sort; the Cooling Castle gatehouse (9), however, dates from the days of Richard II.

When we were talking about the wooden castles of William the Conqueror and his barons, we mentioned that there always had to be a bridge crossing the ditch, and that this was usually arranged so that part of it in front of the entrance gate could be taken away during a siege. This was rather an awkward arrangement and it was found far better to have a bridge which could be taken away quickly and put back again as easily. When they began to take away the woodwork of castles and replace it with stone, the wooden bridges were taken down and stone bridges built instead. Just where the stone bridge reached the entrance gate there was always a gap; generally a deep pit lined with stone. Across the top there was usually a wooden bridge, balanced on a beam like a see-saw, so that it could easily be tipped up on end in the pit, which the enemy had then no means of crossing until the bridge was tipped down flat again. Sometimes the end of the bridge was drawn up by chains wound up into the room in the tower above the entrance passage; another invention was to have this fixed to the top of a heavy door, called a 'portcullis', which slid down grooves in the side of this passage and blocked it as the bridge outside rose into the air.

We have now seen how castles were founded and how their wooden stockades became high walls and towers. Nearly all the castles we have been talking about so far were originally built in the days of the Normans. In another chapter we shall see how the changes in the ideas of castle-builders caused them to build entirely new castles, of a different sort, and in different places from the simple ditched kind that the Normans had used.

The Coming of the Castles

However peaceful the English castles may seem to us to-day, with their broken walls and towers rising above green turf and flowers, let us always remember that in their day they stood for war. They were quite different from the peaceful abbeys, palaces, and mansions; the castles always had to be ready for a sudden assault. They never had large garrisons; only a few men to act as caretakers. But when war broke out, the soldiers—most of these just country people—flocked to defend or attack them. Generally, the besiegers would try to starve the garrison out; there was not much hurry in those days, and nobody really wanted to get killed if he could help it. If the defenders decided that they could not hold out, they asked for a truce of forty days, in order that they could send a message to the leader of the side on which they were fighting, asking for permission to give up the castle.

Once a castle was taken the besiegers had to decide whether they wanted to garrison it themselves. If they did not they usually 'slighted' the castle. This meant doing something to it which would make it impossible for the opposite side to use it again. With an earthwork castle surrounded by wooden stockades, they just pulled these down and burnt them; then they set the local people to work on the earthwork, making them throw the earth of the ramparts and mounds back into the ditches again. They did not trouble to treat the whole castle in this way, but just that part of the defences where they were most easily attacked by a besieger. Stone walls were undermined and thrown down, and the corners of keeps cut off. Corfe Castle in Dorset shows us what the Roundheads did to castles after they had surrendered.

CHAPTER V

VILLAGE CHURCHES

In another chapter, we have explained how the Christian religion was spread throughout England by bishops each of whom looked after the people of an Anglo-Saxon kingdom or tribe. As the country people became Christians, they began to want their own particular priests, and each village had to have its own church in which the villagers could worship. As churches came to be built, the bishops began to give each of these a district, in which the priest was supposed to look after his people and see that they came to his church. These districts were known as 'parishes'; it was during the eighth century after the birth of Christ that England became divided up into the country parishes that we know to-day.

We have spoken of the churches which St. Augustine built, and how, a hundred years after his day, St. Aldhelm and St. Wilfred were building theirs in Wessex and Northumbria. From time to time, colonies of monks settled down in the countryside, and the bishops often set up their 'sees' in the monks' churches. But it was not until the parish priests came to divide up England among themselves that the real parish churches began to appear all over the countryside.

In the west and north, where the people had been Christians for centuries, they knew how to build little churches of rubble stone, each just a simple nave with a tiny chancel at the east end to hold the altar. But most of Anglo-Saxon England built its churches of wood, in the tower-like style with the four great posts, which we described in Chapter II. In the same chapter, however, we explained how the Anglo-Saxons were gradually learning how to build in rubble stone, which they collected in those places where it could be found, and which they used to rebuild the tower-like 'naves' of their churches; so that the terrible Norse pirates, who were raiding the countryside throughout the ninth century, could not burn them down. Each of these sturdy stone towers had, of course, the usual small 'chancel' built out from its east wall.

The trouble about these churches was that no one knew how to make them larger when the people of the parish increased and the church became too small for them. One way was to build three other small buildings, like chancels, one on each of the other three sides of the tower, with narrow arches leading to them. This, however, was very awkward, as no one in the side portions, or 'transepts', could see what the priest was doing in the chancel; so these could really only be used as small chapels.

It was monks coming from Rome who taught the Anglo-Saxons how to build churches in the Roman style: with long naves, like those which St. Augustine had built centuries before. So the parish churches began to have naves of this sort added, on the side of the tower opposite to the chancel, so that large numbers of people could gather together in the body of the church and all see clearly what was going on.

This is how great churches like our cathedrals and abbeys came to be planned. But you must remember that the monks had their choir under the central tower, and that the nave, which had its own altar at the eastern end, was quite cut off from the monks' part of the church, so that the people could not see this.

Now that the parish churches were all beginning to have long naves of the Roman type, the Anglo-Saxons began to stop building high tower-like churches. A tower in the middle of a church was really rather in the way. The tower arches were quite small, nothing like the great wide arches of the cathedrals; people found they could get a better view of the altar of a parish church if the nave went right up to the chancel arch, so they gave up building central towers such as the monks had in their churches.

So the parish churches went back, once again, to the old idea of having just a long nave and a chancel, as the people of the north and west had been doing ever since the days of the Romans. The monks' churches still kept the central tower, and the 'transepts' on either side, but by the time the Normans arrived, the parish churches were giving up their transepts so as to have simply a nave and chancel.

For several hundred years after this time, the little village church had just these two parts. Often the villagers widened their nave by taking away one of its walls and building it anew on a row of pillars and arches, so that an 'aisle' could be built alongside it; sometimes an aisle was added on each side of the nave. Sooner or later, all except the very smallest parish churches had a bell-tower built at the end of the nave opposite to the chancel; the tiniest had a little turret or 'bell-cote' perched on the end of the roof instead.

When the Normans came over here, they did not settle in very large numbers. Most of the men who came were either soldiers or monks. The soldiers, who arrived first, set the Anglo-Saxons to building castles for them; and then the monks made them build great monasteries. For a hundred years this went on, so that the Anglo-Saxons were unable to do anything much about their own buildings.

But during the long years when our ancestors were working for their Norman conquerors, they managed to teach themselves a great deal about the art of building in stone. They learnt how to make walls of properly cut stone, or 'masonry', instead of the roughly squared stones they had been using. When they were at last free to turn to their own neglected parish churches, they were able to rebuild these in a much finer fashion than before.

After the first rush of church and castle building, there was a slowing down during the troubled period when the followers of King Stephen and his rival, the Empress Matilda, fought up and down the country. Then came the reign of Henry II—one of the greatest of our kings—who brought peace to the land, and gave the country people a chance to get on with their building.

During the hundred years following the Norman Conquest, many Englishmen had been to the Crusades, where they had seen for themselves some of the fine churches of the Byzantines. They began to realize that they had been too quick to give up the central towers of their parish churches, and began to build them again. The picture of Shipley church (19) in Sussex shows the kind of church they built. You will notice, however, that they did not build 'transepts' beside the tower; these were all very well for the churches of the monks, who needed small chapels for special services, but they were of no use in small parish churches.

In an earlier chapter we spoke of the round bulges, or 'apses,' which the Romans, and also the Byzantines, always placed at the east ends of their churches to hold the altar. As it was difficult to make this sort of thing in woodwork, the Anglo-Saxon builders had not used it much, and it had gone out of fashion except with the monks, who always had apses at the east ends of their great churches. Some of the chancels of the parish churches built after the Norman Conquest had the ends of their chancels rounded off, so as to give them the shape of an apse; in Henry II's reign, however, church builders gave up apses altogether and went back to the square-ended chancel which had always been the really popular arrangement in this country.

The Roman churches always had their doorways at the west end, so that people could see the altar as they came in. But the short Anglo-Saxon churches always had the door at the side; in this climate, it was far less draughty. The churches built in the Roman fashion, with the doorway at the end, were so uncomfortable in winter that the builders found it a good idea to make a porch outside the door which would help to keep some of the draughts away.

One of the most important things connected with a parish church is the bell which calls the country people to church. Every church had to have a place for hanging a bell. With the tower-like churches, it was easy to find a spot high up among the beams at the top of the tower, but when the parish churches became long, low buildings, another place for the bell had to be found.

What the builders did was to raise the walls of the porch at the end of the nave so as to make a tall, thin tower, at the top of which they could hang their bells. Long after the porch at the end of the nave had gone out of fashion, the bell-tower remained there. Most of our parish churches have one, often very tall and magnificent (A) at the end of the church away from the chancel.

The Anglo-Saxons thought it so important for churches to have bell-towers that any big landowner who had a church with a bell-tower on his lands was given the noble title of 'thane'. Those who could not build stone towers built timber ones. In Norfolk and Suffolk, where there was neither stone nor timber, they built flint towers, making them round for the reason which we talked about in another chapter.

Once the bell-tower had taken the place of the porch at the

end of the nave, and it was agreed that churches should always be entered at the side, the doorways there often had porches as well. Churches usually have their doorways on the side nearest the village; if the village is all round the church, or at one end, the main doorway is generally on the south side to keep the church warmer in winter.

The first churches the Anglo-Saxons built were all made very simply, with the nave just a plain building under one roof. As time went on, however, the churches became too small for their parishioners, so that some way of making them bigger had to be found. We saw how the old churches of Rome were made as wide as possible by supporting the walls in the middle of the building on rows of columns. The English builders did the same, but they used arched openings instead, leading to the 'aisles' which ran along the sides of the nave. At first the arches were supported on pieces of wall, called 'piers', left between them; later, however, when the builders became more skilled, they were able to build their 'arcades'—as rows of arches are called—upon properly formed pillars of cut stone.

It was not until French monks began to build their great churches in the west of England that the Anglo-Saxons first learnt about round stone pillars; we can see their work at Gloucester cathedral and Tewkesbury abbey. But by the reign of Henry II, most parish churches of any size had a row of arches down each side of the nave, supported upon sturdy stone pillars (14). In the east of England, however, they still built their cathedral and abbey churches with massive square 'piers', as they had always done; but they made these a little less clumsy-looking by cutting slender round 'shafts' up the corners and on the sides of the piers. After the end of the twelfth century, however, all 'aisled' churches were being built upon pillars: not round, but shaped into patterns according to the ideas of the masons who built them.

The centre part of the nave of a church with aisles soon became raised above the roofs of these, as had been the case with the old churches of Rome; these 'clerestories' had, of course, small windows in them to light the middle of the church. From the time of the Crusades onwards, when central towers were coming back into fashion, large cross-shaped churches were built again with transepts on either side of the tower; the naves of these churches often had aisles on both sides.

Village Churches

But the ordinary village church was nearly always just a simple nave and chancel, with a bell-tower at the west end if the villagers could afford one (and could get hold of enough stone, and masons to work upon it). Many churches, of course, had in the end to be enlarged by an aisle on one or both sides.

Let us take a glance into one of these village churches and see what arrangements there are inside. As the entrance will probably be on the south—the sunnier—side, we shall then have to turn to the right, when we get inside, in order to face the altar. Until the reign of Henry VIII, when what is known as the 'Reformation' took place, altars were always made of stone, and were shaped rather like the 'table tombs' which you can see in our churchyards. But when it became wrong to talk of 'altars'—which were what heathen peoples had used for their sacrifices—and proper to talk of 'communion tables', the altars of English churches became wooden tables just like a dining-room table of those days. If you care to lift the ornamental cloth 'frontal' of the altar in an old parish church, you will often find that there is a fine old table behind.

At the opposite, or west, end of the church you will always find a font for christenings. Often it is by the entrance door-way; for it is by baptism that we enter the Church. The first fonts were like baths sunk into the floor; people got right inside them when they were baptised, as if they had been wading into the river of Jordan. But in England, where the climate was not suitable for this, and a cross made of holy water was all that was believed necessary, the font became a stone tub standing on the floor of the church. This, however, was rather too low for the priest to reach comfortably; so, after the Norman Conquest, the font was raised up on a low pillar so that he could get at it more easily. Instead of a round tub, the bowl of the font was carved out of a square block of stone; the finest fonts of Anglo-Norman days have the corners of the block supported by four little pillars or 'shafts'. As time passed, both the central pillar and the block containing the bowl itself, became eight-sided; the masons and carvers got to work and fitted the two parts together so that the whole font came to be like a carved stone goblet, something like the 'chalice' used at the communion service (16).

Fonts often stand upon several steps, so as to make them look more important. The bowl of the font was always covered to prevent dust from settling in it. As time went on, the woodcarvers who were making the beautiful seats in which the monks sat in their choirs, and the graceful wooden screens by which these were surrounded, turned to making tall spire-like covers for the fonts of parish churches.

When we were describing the great churches of the monks, as the abbeys became more wealthy and powerful, we explained how the abbots began to lengthen the eastern parts of their churches, where the High Altar was, in order to provide more space in which to bury important people, and at the same time to make this part of the church more magnificent.

At this time, however, the parish churches still had nothing more than a little chancel. The parish chancels were not much bigger than they had been when churches were first being built. But more people were going to church, so that more room had to be provided for them by enlarging the naves of the churches. This meant that the chancels were getting too small for the size of the church. So, after the end of the reign of Henry II, finer chancels began to appear; not just little buildings in which to put the altar, as the old chancels had been, but perhaps twice as long, lit by large windows and often ornamented so as to make the chancel the most beautiful part of the whole church. Many of the chancels of the reign of Henry III are so fine that they have been kept just as they were without alteration.

The chancel of a parish church of the Middle Ages nearly always has, in the wall on the south or right-hand side of the altar, an ornamental opening with a stone basin carved into it. This is the 'piscina', where the priest washed the sacred cup or 'chalice' after holy communion. Opposite to the piscina is another opening, with no basin, and closed with a wooden door; this is the cupboard, or 'aumbry', in which the chalice was kept.

Near to the piscina and sometimes forming part of it there is often a row of openings, the bottoms of which form seats. These —which are called 'sedilia'—are seats for the priests; the builders of the Middle Ages were fond of making sedilia very ornamental so that these were often the most charming pieces of decoration in the whole chancel.

The choirs of the monks' churches were always, as has been explained, entirely surrounded by carved screens. At the end of the choir farthest from the altar was the choir screen itself, with a doorway in the middle through which the monks entered from the nave of the great church. Late in the Middle Ages—about the time of the Wars of the Roses—the builders of parish churches were beginning to copy many of the things which they saw in the churches of the monks. In particular they liked to build a screen of carved wood or stone across the arch which led from the nave into the chancel (33). It had a doorway in the centre, just like one of those in the monks' churches. On top of this screen, and filling up part of the chancel arch, they often put a huge cross—or 'rood'; these chancel screens in parish churches are therefore known as 'rood-screens'. They were often finished at the top with an elaborately carved wooden gallery upon which the priest could walk and attend to any candles which might be burning beside the rood. This gallery is known as the 'rood-loft'; it was reached by a spiral staircase built into the wall at one end, called the 'rood-stair'. You may often find the old stairs which once led to a rood-loft destroyed during the reign of Queen Elizabeth.

Spiral stairs may often be seen in old parish churches; especially for climbing to the belfry in the west tower. The church porch which, as we have seen, helped to keep away some of the draught from the main doorway, very often had a room built above it in which church books were kept and where private meetings could be held; these upper rooms also were reached by spiral stairs.

We have seen how churches grew: first by having their naves enlarged to hold more people, and then by having their chancels enlarged to match. The proud abbots, with their great churches, had been all-powerful in the early days of the Middle Ages; the country priests, with their little parish churches, had taken a very unimportant place. But as time went on, and the monks became less popular, the life of the parish churches became more important. The country people were understanding more about Christianity and the Church and beginning to think about these matters for themselves. Instead of going into the monks' churches they took more interest in their own. They liked to hear sermons preached by their own parish priests; they gathered in the churches, not only to worship God but to learn. So the naves of the churches began to be more and more important and, about the time of Edward I, the people of the country parishes were thinking once more of rebuilding their churches still larger and finer. A new architectural style was giving buildings tall, graceful pillars, wide arches, and large windows letting in plenty of light. Many of the naves of our parish churches date from this period (16).

These fine new naves of the days of the first three Edwards were making many of the old chancels look very old-fashioned. Some chancels had been widened by people who had built chapels alongside them in which they and their families might be buried and in which prayers could be said for their souls. The new chancels which were built about the time of the Wars of the Roses were therefore made with aisles on both sides which could be used for chapels of this sort.

The country families at this time were becoming very rich from selling the wool of their flocks. Ordinary farmers, too, were making plenty of money, and merchants in the country towns were profiting from the wool trade with Europe. In the sheep-farming districts, especially Norfolk and Suffolk, they began to build fine new parish churches instead of keeping on enlarging the old ones which had been growing through the centuries. Instead of building a separate nave and a separate chancel they brought the whole church under one roof so that it was like a great wide lofty hall. The division between the nave and the chancel was made simply by having a screen passing across the church; generally crossing the aisles as well, so that the chancel chapels could also be divided off from that part of the church used by the public.

The monks in their churches had encouraged many craftsmen in stone and wood; as the monasteries became less and less popular, and there was not so much for their craftsmen to do in the great churches, these came to work in the parish churches instead. In particular, they filled the parish churches with beautiful woodwork; especially in the screens round the chapels, and, of course, the great rood-screen itself (33).

Throughout most of the Middle Ages, the worshippers in the churches had stood or knelt during the whole service. With everyone getting rich and comfort-loving, the people who worshipped in the parish churches felt that they should have seats to sit on, as well as the monks in their choirs. So the joiners began to make for them beautiful carved pews; many of which to-day, five hundred years later, we can still find in our churches. As sermons grew longer and longer, people were very glad to have these pews. After the Reformation, when Henry VIII made many changes, sermons became the most important part

of the church service. In the Middle Ages the priest had usually preached from the chancel steps, but by the time of Queen
Elizabeth he generally had a beautifully carved pulpit, raised
high above the heads of his congregation. Many of these fine
pulpits remain to this day.

In an earlier chapter we explained how bell-towers first came
to be built at the west end of the naves of the parish churches.
A bell-tower was always very expensive to build. It needed a
great many stones; as the tower grew ever higher, these had to
be raised with much difficulty to the scaffolds where the masons
were laying them. As a tower might cost as much as the whole
of the rest of the church put together, it is no wonder that we
do not find many old church towers, compared with the hundreds of ancient churches that we still have left. It was not really
until the wool trade brought riches that the country people
were able to afford to have towers to their churches; but then
they certainly made up for lost time. In the wealthy sheep-
farming districts of the east of England, and in Somerset, no
expense seems to have been spared in raising tall and beautiful
towers at the west end of parish churches (A).

At first, towers were covered at the top, like any other building, with a steep roof overhanging the face of the wall. In the
south-east of England, they liked to have a tiny wooden spire
perched on the top of the tower roof to finish it off. About the
time of Henry III, these little wooden spires got larger and
larger until they took up most of the roof of the tower. In other
parts of England, where there was not so much wood for building, and where they were not so clever at making things with
it, people began to wish they could have spires like this also.

The masons of Northamptonshire and Lincolnshire have always been among the best in this country; this is because they
lived in a place where they were always able to collect plenty of
rough stone with which to build rubble walls. Later, when they
discovered that they also had very good building stone lying
beneath their fields, they learnt how to quarry this out of the
ground, cut it up into blocks, and build fine stone churches
with it. By the reign of Edward I they had taught themselves
how to copy the wooden spires of the south-east in stone; most
of the churches of the two great masonry counties have beautiful
stone spires on their church towers.

At the beginning of the Middle Ages, all English roofs were

very sharply pointed; it has already been explained that this was so that snow would not lie upon them and drift in amongst the thatch or shingles. In Derbyshire, however, there are mines in which lead ore can be found. Lead can be cast into sheets for roofing buildings; the Derbyshire mines have been sending their lead for roofing the buildings of Europe since the days of the Anglo-Saxons.

As time went on, the plumbers who laid the lead became very skilful at making watertight joints between the pieces they were using; this meant that there was no need to worry any more about having steep roofs. As a matter of fact, lead is very heavy; if you try to make it lie on a steep roof, it is apt to slip off. About the time of Edward I, therefore, builders began to make their roofs much flatter.

The old roofs had overhung the face of the wall, making what is known as 'eaves'. It is difficult to do this with lead roofs, because it is difficult to finish off the edge of the lead properly. It is much better to build a stone parapet on top of the wall and let the lead finish behind this. In the last half of the Middle Ages—say from the end of the reign of Henry III—all lead-roofed buildings had parapets. Many of these were 'battle-mented', in imitation of those on the tops of castle walls. In the end, parapets became very richly ornamented, often in imitation of wooden panelling.

As parapets prevented the rainwater from falling straight off the roof, openings had to be left in the parapet wall for this purpose. The rainwater was generally led through a stone spout or 'gargoyle'; you have probably often seen these—carved into amusing faces or weird-looking animal heads—peering out from the tops of the walls of churches.

As all important buildings of the later part of the Middle Ages had parapets, all towers had to have them as well. Thus you will find that most English spires are built up not from the faces of the tower walls, as the old spires used to be, but from behind a parapet.

We have explained how a parish church has two main parts: the nave for the people and the chancel for the priest and his altar. The priest had to look after the chancel and the parishioners took care of the nave. There is one kind of church which has, however, no parishioners; this is the building which we call a chapel. Chapels have neither naves nor chancels; there is simply the one building with an altar at the end. During the Middle Ages there were many hundreds of chapels, built for all sorts of different reasons. Castles had them; also the palaces of the king and the great houses of the chief men of the land. There was always a fine chapel in a bishop's palace.

There were many wayside chapels, often built by someone in order that prayers might be said in it for his soul after he was dead. These prayers were called 'chantries'; you may often see tiny 'chantry chapels' built over the tombs inside our great churches. At the end of the Middle Ages, the chantry chapels were the most beautiful things the masons and carvers worked upon; even when the great churches themselves had seen the last of the monks who built them, people still took great pride in their family tombs.

Chapels were founded for all sorts of reasons besides the saying of chantry prayers. We have said that great houses and palaces had chapels; colleges founded for the education of students always had one. Some of the Tudor chapels are very fine indeed; the most famous of all is probably that at King's College at Cambridge (13).

At the time of the Reformation in the reign of Henry VIII, the Church which had been so important and powerful during the Middle Ages disappeared altogether. In another chapter we shall see how Gothic architecture in England came to an end; to be followed by another architecture which for a long time nobody understood properly. New parish churches were built just as plain square boxes, with little that was beautiful about them. Fortunately, however, there were still left in the country many hundreds of fine old buildings, with centuries of the history of England lying with the stones of their ancient walls. It is indeed lucky for us that, when Henry VIII pulled down the great abbeys, he left to us our little village churches.

CHAPTER VI

'NORMAN' ARCHITECTURE

Everyone has heard of Norman architecture. Until about a hundred years ago it used to be called 'Saxon' architecture; but writers about architecture in those days decided that they would call everything built after 1066 'Norman', and only what was built before this date 'Saxon'. This is very unfair to a great many Anglo-Saxons who were still continuing to build long after the Normans came. For the same reason, it is really quite wrong to call the architecture which came after the Conquest 'Norman'; for the only Normans who came over were either people who became landowners, or who founded or entered monasteries. The life of Anglo-Saxon England and its craftsmen still went on as before. A baron or an abbot might set out the general idea of a new castle, or a great church; but it was Anglo-Saxon builders who actually did the job. For centuries they had been teaching themselves new ideas in architecture; the Normans taught them very little more. All the invaders did was to make people work on castles and abbeys, when they ought to have been doing something to their own houses and churches. It was not until about the time of Henry II—by which time most of the castles and abbeys had been built—that the Anglo-Saxons were able to get on with their village buildings. We call the architecture that they used 'Norman'; it is a pity, but there it is.

In another chapter we explained how, while the Anglo-Saxons were really at their best when building in timber, they at last taught themselves how to make walls out of rough pieces of stones they found lying about. It was a long time, however, before they discovered that there was a strip of England, running roughly from the Wash to Somersetshire, beneath the soil of which there was very good stone which could be quarried out and cut up with axes into square blocks for making good walls.

Walls of this sort, made with properly squared stones, are called 'masonry', and the men who make these walls are 'masons'.

In those days it could not have been an easy matter getting the large pieces of stone from the quarry to the place where the actual building was being done. Wherever possible boats were used; on the eastern side of England there are plenty of rivers upon which stone could be carried. The last part of the journey from the banks of the river had to be done by ponies carrying the stone slung across their backs. When it at last reached the place where building was going on, the stone was handed over to the masons. These men worked in rough shelters, called 'lodges', made out of poles and roughly thatched. First of all, the lumps of stone were roughly hacked into square blocks by chipping them with axes. Until about the reign of Henry II this was all that could be done in the way of 'working' the stone; in early buildings you can still see the marks of the axes. By the reign of Henry III, however, some masons were using a sort of very wide chisel, which they held to the sides of the block of stone and hit with a heavy mallet. In this way they smoothed off all the axe-marks from the stones, leaving instead scores of tiny parallel lines, each being the place where the wide chisel was hit by the mallet. As the masons cutting the stones in the lodges finished each one ready for use, they often made their marks upon it, so that the 'master mason' could tell who had made each stone and could complain if one was the wrong size or shape. Each mason had his own mark, and his apprentices or sons would take this over and add a tiny alteration; there are hundreds of these marks to be found in the stones of our ancient buildings.

When we are walking round a great cathedral of the Middle Ages and looking at its architecture, we must not forget all the men who have helped with the finding, carrying, cutting, and building into that cathedral of all the thousands of stones of which its architecture is made. We must also remember that each stone is set into mortar, the making of which is itself a skilled task. Mortar is made by burning limestone—probably at the limestone quarry itself—until it becomes quicklime; then it is mixed with water, and sand is added to make the sort of stuff you have seen builders mixing up beside houses they are building. So in the Middle Ages there were the men who quarried limestone, and those who mixed the mortar, and also those very humble people who just carried it up to the scaffold, or hauled it up in big pots, to where the men were laying the stones. There had to be a great deal of fetching and carrying in those days; poor men had to lug up heavy stones on to the scaffold as fast as the builders needed them. Later on they were able to use a very simple arrangement of a rope and pulley to help them lift heavier stones; you will be able to see that, all through the Middle Ages, stones were getting larger and larger, as people found better ways of hauling them up on to the scaffold.

The most important work of all went on where the stones were actually being laid in their beds of mortar, under the orders of the master mason himself, who would all the time be calling down for special stones to be sent to him, and always keeping one eye on the masons building the wall. Walls made of worked stone—that is to say 'masonry'—are built in a particular way. When the thickness of the wall has been decided upon, it is built up in *two thicknesses*, one of which has its neat smooth 'face' showing to the inside, and the other to the outside of the building. In the middle of the wall, the masons tipped all the bits cut from the stones, mixed with mortar to hold them together. In very bad building they sometimes used mortar with so little lime in it that it was nearly all sand or stone chippings; sometimes they even used earth.

Some of the more important parts of the building—such as the pillars or arches—had to have their stones specially cut in the lodges by masons who were more skilful than those who were merely cutting square stones for the wall. These masons used fine chisels, for they had to cut and make perfect all the complicated 'mouldings' which passed round arches, doorways, and other kinds of openings through the wall. The most skilful workmen of all were the carvers who cut the beautiful ornamentation, for example, capitals; the stone-carving of the Middle Ages is very beautiful and there was a time when it was spreading to all parts of the building, especially in great churches.

But as well as the masons, there were also our old friends the carpenters. Some of these were making scaffolds of poles, beams and planks; in many old buildings you can still see the holes where the ends of the scaffold beams used to rest when the building was going up. Another job the carpenters had to do was to make wooden frames upon which the stones forming an arch had to be laid; these frames, like the scaffolding, were taken away when the work was finished. When it came to roof-making, of course, the carpenters took the building over altogether. In England roofs were always made of wood, and carpenters of the Middle Ages became more and more skilful in the making of beautiful roofs (17). Sometimes they copied the designs that the masons were using for the stonework; more often, perhaps, it was the carpenters who gave the masons ideas for new designs.

So we have seen that a great many men gave their help in the building of the fine churches of the Middle Ages. When the carpenter had finished, the plumber had next to appear; casting his sheets of lead, hauling them up to the roof, and laying them with all the great skill of his trade. A very special job the plumber had to do was to make the little lead strips in which the painted glass of the windows was set; he had to work hand in hand with the glazier who actually fixed the glass in position. In a big window of the Middle Ages the leaded glass could not be made strong enough without a number of iron bars let into the stonework for the glass to be fixed to with wire. The smith had to come along and make these bars; he also had to make the iron 'hooks and bands' for hanging the doors, and all kinds of bolts and bars and catches for fastening doors and windows. The smith's most important job was sharpening the masons' tools; the work was hard on the edges of the chisels and axes, especially with certain kinds of stones.

All these people who were busy building the large cathedrals of the Middle Ages usually came under the orders of the master mason. The master carpenter was also a very important man; the master mason had probably to be very careful to keep on the right side of the master carpenter. It was really these two men together who gave us the architecture of the Middle Ages.

In early days, however, they did not actually design the main lines of the buildings, especially in the case of large churches or castles. It would have been the great man himself who had ordered the work who would explain what he wanted, and would give the master mason a general idea of what he had in mind. A Norman baron might possibly have had very few ideas on building matters; a powerful abbot, however, might very well have studied something of the design of great churches. If not, he would probably be able to get hold of somebody—possibly a monk—who had travelled about a great deal, so that, between them, they would rough out the main lines of the church. During the reign of Henry II, Alnoth, the king's engineer who helped the king when he was besieging castles, became so interested in buildings that in the end he was actually designing the king's castles and palaces for him. Alnoth was one of the first English architects.

But by far the greater part of the design of buildings was left to the master masons. As time went on they began to make their own sketches of various parts of the building. The master mason generally designed all the 'mouldings', marking them out exactly as he wanted them on a piece of board, and giving it to the stone-cutters in the lodges to cut their stones by it. These full-size drawings of architectural 'details' are known as 'templates'; Gothic architecture was at times being carried about England by masons stealing each other's templates.

It was during the Golden Age of Anglo-Saxon England— that is to say, the hundred years before the Norman Conquest —that the Anglo-Saxons learned the art of masonry. As we have already seen, the coming of the Normans made little difference, although they certainly encouraged the Anglo-Saxon masons to build fine churches and castles. It was, however, still the Anglo-Saxons who were doing the work; to-day, nevertheless, we call the architecture that they turned out after 1066 'Norman' architecture.

This architecture was really very simple in its general lines. All the arches, for instance, were just plain half circles. In the wooden buildings that were being made at the same time, the carpenters were using wooden arches which were made out of two curved timbers meeting at a point. But it was not until a hundred years or so after the Norman Conquest that *stone* arches became pointed.

We have already explained that if you want to make a stone arch you must first make a framework of wood to build it on. When the Anglo-Saxons first began to build arches, they used a framework which was as wide as the whole thickness of the wall in which the arch was to be made; this was the Roman way of doing things; it just left a plain underside to the finished arch. But this way of framing up the arch timbers used a lot of wood; as it all had to be thrown away afterwards this was rather a wasteful way of doing things.

'Norman' Architecture

So a better way was invented. The carpenters made a much narrower framework· just enough to take one 'ring' of arch-stones. They used this ring of stones to carry another which was a little wider than the first one; then they went on adding wider rings until at last they had a ring of arch stones which was the full thickness of the wall they had to support. The kind of arch this made can be seen in the picture (14) of Hullaving-ton church. The rings of arch stones are called 'orders' (this must not be confused with the 'Orders of Architecture' which were used by the Greeks and Romans when they were design-ing their columns).

The pieces of wall that are left between the arches in a row of arches (or 'arcade') are known as 'piers'. The Anglo-Saxons made the sides of their piers match the 'orders' of the arches above. After the Norman Conquest, the masons used to cut little columns or 'shafts' on the angles of their piers as a kind of ornament.

At the time of the Conquest it was the eastern part of Eng-land which was doing most of the building; the west was still very much behind the times. But with the Conquest many French monks came into England, and these started to build monasteries in the west. In France, at this time, they were not building their arches upon the square 'piers' that the Anglo-Saxons were using, but had round pillars rather like a clumsy copy of the columns of the old temples. So these French monks brought with them into the west of England the idea of using round pillars. If you go to Gloucester cathedral or Tewkes-bury abbey you can see the enormous fat round pillars which were some of the first of their kind to be built in this coun-try. A hundred years later they had become much smaller and neater. By the time of Henry II, even the humble parish churches were having their arches springing from slender round pillars (14), each finished off at the top with a rough copy of the 'Corinthian' capital that the French monks had also brought to England.

In the hundred years before the Conquest, the Germans were building their great churches with both piers and pillars next to each other in the same arcade; first one and then the other. The fashion spread to eastern England; even a hundred years after the Norman Conquest, you can still see churches built with their pillars not all the same. Generally they are first round

75

and then eight-sided. You can see the German kind of arcade even better in some of the great cathedrals of the east, especially at Durham (7).

We have mentioned before that the great churches of the Normans had aisles in two stories. The floors of the upper galleries were not wooden boards but stone slabs; these had to be carried on stone arches. The arches were all joined together, so that the whole of the ceiling of the aisle beneath was arched. A stone ceiling like this is called 'vaulting'. The simplest kind of vaulting is the long stone arch which reaches from one end of a building to the other; this tunnel-like arrangement is called 'barrel-vaulting'. A stone ceiling like this, however, is rather dull and gloomy; it also makes it very difficult to cut any arches or windows at the sides. So the builders arranged for every barrel-vault to be cut across by a number of short pieces of barrel-vault; one opposite each main arch of the building. This is called a 'cross-vault'; you will see many examples of it in our ancient buildings. The sharp edges where the long vault and the cross-vaults meet each other are known as the 'groins', so this vault is sometimes called a 'groined vault'.

A stone ceiling like this was a very difficult thing for the early masons to build. It had all to be pieced together on a strong wooden framework and the stones all had to be carefully cut and fitted. Obviously they could not make enough wooden frameworks for the whole church at once; it would have used far too much wood, all of which would have been wasted afterwards. The thing to do was to make one piece of framework which could be used again and again all down the church. This meant that the church had to be designed so that each bit of the 'vaulting' was the same size in order that the same piece of framework could be used for any part. The simplest way of arranging for this was to make the framework square and have the church set out as a number of squares of this size. This is what the old builders did, making the aisles of their great churches in square 'bays'. It was much easier to set out a church on the ground in this way. They could tie four poles of the right length together in a square, and just move this frame about on the ground, marking out with pegs each place where it rested, until they had the plan of your church all laid out. Very often they made the central part of the church just twice the width of the aisles in order to make things still easier for the builders.

'Norman' Architecture

During the Middle Ages, our great churches were all set out in 'bays'. Each of these is the distance between the pillars of the great arcade which supports the main part of the building; or, if there should be no aisles, the distance between the 'buttresses' which support the main walls. As time went on, and the builders became more clever at throwing wide arches across from pillar to pillar, the 'bays' became wider. In the Norman abbey churches, however, the width of the bay was usually about half the width of the main part of the building.

All this was first invented so that the heavy stone vaulting which supported the floor of the gallery could be built as easily as possible. After the Normans had been here for some time, however, the masons discovered a new way of building a vault without having to use the complicated wooden framework that they had needed for a groined vault. They used the same method as they had done in the case of the main arches; building two stone arches which crossed each other along the lines of where the 'groins' would have been in the case of a groined vault. On these stone arches, or 'ribs' as they were called, they were able to build their vault without using any more of the wooden framework. This is the origin of the beautiful vaulted ceilings that we see in our great cathedral churches (1, 7, 8). Once the masons had discovered how to build vaulting with ribs, they were able to give up using squares when they were setting out their buildings; thus it did not matter how wide the main arches were, compared with the width of the aisles, for the builders could cover any shape they liked with a ribbed vault.

The windows in the days of the Normans were still very simple; hardly less so than before the Conquest. In the great churches, however, more glass was being used, so that the windows could be made much bigger and yet keep out the rain and wind. In the great churches, the largest windows of all were in the aisles; there was a smaller row lighting the galleries, and, high above all, the windows in the 'clerestory' above the aisle roofs. So as to be able to get at these clerestory windows to clean them, the masons always arranged for a little passage to be made in the thickness of the wall along which the window cleaners could walk (6, 7); on the side of this passage towards the church there were usually three little arches to each of the windows. These arches were supported by small round 'shafts' or tiny

77

columns. When the masons wanted to make a very wide window; you may often see them at the tops of church towers, arched tops supported by a round shaft like this. A window having two openings side by side is called a 'two-light' window or 'bifora'; this kind of window, which was used by the Byzantine architects, may be found in the belfry stories of some of our very early church towers, even before the days of the Normans, and it came into fashion again for belfries a hundred years after the Conquest.

Like their windows, the doorways of the days of the Normans always had a half-round arch. The trick of building arches in 'orders' led to the same method being used for doorways. In the case of the large arches, the lowermost ring of stones was always in the centre of the thickness of the wall. With doorways, however, it was always on the inside of the wall, so that all the 'orders' showed on one side of the arch only, making the doorway look as fine as possible from the outside. Each order was carried down to the ground—as had been the case with the arch piers—and the Normans were just as fond of having ornamental shafts on their doorways as they had been in the case of the piers inside their churches. The line of these shafts was often carried up and round each of the orders of the arch. It was here that the carvers set to work. Most of you must at one time or another have seen one of the beautiful carved doorways that date from the days of the Normans.

We still do not know how the carvers got all their many hundreds of patterns—possibly some of them came from as far away as the East—but they certainly spared no pains to make the entrance to their great churches as beautiful as they could. Sometimes the patterns were made with leaves and flowers, and even animals and men and women. On the other hand, the designs were sometimes very simple and roughly cut; but even then the carvers made up for their lack of art by the pains they took to leave not an inch of stone without some kind of ornament, however humble. A very popular trick was to carve each of the arch stones into a shape like the head of a dragon; possibly they got this idea from the Danes. But the most common design of all was simply to cut notches in the edges of the stone, so that the notches made a zigzag line running right round the arch. They tried all sorts of different ways of using this zigzag line (which is called a 'chevron' and is something like the stripes on a policeman's sleeve); it may be seen in some form or another in most of the buildings of Norman days (7).

There had not been many arches in the first stone churches of the Anglo-Saxons; the entrance door and the chancel arch would probably have been all there were. Even by the time of the Norman Conquest, only the largest churches had aisles with rows of arches separating these from the main body of the church. But as time went on, and the English builders began to think less of carpentry and more of masonry when setting to work on their more important buildings, they began to learn more and more about arches. The 'ordered' arch was a great discovery, especially when the builders saw what a fine effect it gave when used on doorways. They came to love the long rows of arches—the 'arcades'—which lined both the ground and gallery floors of their great churches. In the end they began to use arcades simply as an ornament, built into the face of the wall. They used small arches, sometimes criss-crossing each other as if they had been wooden struts, both inside and outside the building. In some of the great eastern churches, such as Peterborough or Norwich there are rows of these small arcades making bands all round the building. Towards the end of what we call the Norman period, that is to say during the reign of Henry II, when more and more towers were being built—to churches as well as in castles—the masons delighted to finish off the tops of these towers with rows of arcading.

At the time of the Norman Conquest, there were two kinds of church towers in England. The great churches, and some of the more important of the parish churches, had low 'lantern' towers in the centre with windows in them to light the church at this point. Some churches had, at the western ends of their naves, tall towers to carry bells. We have explained how the arcades inside the churches were changing in appearance as the arches grew ever wider and the clumsy piers still more slender. The most important part of a great church was the 'crossing' which lay beneath its central tower; one of the oldest and finest is that at St. Albans abbey (6). If you look closely at this or any other crossing, you will see that the tower over it is supported upon four very tall arches leading into the four arms of the church. The sides of these high arches are being pushed in, all the time, by the lower arches on either side. The builders of the great Norman churches were never able to understand why it was that their low lantern towers were always collapsing; it was, however, because of the bursting of the sides of the tall arches which supported them. At the very end of the Norman period, however, the abbots were starting to make their central towers higher, by building a belfry story on top of the 'lantern' in which were the windows lighting the church below. Towers which were raised in this way did not fall down, as the weight of the upper part of the tower kept it steady, so that the side arches were not able to burst the four big ones. It was not until a great many years afterwards, however, that English builders began to realize that the more weight they put upon the four pillars of the crossing, the less chance there was of these collapsing. Then it was that we got our beautiful central towers of which we are so proud today (2, 18).

The chief buildings that remain from the days of the Normans are of course the great churches. There are, as well, quite a fair number of fine castle keeps, some of them—like that of Norwich for instance—were as beautifully ornamented as a fine church. Nearly all the rest of the buildings in England were, however, still of timber. They have nearly all disappeared; but just a very few are left to show us that the wooden halls of the Anglo-Saxons were still being used long after the Norman Conquest. At the very end of the Norman period, some of these halls were being rebuilt with stone pillars and arches instead of the old wooden posts and beams. There were some very fine halls of Norman days; Westminster Hall, the greatest of them all, was built by William Rufus. The picture (15) shows the hall of Oakham castle in Rutland; it dates from the very end of the period.

Although the homes of the people were simply huts, there were a few very small stone houses being built during the Norman period. Some of these were in castles, some in the palaces of the king and those of his bishops. The little houses, which did not begin to appear until about a hundred years after the Conquest, were, however, very humble buildings. It is true that they had two stories. Some of them even had the upper floor supported on stone vaulting like the floors of the galleries in the great churches. But each house was no bigger than a stable for half a dozen horses with its hayloft over. Yet in their day, they were the finest houses in Norman England.

CHAPTER VII

GOTHIC ARCHITECTURE

After what we told you at the beginning of the last chapter, it will seem strange enough to you that the architecture which the Anglo-Saxon masons used after 1066 is to-day called 'Norman'. It is still more difficult to understand why the architectural style which was used in England throughout most of the Middle Ages should be called 'Gothic'. The Goths, after all, were people who lived in eastern Europe; they had no architecture at all and, anyway, had been forgotten centuries before the days of the Gothic cathedrals.

Gothic architecture—as we shall see later—died out at the time of the 'Reformation' which took place in Tudor days. It was followed by an architecture which was, in fact, the old architecture of Rome, brought back into England by learned men who had studied it abroad. These scholars despised the architecture of the Middle Ages, which they said was uncivilized and only fit for barbarians such as the old Goths. So they called the style in which our most beautiful buildings had been raised—'Gothic'!

As probably many of you already know, the great difference between Gothic architecture and what we call Norman is that whereas 'Norman' architecture always uses a simple half-round arch, the Gothic architects used instead, a stronger kind of arch which was pointed in shape. As a matter of fact, the timber builders had been using a wooden arch, made out of two curved struts meeting at a point, even before the Norman Conquest; but the people who, two hundred years or so ago, began to study English architecture, took no notice of timber buildings and only interested themselves in those of stone. As we talk about Gothic architecture, we shall find that it is only the stone buildings which have been arranged into 'styles'; wooden buildings have been left out altogether.

Pointed stone arches first began to be built at the end of the reign of Henry II. From then until the end of the century, is a period during which the general architectural style is 'Norman', but the arches are pointed instead of being half-round. This short period is sometimes called the 'Transitional', because it links up the 'Norman' with the 'Gothic'.

Gothic architecture in England was used roughly from A.D. 1200 to 1500. The architects who studied it a hundred years or so ago discovered that by taking these three centuries they could divide Gothic architecture up into three 'periods'. It was not a very good arrangement, but we have got so used to it now that it is best to stick to it. These three periods are some-times simply called the thirteenth, fourteenth and fifteenth cen-turies. The architects we have referred to, however, gave a name to each of the three: calling them 'Early English', 'Decorated' and 'Perpendicular'. It is these three periods that we shall now talk about.

The difficulty is that buildings which seem to be in the same architectural style may not have been built at the same time; this is either because one was more important than the other and had better men designing it, or because it was in a part of the country that was more up-to-date in its ways of building. If somebody had a new idea while he was building a cathedral, it might be fifty years before somebody borrowed that idea when he was building a parish church. If somebody invented a new kind of window in London, for example, it might take a very long time for the idea to reach, say, Carlisle. So it is very difficult to try to discover the actual date at which a building was designed; all you can do is to say that it belongs to a par-ticular 'style'. Roughly speaking, the three styles we have just mentioned—Early English, Decorated, and Perpendicular— fit in with the thirteenth, fourteenth, and fifteenth centuries where parish churches and country buildings generally are con-cerned. In the great cathedrals, however, the style comes in about half a century earlier in each case; so it is not always pos-sible to call a 'Decorated' window, for example, a 'fourteenth-century window', as it may in fact date from the end of the thirteenth century. So it is probably safer, when you are looking at a building, to try to recognize which of the styles it belongs to, rather than to try to guess the date at which it was built.

Possibly the most beautiful period in Gothic architecture is the first of the three, which we have come to call the 'Early

English'. From the simple half-round arches of Norman England, we suddenly began building very sharply pointed ones; so that in a few years English buildings changed from being sturdy and rugged-looking, and began to arrange themselves into far more slender and graceful shapes. The old-fashioned galleries were left out of great churches; when this happened, the main arcades became, as it were in an instant, much taller and lighter. The side aisles of the building were able, as they took in the space where the galleries had been, to become much taller; the main windows, also, grew larger. As the galleries disappeared, the clerestory became higher; as its windows, too, became larger, the whole of the inside of the building changed from being dim and gloomy to being light and fairylike.

The ribbed vaulting—which had been, first of all, invented to support the gallery floors—became a stone ceiling, with slender graceful ribs making a pattern upon it. So clever had the vault-builders become, that they could now cover the main part of the church with a stone ceiling like this, so that the ugly tangle of wooden beams supporting the roof were now hidden from view.

In the last chapter, we explained to you how the masons had taken to building their arches in rings of stone called 'orders', and how the piers supporting the arches were being built in orders to match them. The effect of this was rather clumsy, so the masons had begun to make the edges of each 'order' look a little more ornamental by cutting a slender little column, or 'shaft', up each angle. Then they made this little shaft run all round the edge of the order of the arch above. This kind of ornament which runs along the edge of a piece of stone or wood is called a 'moulding'; all through the Gothic period, the masons were inventing different kinds of mouldings with which to ornament the orders of their arches. By the reign of Henry III, the whole arch had become a cluster of hollows and ribs, so that you could no longer see where the orders themselves were (8).

Then the old sturdy piers, and even the round pillars, began to lose their shape as the mouldings began to creep down them to the ground; sometimes the pillars were surrounded by clusters of slender shafts, each with its tiny capital carved with small leaf-like designs. By the Decorated period, however, the shafts had gone and the whole pillar was a cluster of mouldings like those of the arches above.

Gothic Architecture

When the arches changed from half-round to pointed, the tops of the doors and windows changed to match; here, too, the clustering mouldings grew ever thicker. It was during the Early English period that the finest mouldings were being cut; afterwards, the masons seem to have taken less trouble with this kind of ornament. Everything during the Early English period was as tall and graceful as the builders could manage to make it; they seemed to be trying to get as far away as possible from the sturdiness of the old 'Norman' architecture which had just passed. Although the roofs of important churches were all by this time covered with lead, they were even more steeply pointed than before, like the arches beneath them. In a large building—such as, for example, Salisbury cathedral (2)—there is no mistaking the Early English style when you see it; in a small building such as a parish church, however, all you have to go on is the sharply pointed tops to the doors and windows.

There is one small thing which may sometimes help you to guess the date of a building. Just where an arch rests upon its support, the place where the two meet—known as the 'springing' of the arch—is often marked by a moulding. This moulding may be just the top of a capital, or it may be the 'impost' where an arch springs from a wall instead of a pier or pillar. Sometimes the 'impost moulding' is taken along the wall of the church to make a thin line of ornament joining the tops or bottoms of windows; a moulding like this is known as a 'string-course'. You will see that this kind of moulding—capital, impost, or string-course—is not like those passing round an arch or up a pillar, but runs at a level, parallel with the floor of the building.

It is the *top edge* of a moulding of this sort which may often give you a clue to its architectural period. In an Anglo-Saxon or 'Norman' building the top is just square; in fact, just the corner of the stone from which it was cut. In the Early English period, the top is rounded off so that it looks, in the case of a round capital, something like a smooth bicycle tyre. In the Decorated period, it is also rounded off but is generally ornamented, in addition, with a little rib or perhaps just a slight cutback to make it less simple than it had been in the Early English period. In the Perpendicular period, what was the square edge of the stone is simply sliced off at an angle.

It was during the Early English period that a number of our

great churches had their eastern arms or 'presbyteries' made longer, for reasons which were explained in Chapter III. A number of the churches built by the Cistercian monks also date from this period; but these are always very simple and plain, because the Cistercians were not allowed to have any ornament in their churches. Very few great Benedictine abbey churches date from this period, because they were mostly already built; but it was during this time that the bishops began to build fine churches to imitate those of the monks. Salisbury (2) and Wells cathedrals are examples of Early English great churches.

During this period our castles were having their old palisades all replaced by stone walls; as these were now of no use unless they were very tall, castle walls of the Early English period always had a number of wall-towers to protect them. Keeps had, of course, gone out of fashion. Although they must have looked very fine when they were rising behind palisades or low stone walls, their day was now over; the money and labour that used to be spent on them was now better spent on improving the defences of the castle.

Both inside the fortifications of the castle and also on estates which had no defences, the old wooden halls were still being built. Stone halls with slender pillars and wide arches like those of a church were also coming into use; but, as we shall soon see, the days of all these rambling old buildings were coming to an end. What people were more interested in were the two-storied houses of stone, upon the upper floors of which they could live in peace and comfort, away from the noise and dirt and rubbish of the ground below.

The end of the Early English period for important buildings is about the time of the battle of Evesham in 1265, but it was not until the end of the century that the style ceased to be used for parish churches and country buildings. The old England of the Anglo-Saxons, Danes, and Normans, was passing away; so was the Feudal System, which saw the country squires living, surrounded by their peasant labourers, on their large farms, each with its wooden hall. The country was much more peaceful and settled. People were worrying less about the need for huddling together for safety and were thinking more about living in comfort in their own homes.

But those were the days of Edward I's frontier wars against the Welsh and Scots; there was still the need for keeping the country free from invasion by these rather savage peoples. To move his armies about the country Edward began to make good roads, such as had not been seen since the days of the Romans. William the Conqueror had built castles to keep down the Anglo-Saxons; Henry II had built them to keep down his rebellious barons who were troubling the peace of the land. Edward I built them to keep the country free from the Welsh (10) and Scots.

With Edward I, there comes into the architecture of the great buildings of the land that style which we call the 'Decorated'; this, when it reaches the village churches, covers, roughly speaking, the fourteenth century.

While it is always much more interesting to talk about the beautiful buildings of the Middle Ages, we must not forget that there were only a very few of these and a great many quite ordinary buildings of a kind we do not take the trouble to look at nowadays. The countryman was still living in just the same miserable hut that he had been in in the days of the Anglo-Saxons. But for middle-class people there were the smaller halls; there were also plenty of quite humble village churches, with, however, very little architecture about them. All these simple kinds of buildings would still be covered with roofs of thatch, shingles or some such material. But the large and important buildings were by this time all being covered with lead, the use of which—as we have already seen—forced the carpenters to make their roofs very much flatter.

Inside the large churches and halls, which had aisles, the arches were becoming much wider as the masons became more skilled at building them. If you build a very wide arch you have to make the supporting pillars tall, otherwise the arch is apt to look dumpy. But if you still keep the arch itself very pointed, as was the case in the Early English style which we have just talked about, the whole arch becomes very much bigger and taller than you can manage. So the arches became less pointed as time went on; it so happened that this new arrangement fitted in very well with the flatter roofs above. Not only main arches like chancel arches, or those forming part of an arcade, but the arches of windows and doorways too, all became flatter and less pointed.

The builders of the great churches were now covering these with a stone ceiling or vault. This was being carried on very cleverly built arches or ribs; the masons were making their ribbed framework much stronger by building a lot of small ribs across between the main ones, so as to stiffen up the whole arrangement before they actually laid the stone slabs which formed the vault itself. The vault of the presbytery of Norwich cathedral (1) gives you some idea of the beauty of these stone ceilings; notice the carved stone 'bosses' which the masons put wherever the ribs met.

It will be easy for you to understand that a stone ceiling of this sort was an enormous weight for the walls below to carry; beside which, the vault, being made of a lot of very wide arches, was all the time pushing against the walls and trying to topple them over. So it was becoming absolutely necessary to prop up the walls with heavy 'buttresses' jutting out from the building where the main arches of the vault came down upon the walls. This was easy enough to do when the building had no aisles, but when the high walls were carried upon pillars and arches there was no place left in which to build the buttresses. The masons had therefore to build them against the walls of the aisles; making arches called 'flying buttresses' (11) across the aisle roofs to push against the vaulting of the main part of the church.

There is an old saying that 'the arch never sleeps'. When you are using a slab of wood or stone as a beam, its weight is being carried quite simply by the supports at either end; but if you build an arch of a lot of small stones propped up on a wooden framework, as soon as you take the framework away all the stones try to drop down on the ground. As they do so, they try to push the supports of the arch outwards so that these begin to topple over.

There are two ways of preventing this from happening. One is by making the supports of the arch so wide that they cannot be toppled over; that is why buttresses were used. But there is another way; you can keep the supports quite slender, but make them so *heavy* that the arch is not strong enough to move them at all. You do this by piling up stones on top of the supports; the more and more stones you add, the heavier the supports will become. It was not until the Gothic period that the English masons discovered all about this business of adding heavy weights on top of the supports of arches. Once they had done so, however, they made great use of the idea. The beautiful pinnacles that you see perched on the tops of the walls and buttresses of Gothic cathedrals are not there only for ornament; they are really huge stone weights keeping the arches that are inside the building from falling down.

In this architectural period—the 'Decorated'—about which we are now talking, the windows of important buildings were becoming very much larger; for there was now more glass and glaziers were learning more about how to use it. But you cannot have a very large window, filled with small pieces of glass just held together by lead strips, or the wind will very quickly blow all the glass in. Even with the aid of iron bars, the builders found that there was a certain width of window beyond which they could not go. But they wanted more light. First of all they tried putting their windows side by side, with only a small piece of wall between the two. This piece of wall got smaller and smaller until at last it became merely a thin stone division, called a 'mullion'; the two windows then really became one window divided into two. As time went on, the masons divided up their windows with several of these stone mullions; by this means they were able to make their windows as wide as they liked.

The first windows that we had in this country were simply holes cut into the wooden boards of which the walls were made. Later on, the wooden board became a stone slab, and the hole in it became a pattern like the sort of thing that you can make with a compass. Sometimes the old masons put a stone slab like this between the tops of the arches of a double window. Then they made the hole in the stone slab larger and larger, until they had to build it up with pieces of stone instead of cutting it out of one slab. In the end they decided to join up the design of the hole with the tops of the window arches, by building up the whole thing in pieces of stone in the same way as they were doing with the mullion below. Thus instead of a window made in three parts—two side openings and one small top opening—the masons made one window which was divided up into these three parts by stone bars. Because of the geometrical pattern which the old masons made with their compasses when they were designing the upper parts of these windows, this style of window is called 'Geometrical' (3, 12). Later on, when they became still more skilful, the masons designed all sorts of pretty patterns for the tops of their windows. The

Gothic Architecture

stone bars which are used in the tops of the large windows of the Middle Ages are called 'tracery'; the very beautiful windows of the end of the 'Decorated' period are said to have 'flowing tracery'.

Although this word 'Decorated' is perhaps not a very good way of describing the style of the reigns of the first three Edwards, the masons of that day certainly made very beautiful patterns with their window tracery. But the people who did most to beautify the great buildings of those days were the carvers. There were a great many of these in England at this time, and they had been taking great pains with their studies of English trees, flowers, and even animals; all of which they worked into the most beautiful designs, and used in the buildings upon which they worked. The capitals at the tops of the columns were favourite places for them to beautify with their chisels (8). One of the methods the masons used for getting a start for the ribs of their high stone vaults was to raise these upon a capital without any column underneath it but with its underside just dying away into the wall. These 'corbels' were usually beautifully ornamented by the carvers of the day; as were also the 'bosses' which covered the network of ribs in the high vaults above.

The Decorated period was, after all, probably the richest period of Gothic architecture. Not only were great churches with magnificent presbyteries being built; but, at last, comfortable houses were appearing all over the countryside, instead of the stern castles of the days of the Normans. The great halls of these houses were becoming very fine rooms with windows like those of a church. Castles were still being built (as will be seen in the next chapter); these, however, were not so much fortified *houses*, as they had been in the past, but were built simply to be as strong as possible. But the English nobleman could now feel quite safe in a fine house and no longer needed strong walls and towers for his protection.

In August 1349, the England of the great Gothic churches, the banqueting halls, and the mighty Edwardian castles was at the height of its glory. But during that month, at the port of Melcombe Regis in Dorset, a man fell ill and died. A terrible plague had come to England; before long, half the people in this country had died of it. The nobleman in his great house died; the abbot and his monks died also. The peasant working in the fields, and the labourer who helped with the building works, were both carried away by the 'Black Death', as the plague was called. What was still more important to English architecture was that scores of our masons and carvers died of it as well. And in the end this beautiful architectural style which we called the 'Decorated' died also.

Never again were there masons who could work out all the hundreds of mouldings, or carvers to design the beautiful ornament; all this art passed away from England for ever. But all the time that the masons had been working on the great buildings, the village carpenters had not been idle. They had still been working away at the wooden buildings in the villages, becoming more and more skilful in framing up their timbers; so that even the little wooden houses were now becoming much less like hovels than they had been a hundred years before.

You will remember that, at first, these carpenters only used huge timbers and joined them together as posts and beams; the wooden walls being simply made by sticking a row of planks between beams at the top and the bottom. But now the carpenters were using much smaller timbers, and framing them up more neatly, so that they could now make walls of framed-up timbers, filling in each frame or 'panel' with a piece of board, or perhaps getting someone to fill them up with wattling, or rubble stone, or perhaps just mud.

This way of framing-up small pieces of wood to form panelling was becoming very well-known throughout the English countryside at about the time of the Black Death. As the art of inventing the beautiful flowing designs had died away, the English masons copied instead the panelling designs of the village carpenters. So about the time of the Wars of the Roses, architecture had become full of straight lines, all rather plain and dull after the beautiful flowing curves of the Decorated period. The new style, which came into the village churches about this time, is called the 'Perpendicular'.

In order to fit in with these new panelling designs, arches began to lose what was left of their points, and so became very flat. Over windows, the opening often lost its arch altogether and became quite flat. Even if a doorway still kept its arch, this was, more often than not, squared-up on the wall above the opening, so as to fit in with the general straight-line effect which all buildings seemed to be trying to show. As, by this

Gothic Architecture

time, the roofs of all important buildings had become nearly flat, everything was in fact beginning to fit in rather well; but it was a pity that the graceful pointed arches of earlier days had gone for ever.

There was now plenty of glass to be had for filling the big windows that were so popular at this time. The builders of the Perpendicular period cut a great many large windows through the walls of old-fashioned buildings such as the ancient parish churches. These new windows all had very flat arches or straight tops; their stone 'tracery' was now all arranged in panelled designs (13) instead of the flowing patterns of the century before.

Earlier on in this chapter, we saw how the stone ceilings or 'vaulting' of the great churches had become more and more elaborate, as the masons were always putting in more stone ribs so as to make it easier for them to lay the actual slabs filling-in between these. At last the stone framework became so full of ribs that there was hardly any of the filling left. By the Perpendicular period, the masons stopped framing-up the vault with stone ribs altogether, and went back to the old idea of making the whole vault of stone slabs. They built up these slabs, very cleverly, as huge arches crossing from side to side of the building. It is too difficult to explain how this was done, as pictures of this kind of vaulting do not show the main arches; these are out of sight above the vault, which is actually hanging down from them instead of being carried upon them as was the case with the older kinds of vaulting. As the old ribs which had formed such pleasant decoration to the underside of the vaulting had now all been taken away, the fifteenth-century masons carved the stonework into beautiful patterns. The old 'bosses' became very large stones hanging down a long way below the vault and carved into queer shapes. This kind of vaulting is known as 'fan-vaulting'; you can see from the picture (13) of the inside of King's College Chapel at Cambridge how the vault seems to spring from the wall like a row of opening fans.

While talking about these beautiful stone ceilings of the great Gothic churches, we must not forget that the ordinary parish church never had anything of the kind and so had to make the most of the timbering in its roof. All roofs are made of slanting pieces of wood, called 'rafters', which rest upon the tops of the walls and lean against each other at their tops. Sometimes there is a piece of wood, running along the 'ridge' of the roof, against which all the rafters lean. This is always so to-day; but, in the Middle Ages, rafters were usually built up in pairs leaning against each other. Each pair of rafters usually had a piece of wood joining them together somewhere near the top. Throughout the Gothic period, it was usual to add other pieces of wood to stiffen up the joints between these three timbers; this smoothed off the shape of the roof when you looked at it from underneath. Sometimes—especially in the sleeping chambers of private houses—the undersides of these beams were covered-in with wooden boards to make a kind of rough timber copy of a stone vault (only, of course, these wooden ceilings were quite plain, and ran from one end of the building to the other without any cross-vaults or ribs of any sort).

Although it was fairly easy to stiffen up the rafters of a roof so that it could not fall down sideways, it was sometimes more difficult to prevent it from being blown end-ways. Particularly in the west of England—where the winds are very strong—they used to add a lot of other timbers in the sides of the roof, between the rafters, so as to stiffen it up to prevent this happening. They liked to use curved pieces of timber, often cut into flowing shapes so that they could make patterns with them.

Although the carpenters of the west of England have always been very skilful, this part of the country was never so rich as was the east. The churches of the west of England still used thatch or stone slates for their roofs for some time after the east of England was using lead. In the east, therefore, roofs became flatter at a much earlier date than they did in the west. With a flattish roof, it is not nearly so easy to lean your rafters together in pairs; it is much better to have that small beam called a 'ridge', and to prop this up from underneath if you can. What they did in the east of England was to have, every now and again across the length of the building, a strong beam called a 'tie-beam', from which they could prop up the ridge.

The eastern carpenters sometimes did their propping, not with a post, but with a kind of Gothic arch made of two pieces of wood resting on the tie-beam. This meant they could leave out the middle of the tie-beam altogether, and merely use its two ends with curved wooden struts or brackets underneath these. A roof of this sort is called a 'hammer-beam' roof; sometimes the eastern builders, especially in Norfolk and Suffolk, were so skilful that they could have several rows of these short hammer-beams, one on top of the other, and in this way they got an exceedingly beautiful effect, which was very popular amongst the builders of great banqueting halls (17).

In the case of small buildings, it was a simple matter to have a roof which was almost flat, with just enough slope for the rain to run off. The carpenters then set to work to ornament the undersides of such roofs; in other words to make a carved ceiling. It was during the Perpendicular period that carved wooden ceilings began to be popular, especially for the living rooms of houses. We shall see in the next chapter that the ground floors of houses were now being lived in. This meant that the timbers carrying the floor above could be used to make a fine ceiling for the room below.

Not only in the buildings themselves did the carpenters and joiners of the Perpendicular period make full use of their skill. They had come a long way since the days of great posts and beams and were now quite able to make graceful furniture. Many of our great cathedral churches are full of beautiful seating—known as 'stallwork'—which the fifteenth-century joiners made to furnish the choirs of the monks as, for example, at Chester. Even the parish churches were beginning to have seats for the humblest villagers to sit upon. The ends of these 'pews' were usually covered with fine carving; once only done by stone carvers but now from the chisels of the village woodworker. The most graceful work these craftsmen could turn out we can see in their delicate screens, which filled the parish churches as well as those of the monks. Above, they are light and graceful; in the same style as the windows and, in some cases, the stone panelling with which the walls are ornamented. The lower parts of these screens, however, are generally filled with boarding painted with the figures of saints. In the west of England, where the woodworkers were always as good as the masons, the joiners took to making imitation wooden vaulting to carry the galleries or 'lofts' above the chancel screens (33).

To go back to the buildings themselves: there is one particular kind of object which belongs above all to the Perpendicular period. This is the bell tower. In an earlier chapter we explained how difficult and expensive it was to try to build bell towers. We have also talked about the trouble that the builders of the great churches had over the matter of the collapse of the four tall pillars in the centre of the church where the crossing came. When the Gothic builders discovered that they could stop arches collapsing if they put enough weight upon the pillars supporting these, it suddenly occurred to them that the way to stop these disasters was to make the tower in the centre of the church much higher. So, during the second half of the Gothic period, the low 'lantern' towers of the great churches came to be raised to what must have seemed to many people at that time a most dangerous height. In actual fact, of course, it was the very height of these towers which made them safe. And that is why we have in England to-day the most beautiful towers in the world; such as, for example, those of the cathedrals of Canterbury (18) and Lincoln. A fashion for tall towers began to arrive in England during the so-called Perpendicular period. The country was at this time becoming very rich, owing, as has already been explained, to the profits from the wool trade. Even the villagers were now able to afford bell towers for their parish churches; they lost no time in setting to work to build these (A).

The two richest parts of England at this time were the sheep farming districts: Norfolk and Suffolk on one side of England, and Somerset on the other. All the finest church towers are found, therefore, in those parts. Although the Black Death caused much that was beautiful to pass away from Gothic architecture, the great wealth of the country was now playing its part by allowing the masons to spare no expense in trying to make buildings as ornamental as they could. There were no more graceful windows or beautifully carved capitals, but there was plenty of carved panelling to go on the walls; on the tops of these, and on the tall towers, the pinnacles were piling ever higher and higher. Inside the great churches, wealthy people spent much money on their tombs; around these, also, pinnacles began as it were to climb into the air and cluster thickly in the canopies above.

But on the whole, the churches were less popular than they had been; even more attention was being paid to people's houses. After the church, the finest building in the land was the nobleman's banqueting hall. This was generally very tall, with fine large windows, and a roof as magnificent as that in any church (17).

Public buildings, also, were beginning to appear in England. The old village crosses, on the steps of which the country people had gathered to sell their eggs and butter, were now being given roofs supported on pillars and arches; sometimes—as for example at Chichester in Sussex—beautifully ornamented. The rich tradesmen and craftsmen, who had already formed themselves into companies or 'guilds', were building halls in which they could meet together.

People were not nearly so ignorant as they had been at the beginning of the Middle Ages and they were for ever anxious to learn still more; thus it came about that wealthy colleges were being founded in the university cities for this purpose (22). So with the rich, proud, but not very beautiful Perpendicular period the Middle Ages in England come to an end.

CHAPTER VIII

HOW THEY LIVED IN THE MIDDLE AGES

In earlier chapters we have more than once reminded you that, during the Middle Ages, the home of the poor person was nothing better than a hut. Until about a hundred years after the Norman Conquest, the only houses—with the exception of the great stone towers of the Norman castles—were the barn-like halls which we have already described. Even the king's palaces had halls like these; with, however, stone walls instead of boarded ones. But the families of the Norman barons wanted their own houses to live in; and they wanted them made of stone, each with an upper floor upon which to sleep and a strong room underneath in which the great man could keep his treasures.

During the reign of Henry II, such houses began at last to be built. They were very small indeed, with just one room upstairs and one room downstairs. At first the floor was of wooden planks resting on beams; this was called a 'solar' (pronounced 'soller'). Later, however, they had a stone floor, supported on vaulting like the galleries above the aisles of the great churches. Inside the ground-floor room—which had tiny slit windows, no outside door, and could only be reached by a stair from the floor above—the owner of the house kept all his property. It was in the room above, small though it was, that he and the whole family and some of his servants lived. At one end of it was a doorway; from outside this, a stair—either of wood or stone—led down to the ground. At the end of the room farthest from the entrance doorway would be the rough beds of the owner of the house and his wife; the young children and their nurse and a maidservant or two might sleep at the opposite end near the entrance. The older children would have to find places to put their beds wherever they could. Although this arrangement seems very cramped and

The greatness of England is said to have been built upon sacks of wool. This fine Cotswold church tower was paid for out of the profits of the wool trade

1.

The choir of Norwich Cathedral looking towards the eastern apse

2.

The Early Gothic cathedral of Salisbury

3.

The cloisters of Salisbury Cathedral

5.

Wall-towers protect the high curtain walls of
Ludlow Castle

4.

The great keep of Rochester Castle

7.   The nave of Durham Cathedral

6.   Under the central tower of St. Alban's Cathedral

8.

The Gothic nave of Lincoln

9.

Through the 'machicolations' at the tower-tops of this castle gatehouse the garrison could see what was happening at the foot of the wall

10.

The grand Edwardian castle of Harlech looks out over the sea

11. Flying buttresses at Westminster built by the Gothic engineers

12. The chapter house of York Minster

13.

The fan vaulting of King's College chapel at Cambridge

14.

Twelfth-century arches in a Wiltshire parish church

15.

The great hall of Oakham Castle

17. Henry VIII's great hall at Hampton Court

16. Blakeney Church in Norfolk 'founded upon sacks of wool'

18.

Above Canterbury Cathedral rises its Angel Tower

19.
Its east window was made in the fifteenth century but the church was built at the time of the Crusades

20.
The vaulted basement of a thirteenth-century house at Guildford

21.

The porch and bay window of a great hall of the fifteenth century

22.

The quadrangle of Magdalen College at Oxford

23.

A Tudor gatehouse welcomes the visitor to the courtyard of Cowdray

24.

Across the courtyard is the grand front of the mansion with its porch and bay window

25.

Notice the huge bent 'crucks' in the gable end of the nearest of these sixteenth-century houses

26.

The close spacing of the timbers in the Suffolk yeoman's house show that it is older than the ones seen above

27.

A sixteenth-century 'skyscraper' in the 'magpie' style

28.

A great barn of the seventeenth century

29.

Burghley House: a palace of the Elizabethans

30.

Blenheim Palace, begun in 1705

31.

An Elizabethan E-shaped country house with its porch and wings

32.

A Georgian country house with its colonnaded portico

33.

A fine 'wool church' of Devonshire with its richly-carved rood screen

34.

Columns of the 'Roman Doric Order' support the plaster vaulting of the Georgian cathedral of Derby

35.
The Stuart windows of Brympton D'Evercy look out over a wide terrace

36.
Inigo Jones's banqueting house at Whitehall Palace has had its windows altered to Georgian 'sashes'

37.

A village church of the Renaissance

38.

Inside a Renaissance village church it seems as though we were still in the days of the Puritans

39.

The seventeenth-century farmhouse is built round its great chimney stack

40.

In the West Country they like a little porch set between a pair of gables of the attic windows

42.

The Georgian church-builders put steeples like
this on their towers instead of Gothic spires

41.

Over London towers Wren's great dome of
St. Paul's Cathedral

43. Charles II's gatehouse to the citadel of Plymouth

44. A Renaissance market house with the town hall above it

45.
Next to the church stands the house of the Georgian squire

46.
'Clap-boarded' cottages like this were built in great numbers in the new American colonies

48. A Georgian shop-front

47. The Corinthian portico of Claremont

49.

The last house in a Georgian 'terrace'

50.

The Royal Crescent at Bath

51.

A Regency terrace on the sea-front at Brighton

52.

Regency bays and balconies at Hastings

53.

A Classic Revival country house

54.

A Gothic Revival country house

humble, it was, of course, absolutely magnificent compared
with the wretched hovels in which the ordinary man lived.

There are not many of these old stone houses left in England
to-day; but quite a number of our ancient cities still have the
ground floors of some of them left hidden away amongst more
modern houses. You can tell them by their vaulted ceilings
(20). People will often tell you that they are 'crypts' but they
are, of course, nothing of the sort. The reason why they now
seem to be cellars is because all through the Middle Ages—
when rubbish was not collected and taken away as it is now
but simply thrown out into the street—the level of city streets
was always getting higher and higher as more rubbish was
thrown out.

One of the reasons why the Norman house-builder liked to
have a stone floor to the sleeping chamber instead of a wooden
one was so that he could build a fire on it. But as the room
was so small, the fire-hearth rather got in the way, so the
builders soon learned to make a fireplace in the wall. At first
these were simply roughly-made openings, with an arch over
and a hole high up at the back for the smoke to escape by; it
was a long time before builders discovered how to make a stone
pipe or 'flue' reaching up through the thickness of the wall to
the top of the building as nowadays. In the old days, probably
as much smoke came into the room as managed to get outside;
but there was usually a kind of canopy of wood built out over
the top of the fireplace arch to gather in as much smoke as
possible. Later on the builders made these canopies with stonework and supported them on stone brackets.

The timber halls were all built as it were round the large
fire building in the middle of the floor. These early halls, as
explained before, were generally squarish and had their roofs
supported by four large posts. Later on, when they wanted
halls which would hold more people, they began to make
them longer. Important halls, such as those of the king's palaces,
were built with stone walls; towards the end of the reign of
Henry II, when the period of building great churches and
castles had come to an end, the masons were able to turn to
building stone pillars and arches instead of the old posts and
beams. You can see the sort of thing at Oakham castle (15) in
Rutland.

Let us try and imagine a royal palace of the days of Henry

II. The centre of it would be the hall: a stone building with low walls and its roof propped up inside by two rows of round arches each supported by two or three round stone pillars. The whole building would have been much lower than a large church of those days; like the village churches it would have no 'clerestory': nobody would worry much about light and would far rather have the hall as warm and draught-proof as possible. Scattered about all round the hall would be little stone houses, each two stories high with staircases leading up to the living room on the first floor. The king would live in one of these houses. As the king and the queen did not always travel about together, she might very probably have her own house in which she and her maids could live. There might be houses for some of the great officers of the king's household and their families; possibly one of the king's married sons might have his own house. You can imagine the well-worn paths leading from the foot of the stairway of each house to the entrance doorway of the great hall in which everybody in the palace would gather at mealtimes. The paths from the king's and queen's houses might be covered by roofs, supported on posts like those of the first cloisters the monks made, so that the king and queen could go from their houses to the great hall without getting wet.

In the Middle Ages, all buildings had their doorways near one end. This end was called the 'lower' end; the other, the 'upper' end, was the best part of the building. In the early great halls, the main entrance doorway was always placed near the end of one of the long walls; opposite to it was the back door leading to the yard where the cooking was done. In the king's palace, the food was probably cooked over fires made in shelters of some sort which were later made into stone buildings with holes in the roof for the smoke to escape by; in a less important hall, the cooking may have been done over the fire burning in the centre of its floor.

By the time of Henry II, however, more attention was being paid to the problem of feeding all the great number of people who had to take their meals in the hall of a large house or palace. The chief food was, of course, bread; as time went on, therefore, every hall had a proper room—called, from the French word for bread, a 'pantry'—built against the lower end of the hall. There was also another room built close to the pantry; this was the 'buttery', the place where the bottles of wine were kept. Sometimes in the 'lower' end wall of a hall you can see two openings called 'hatches'; one of these opened into the pantry and the other into the buttery. You can imagine the bread and wine being passed through these hatches to the servants who carried them to the people eating in the hall. These two hatches often have between them a doorway leading down a passage into the kitchen where the food was cooked; it was usually here that the proper stone kitchens came to be built.

It is difficult to imagine what these barn-like places were really like a hundred years after the Norman Conquest. Their floors were simply of earth covered with a very rough carpet of straw or reeds, upon which everyone just threw away anything he happened not to want. He was quite capable, for instance, of throwing his soup on the floor. Scraps of food thrown away were eaten by the house dogs, who also added to the mess on the floor; this was, in fact, always in a perfectly dreadful state and was, understandably, known as the 'marsh'.

˙ The king and all his great men took their meals in a building of this sort. So it came about that they had provided for them, at the 'upper' end of the hall, a raised platform, paved with stone, which could be kept cleaner than the rush-strewn earth of the 'marsh'. This platform was called the 'dais'; throughout the whole of the Middle Ages every hall had one upon which the owner and his family and important visitors took their meals.

When all is said, then, these halls really were little better than barns, with a few rough tables and benches in the middle. Many of the servants of the great house actually slept in the hall on their rough beds—or more probably just piles of straw —laid in the darkness of the aisles outside the posts or pillars. Since most of these halls were made of wood and had so much straw lying about, with a sort of bonfire burning in the middle of the floor, it is not surprising that none of them are left to us to-day; they must always have been catching fire.

Even when we see a fine stone hall like the beautiful one at Winchester castle with its graceful pillars and arches like those of a church, we must try to remember that a building like this looked very different in the days when it was being used. The masons of the Middle Ages always did their best—they wanted their buildings to be as beautiful as they could make them—and when they had finished Winchester Hall it must have looked much as it does to-day. But then imagine the rough people with their humble manners who used that hall for their meals. Imagine the thick squelching mass of straw on the floor and the dogs fighting over scraps of food. Think of people sleeping all along the walls on their straw beds, the whole place filled with dense smoke from the fire and probably smelling like a rubbish heap. However beautiful these buildings may seem to us to-day, at the time they were built they were after all little more than stone barns, like the many hundreds of wooden halls that must have existed around them in the villages. Some of the more important of the officials who looked after the feeding arrangements in the hall—such as, for example, the 'butler' who was the man who took care of the drinks—may have made little cubby-holes by fixing up wooden partitions round their beds in the aisles of the hall; at all times there were probably all sorts of odds and ends—weapons, broken benches, sacks— lying about. In these days we have nothing left to remind us of the life which went on in the feudal hall. But whether it was a palace or a squire's house, the hall of the Middle Ages was the centre of everything.

We have now dealt with the two chief kinds of buildings in which people lived during the earlier half of the Middle Ages: the houses and the halls. By the end of the twelfth century, everyone who could afford to build himself a house did so; but he did not always need a hall, which was really a building used on a big farming estate and served therefore no purpose in the life of towns. The town of the Middle Ages had its narrow streets lined with small two-storied houses, with their steeply pointed gables facing each other across the way. In the country, however, a man owning a house of this sort would usually be a farmer who would of course need a hall as well in which to feed all his farm servants.

We saw how the royal palaces of the Norman kings had their houses scattered about all round the hall. The Norman farm-houses would have just the two separate buildings: the hall and the house. As time went on, however, it occurred to the farmers that they might just as well build their house on to the end of their hall so that they would have a shorter distance to go between the two. It was not always easy to do this, as the hall was a big, low, barn-like building and the house was a small high building of two stories. The living-room of the house was on the upper floor and had to be reached by an outside staircase. But the builders took the matter in hand and at last succeeded in joining the two buildings together so as to form one. In this way we invented the kind of house known as a 'manor house', that is to say, a large country house containing a hall.

Manor houses of this sort first came to be built towards the end of the reign of Henry III. Although the two-storied house part was usually built of stone, the hall was very often still a timber building. You may sometimes see to-day a small stone house which may at one time have been part of a manor house but has long ago lost the timber hall against which it was built.

One of the first improvements to be made in the planning of the new manor houses was to put the stair leading up to the 'chamber' *inside* the end of the hall; the owner of the house could then get to his table at mealtimes without having to go outside in the wet. It was now quite safe to have a doorway on the ground floor leading into the important storeroom underneath the chamber; where the house was joined on to a hall, the storeroom door could lead from the upper end of this, near the foot of the stair. In this position there would be no fear of burglars getting in, because they would first have to pass through the hall with the farm servants sleeping about its floor.

During the thirteenth century, manor houses were being built all over the country. Most of them were quite small, with wooden halls and a stone wing at one end. But some of the better manor houses were all built in stone. It was now not such a difficult matter to build a stone hall; for the carpenters were much better able to build wide roofs without having to prop these up with posts or pillars. This meant that, unless the hall was very wide, it need not have aisles to it as had been the case with the old halls. The manor-house hall of the thirteenth century therefore was simply becoming a large room with a high roof. Now that building in stone was better understood, the masons were able to provide much higher walls to support the wide roofs above. It was a good thing to have these high walls because it meant there could be large windows in the sides of the hall to let in plenty of light, and it was becoming fashionable at that time to have large windows like those in churches (21), sometimes even with painted glass in them.

You will usually find, however, that the windows of buildings in which people lived are slightly different from those of churches; the first kind usually have a stone bar, called a 'transom', passing across the window near the bottom. The reason for this is so that the parts of the window below the stone bar could be filled with glass fixed to hinged iron frames or 'casements'; in other words, house builders were now able to provide windows that would open and shut.

The finest houses of all—that is to say the palaces of the king, his great nobles and the bishops—all had fine stone halls. The house part at the upper end of the hall, however, was not always built on quite so simply as was the case with the smaller houses. The old-fashioned straight staircase, which took up so much room, had given place to a spiral staircase running up inside a little tower or 'turret'; this kind of stair was found to be a much better way of reaching the chamber above from the hall. So instead of having a straight stairway rising up the end wall of the hall there was a spiral stair rising in one corner. This meant that the house part of the palace need only be joined on to the hall by one of its corners; this of course would be the one in which the staircase had been built. Bishops' palaces sometimes had two houses. One of these had on its upper floor the bishop's great chamber; the other, his council chamber. These council chambers of the bishops were sometimes known by quaint names such as 'Paradise' or 'Heaven's Gate'.

The manor house is, of course, a kind of house which would not ordinarily have had any sort of defences (although, as a matter of fact, at the end of the thirteenth century quite a number of them were being provided with wide water-filled moats, with bridges at the entrances). Ever since the days of William the Conqueror it had been unlawful to build any sort of castle without the king's permission; but from time to time—during such troubled times as the reign of King Stephen for instance —people often took no notice of this, and built castles both for their own protection and in order that they might raid their neighbours' lands. But, all the same, the idea was that no one should build a castle without the king's permission, and during the thirteenth century—by which time law and order had come back to the country—this rule was being faithfully carried out. But there were still people (especially those living in parts of the country where they did not feel too safe) who wanted to build castles. By the sea coasts, many were afraid of raids from the French; to the north and west the Scots and Welsh were always giving trouble. So the owners of quite a number of these country manor houses got permission from the king to surround them with stone curtain walls and towers, and so turn them into castles.

The reign of Edward I was a great time for castle building. It is true that the old castles of William the Conqueror had now ceased to be of much use; only those castles in which the most powerful nobles still lived were being kept in proper repair. But the king was doing his best to protect his country from raids by the Scots and Welsh, and one of his ideas was to build great castles along the borders of his realm. These castles were quite different from the kind of thing that had been built up till then. The old castles had been growing through the centuries, from earthen banks to stone walls and towers, on the sites where the Norman nobles had first founded them. But the king could build a castle where he wished; he could start on a fresh site, so that he would not have to trouble himself about old ditches or walls or towers which were already there.

You will remember that we explained how very much afraid castle builders were of being undermined. The first castles had all been perched up on high ground where it was difficult to assault them but where they were very easily got at by miners. Unless the ground was very rocky, therefore, so that miners could not work, the king founded all his new castles on low ground in order that he could surround them with a moat. A moat is quite a different kind of defence from the dry ditch of the Norman castle; while this was always made as *deep* as it could be, the moat was made very wide, so as to keep the besiegers as far away as possible from the high wall behind it. No miners could reach the walls of a moated castle without running the risk of being drowned by the water of the moat seeping into their tunnel. In some of the great Edwardian castles, the engineers would actually build a dam across a valley so as to flood this and surround the castle with a wide lake. They then had to make certain that the dam itself was well defended by walls and towers, or else the besiegers might cut through it and let all the water out.

Inside the moat, King Edward's grim castles rose four-square with a tower at each corner. No keep was necessary; indeed it would have looked rather smothered behind such high towered walls. The gate-house, however, with its two big half-round towers protecting the entrance passage, was often made into a fine house in which the constable of the castle could live; on one of the upper floors there was often a large hall and, above this, his sleeping chamber.

The castles of the Edwardian period were the largest buildings of the great days of the Middle Ages. They were built for soldiering and all the pomp and excitement of 'chivalry'; within them was much clanking about in armour and waving of banners and blowing of trumpets. All over Europe, the towns and castles were always being besieged by somebody or other. The old days of the stone-throwing engines had now gone; the assault of castles was becoming much more of a hand-to-hand affair. The castle had become a very strong place indeed and it was no good merely hurling stones at it; you had to get right up to the walls, and either capture or destroy them.

A number of new kinds of siege-engines had been invented to help in the assault. There was the 'ram', which was a beam having a heavy head that butted the base of the walls and tried to smash the stonework. There was the 'mouse', which had a sharp point for pecking out the stones of the wall after the ram had butted them loose. And there was the 'cat', which was simply a long low house full of miners; it was rolled up on tree trunks to the foot of the walls and inside it the miners worked away protected by the roof above them. The most fearsome animal of all was the 'bear', which was a great wooden tower built as high as the walls it was assaulting and also rolled up to them on tree trunks; it was full of soldiers ready to attack the garrison on the walls from the top of their 'bear'.

With engines like these against them, something had to be done by the castle builders to make it still more difficult for the enemy to reach the walls. The moat, of course, was a very good defence but it was sometimes possible for the besiegers to fill it up. So the castle people often built round their castle yet another wall (10), which the attackers would then have to get through before they could bring their engines up to the great 'curtains' themselves. The space between these two walls was known as the 'lists'; it was there that the garrison held its tournaments.

This England of the end of the thirteenth century had become very wealthy through trade with the Continent, so that

our cities were steadily filling up with numbers of busy tradesmen and merchants. Although we were such a small country,
we were even then so safe from the wars which were always
taking place on the Continent that there was nothing for our
townspeople to do but to get richer. It was the fashion of the
times to surround your town with a city wall, with high curtains
and wall towers just like those of a castle of the period; so, although there was really little need to do anything of the sort,
many of the English cities spent large sums of money in building fine walls round themselves.

Except for the improvements in the design of the manor
houses—that is to say the chief house in each village—the life
of the countryside must have gone on very much as it had always done; with the peasant still living miserably in his wretched
hovel. But it was during the Edwardian period that people began thinking more of public works. The king himself was very
keen on having good main roads, along which he could move
his army if he needed to defend his frontiers against the Scots
or the Welsh. A very important part of road-building is the
crossing of streams and rivers; it is no use marching an army
with all its stores of war along a good road and then finding it
stuck for days because of a flooded stream. The first stone-
arched bridges had been built in Henry II's reign, but it was
not until the end of the thirteenth century that we began to
have well-built stone bridges provided along our main roads,
especially where these entered large towns and the townspeople could look after the bridge.

The large towns all had, of course, their proper places for
markets, where merchants and tradespeople came along and set
up their stalls. The larger villages of the countryside used the
steps of the village cross; during the Edwardian period, masons
began to pay attention to the design of these village crosses. It
will be remembered that Edward I had crosses built to the
memory of his wife in every village where her body rested for
the night on its journey from Nottinghamshire to burial in
Westminster Abbey; the most beautiful of these is at Gedding-
ton in Northamptonshire.

CHAPTER IX

TUDOR PALACES

In the last chapter we saw how wealthy and comfort-loving the English people (excepting, of course, the poor peasants) were becoming at the beginning of the fourteenth century. In those days, there were really two Englands. On the one hand there were the new towns and cities which were rising as a result of the growth of English trade. But outside the walls of these cities there was still the old England of powerful nobles ruling the peasants who worked upon the great estates. The nobles, of course, were also sharing in the wealth of the towns; for much of the trade that these were enjoying was the result of what was going on all over the countryside in the way of growing corn and rearing sheep for wool.

During the fourteenth century, the great landowners were becoming so wealthy that they were beginning to set themselves above the king, as they had done in the bad old days before Henry II had brought them to heel. The halls of their great manor houses and palaces were no longer those barn-like buildings in which the farm servants had slept. They were now magnificent rooms—as large as many a church—and were being built to display the magnificence of their owners. These powerful lords were surrounding themselves with small armies of servants—and even soldiers—who all feasted together in the great hall; on the dais at its upper end, My Lord would take his meals well pleased with the signs of his wealth that he could see displayed before him. The farm servants had long ago been banished from their straw beds in the hall, to their own poor hovels, somewhere in the world which lay outside the buildings of the great house.

The day of castles was really over, for the iron cannon had come to batter down their high walls. But the nobles who lorded it over England at the end of the fourteenth century were determined to have something of the sort; so they took to raising great tower-houses, many stories in height, from the tops of which they could overlook the lands they ruled. At Tattershall in Lincolnshire you can see the sort of thing they built.

The result of all this was bound to be that sooner or later these proud feudal lords would actually suppose that they had the right to decide who was to be king. This, of course, could only end by their fighting among themselves. They had already collected the private armies with which they could fight each other, and at last formed up on two opposing sides, one of which wore the badge of a white rose and the other a red rose. While the merchants in the cities carried on with their trade as busily as ever, the nobles marched with their private armies up and down the countryside, bringing misery to the peasants and, in the end, wearing themselves out in their stupid attempts to put first one king and then another on the throne of England. But in the end they found a king who would stand no nonsense. He was Henry VII, the first of the Tudors; like Henry II, three hundred years before, he brought peace once more to a much-troubled country.

The Wars of the Roses brought to an end the feudal England of the Middle Ages. With Henry VII began a new period in which the wealth which the English had now gathered in could be displayed by means of fine buildings. The great churches had belonged to the Middle Ages; their day was already over and they were only waiting for another Tudor king to declare that they were finished for ever. But there were still plenty of good builders in England, and good stone for them to work upon and plenty of money to pay them with. So it was clear that some kind of building had to be found upon which they could show their skill.

Since the days of the Norman Conquest four hundred years before, the architectural style of the finest buildings in the country—the great churches—had very much changed. For three centuries it had been getting ever more magnificent; after the Black Death, however, it had begun to lose much of its beauty. By the time the Tudor kings had come to the throne of England the day of the great church had passed away; few important churches were being built, and those which were founded were much smaller than the great buildings of the days of the Normans.

During those four hundred years, however, great strides had been made in the design of ordinary houses. At the time of the Norman Conquest, there may have been only half a dozen mason-built houses in the whole of England; now there were hundreds—many of them very large and magnificent. Obviously some of the skill that the English builders had once put into the great churches of the Norman period was now being employed on people's houses, thus we shall find that after the Middle Ages English architecture is not concerned very much with churches, but rather with good houses in which ordinary people could live in comfort.

The most important part of each great house was still something which belonged to the days of feudal England—the hall. When you go into one of these halls of the Tudor period you might for the moment think you were inside a great church (17). It is as if the masons who were no longer able to raise those lovely buildings were still sighing for them, and so were trying to make the great halls just a little like them. These Tudor halls are very tall and are often covered with as fine a timber roof as the carpenters of the day could possibly manage. The windows are very large like those of a church; they are usually raised well above the floor in order that tapestries might be hung to cover the wall below them. These were not only very decorative but also helped to keep the place warm.

There is one kind of window which you will find in a Tudor hall which you will never meet with in a church. The window which lights the dais, on which was the 'high table' of the owner, was nearly always made to jut out from the wall to form what is known as a 'bay window (24). Such windows were probably the finest that we have ever made in this country; when filled from top to bottom with painted glass they must have looked very beautiful indeed. One pleasant thing about a bay window is that when you are standing within it you can get such a good view of what is going on outside.

Somewhere at the upper end of the hall, next to the dais where the master of the house took his meals, were his private rooms. The chief of these, the 'great chamber', would still be, as always, on the first floor. But a change had taken place in the room below this. You will remember that this had at first been merely a storeroom for the owner's valuables; but now the times had changed and there was no need for a man to look after his property quite so closely as in the past. The Tudor gentlemen found that their old storerooms made very good private sitting-rooms, into which they could disappear when they wanted a quiet chat, away from the noise of the bustle in the hall or the children in the chamber. These private sitting-rooms were given the name of 'parlours' (from the French *parler*—to talk). In another chapter we mentioned that the fifteenth century was a period during which fine wooden ceilings were popular. The carpenters of Tudor days generally made the underside of the floor of the great chamber into a magnificent ceiling for the parlour beneath it.

No expense was spared in making the private apartments of the Tudor noblemen as comfortable as possible. The rough stone or brick walls, even when they were covered with plaster, were not good enough, so the carpenters covered them with wooden panelling like that which they used for partitions and screens. Each of the panels was often carved into a pattern which looked like a folded napkin; this is known as 'linenfold' panelling. In the reign of Henry VIII, when Italian carvers were coming over to work on the great houses, the panels sometimes had heads worked on them.

Except that it was of course getting rather larger, the great chamber itself was still much the same as for the last two hundred years or so. It was still, for example, only one room (although as a matter of fact a great many of these chambers were probably afterwards divided up by wooden partitions into smaller rooms). Even as far back as the days of Henry II, a certain amount of care had been taken to make the window at the upper end—that is to say the end farthest from the entrance —of the great chamber rather better than the others: as if to show to people outside where the bed of the great man himself was placed. From the fifteenth century onwards, a number of great chambers were provided with a small copy of the large bay window in the hall below. Instead of building this up from the ground, however, the bay window of the chamber was usually built out on a big stone bracket from the wall; windows like this are called 'oriel' windows.

The fireplace in the wall was to be found in every one of the great chambers of the Tudor days. One of the difficulties about living in one room—especially if this is entered from an outside doorway—is that every time anyone opens the door you are almost certain to feel a draught. In all Henry II's houses, he liked to have a short wooden screen built out into the room beside the doorway so as to stop this nuisance. These screens were called 'spurs'; after a time, all rooms with outside doorways had them. Towards the end of the Middle Ages, however, when chambers came to be reached by spiral stairs, there was no need to worry any more about the draught from the doorway.

Down in the great hall they still went in for roaring bonfires of logs in winter time. Many halls still kept to their hearths in the middle of the floor; but, once the aisles had been given up so that the hall became a simple room, the builders began to have large fireplaces made in the high walls so that the fire could be in a place where it was less likely to set the building alight. But wherever it was, a blazing fire like this, sending currents of air sweeping through the hall, was bound to cause a great deal of draught inside the building. We have seen already that it was always necessary to leave the hall door open when the central fire was burning, or the smoke might never rise above the heads of the people who were taking their meals. A porch was often built outside the main doorway of the hall to give it shelter from the wind and stop some of the draught (21); in the days of Henry III, the porches of the great halls were often as fine as those of the cathedral churches. Even the country hall might have a porch and the parish church none.

Another way of keeping out some of the draught was to build inside the hall the same kind of wooden spur as Henry II had had fitted up in his chambers. As the hall had two doors opposite one another, each of these had to have a spur. During the fifteenth century, somebody had the idea of making another length of wooden screen which would fill up much of the gap between the ends of the two spurs; there was then, in fact, a draught-proof screen passing right across the whole of the end of the hall and only broken by two gaps for people to go through. At first, the piece of screen in the middle was not fixed but was only moved there during the winter. By the Tudor period, however, the hall-screen had become a fixed partition running right across the hall with two doors in it, one near either end (17). This meant that the hall had now a sort of long inner porch joining the back and front doors; this short passage was known as the 'screens'. The Tudor carpenters en-

joyed making these screens; they often finished them as beautifully as if they had been the rood-screens of great churches. In
very fine halls the 'screens' passage had a floor above it; this was
the 'minstrels' gallery', from which musicians could play to the
company during a banquet.

These great banqueting halls of the Tudor period were really
at first intended to hold an army of servants, such as belonged
to a nobleman of the days of the Wars of the Roses. But the
wealthy, peace-loving, comfort-loving nobles of the Tudor age
began to use them more for entertaining each other; so that
often the hall would be full of somebody else's followers all enjoying themselves at its owner's expense. The most important
guests would of course be feasting at the high table on the dais.
After a while, the Tudor lords began to wish for a place in
which they could take their meals a little more privately and
away from the noise—which must have become pretty deafen-
ing towards the end of a large party in the hall. So they searched
for a place in which they could make a private dining-room.
This place was found to be at the lower end of the hall, beyond
the screens' passage; a very convenient arrangement as the food
for the 'dining parlour' could then be brought straight to it
without having to be carried right up the hall.

This made a very great change in the old manor-house
plan. For the first time an important room was being provided,
not at one end of the hall only, but at both. Soon a 'guest chamber' was being built above the dining parlour, to match the
'great chamber' at the opposite end of the house. This changed
the shape of the ground floor of the house from a 'T' to an 'H'.
That is to say, if you had been walking up to the hall doorway
of a manor house of the Middle Ages, you would have seen in
front of you the long low hall with a tall narrow building at *one*
end; but in the Tudor period the hall might have had a wing at
each end—one as it were balancing the other.

If you had gone in by the main door of a Tudor hall, walked
straight through the screens' passage, and out at the back door,
you would have come into the kitchen yard. In this yard there
would be a jumble of buildings provided for the business of
running the great house. Chief of these would have been, of
course, the great kitchen itself; somewhere near would be the
pantry and the buttery and various other rooms for storing all
sorts of different kinds of foods. There would also be buildings

of different shapes and sizes in which lived the servants of the great house, from the butler at the top to the kitchen boy at the bottom.

In the days of the Tudors, builders were getting much more careful in the way they set out their buildings. No longer did they stick up a shed just on the very first place that came into their minds; they tried to make a proper plan and arrange everything more or less in detail. Edward I's castles had all been set out neatly around square courtyards. This idea of planning buildings round a courtyard was becoming quite a fashion in the days of the Tudors and the kitchen yard was usually planned as a square of buildings, on one side of which was the great hall.

It may seem strange that the owner of one of these fine houses should still have had only one room—it is true that this might have been divided up by wooden partitions—in which he and his family had to live. And surely he must sometimes have wished he could have had a fine council chamber such as the bishops of the Middle Ages had provided in their palaces.

One of the troubles of the owner of a mediaeval house was that there was nowhere for his important guests to sleep. Persons travelling about the country usually stayed in monasteries. Sometimes they slept in a special building called a guest house, divided up into bedchambers by wooden partitions. But generally some of the rooms in the upper floor of the western part of the cloister buildings, where the abbot had his private lodgings, were set aside for important guests. During the later Middle Ages it became the custom to build proper guest houses, with the rooms separated by stone partition walls, in castles as well as monasteries. This is important, as it shows us that the builders were actually trying to plan the inside of a building properly instead of just dividing it up with wooden partitions after the outer walls and roof had been built.

Let us imagine once more that we are standing facing the main door of a Tudor hall. On one hand would be the gable end of the short wing, inside which was the great chamber of the house. The end we should be looking at would probably be the upper end of the chamber, so that this would be as far away as possible from the noise and smells of the kitchen yard behind the house. By the reign of Henry VIII, house builders were beginning to make this wing much longer by building out a row of small rooms joining on to the upper end of the great chamber and providing private rooms for the owner of the house and his family. This meant that the chamber itself could now be used as a council chamber only; everyone could sleep in the private bedchambers in the wing. The troublesome thing about this arrangement was, however, that it would look very untidy unless another wing were built out at the opposite end of the hall to balance things. So the Tudor builders generally provided this also; as it was joined on to the guestchamber over the dining parlour, it could contain bedchambers or 'lodgings' for guests.

You will now see that the house is beginning to have, on the most important side of it, buildings arranged round three sides of a square, the back of this being the great hall, with a wing jutting out on either side. The Tudors liked these 'forecourts'; houses looked very large and important when you were standing inside them. Soon the builders were making the courtyards complete by building a range of 'lodgings' across the front between the ends of the wings.

The only thing that was missing was a tall tower of some sort. As there had to be some way of getting into the courtyard, however, it became the fashion to build, in the middle of the range of lodgings opposite the hall, a fine gatehouse (23), something like there used to be in the days of the abbeys that were now all being pulled down. The finest of these great Tudor gateways is that of Layer Marney in Essex. It is very interesting to notice how all the things which used to be built for the abbots were now being used by the Tudor nobles.

There was another kind of building which, once important, had like the abbey passed away for ever: this was the castle of the Middle Ages. The invention of gunpowder had made them useless; for the iron balls which were being fired from the cannon of Tudor days would very quickly have knocked them into piles of stone. But the Tudor house builders still wanted to make their great houses look a little like castles, a fairly easy thing to do now that houses had come to be built round courtyards, instead of in a straggling line as during the Middle Ages. There had to be turrets here and there to hold staircases to get from one floor to another, so the builders made these look as much like castle towers as they could. And then there were the tall turreted gatehouses to make the entrance fronts of great houses look something like those of the castles of old. It was all make-believe, for the walls and turrets were very thin and flimsy —the windows through them were so large that there would have been no protection for the people inside. You can see the kind of thing at Hurstmonceux castle in Sussex.

During the wealthiest period of the Middle Ages, when there was much trade with the Continent, fleets of merchant ships were always leaving the English ports with wool and other goods for Europe. We were sending out very much more than we wanted in exchange, so that the ships had to come back to this country laden with something which would keep them properly weighted for the return trip. What they usually carried was bricks; a great many of these were being made in Flanders, where most of the houses were built of them. By the Tudor period, the eastern side of England had for some time been building with these bricks and the masons were fast learning how to use them. And as we had the right kind of clay in this country—especially in Essex—we were beginning to make bricks here in large numbers and build houses with them. So a great number of Tudor palaces were being built of this material, so easy to make and carry from place to place, and which does not need armies of stone-cutters to shape it before it is used in the building.

Bricks are made in moulds, and these are all of the same shape and size. This is very helpful to builders, who know just what size of bricks they are going to use, and can plan their walls to suit. The 'red masons'—as the bricklayers were first called— laid their bricks in two ways; either they put them with their long sides showing on the face of the wall ('stretchers') or with the end only showing ('headers'). Each 'course' of bricks was laid differently from the one on either side of it; in this way they made a strong wall. Building a wall with the bricks arranged so that the joints do not come one directly above another is called 'bonding'; the Tudor builders used the 'English bond'.

It was a wonderful thing for English building when bricks came to be made in large quantities over here. At the end of the reign of Henry VIII everyone was building houses. This was partly due to the Dissolution of the Monasteries; for anyone who had been given monks' land suddenly became rich and needed a house to live in. As the abbeys fell away into ruins the English countryside became covered with large new mansions in place of them. The builders used everything they could lay their hands on, trying to provide houses as quickly as possible. There was no time to start quarrying stone and setting masons to work; so when they could not get hold of stones of ruined abbeys they were very glad to set to work making bricks.

During the Middle Ages, most of the teaching of young men had been done by the monks. So when Henry·VIII dissolved the monasteries, he founded in their place a number of colleges which were to carry on the work of teaching. These colleges were designed partly like monastery cloisters, and partly like the great houses of the age. You entered them through a gatehouse; within was a courtyard, on one side of which was the college hall and on another the chapel (22). All round the courtyard were the lodgings of the students.

The most magnificent of all the buildings of the Tudor period were the palaces of the king and his nobles. Nothing like them had been seen in the history of this country. The size of houses suddenly became so very much greater than ever before. Never before had houses been provided with such a number of rooms; the hall and great chamber had been all that the Middle Ages had known. All round these Tudor houses, there were little turrets with spiral stairs inside them; the tops were ornamented with tiny lead-covered domes and pinnacles like those of the old churches. There was much that was still very church-like about them. But the old Gothic arches had lost most of their points; the Tudor arch was very flat, with so little of the point left that sometimes, in windows especially, it had disappeared altogether (24).

Strange new fashions in architecture were beginning to appear. Architects from Italy were coming to England to seek their fortunes; sometimes they were allowed to design an entrance doorway to somebody's house. There were queer new mouldings, and pillars—of a kind which had not been seen in England since the days of the Romans—used, not for supporting walls, but merely as ornament. The foreign architects took great pains over the design of the new doorways, ornamenting them with sculpture and coats of arms.

But what everyone noticed about these Tudor mansions was the fact that English houses were at last being properly heated. Every room had its fireplace in the wall, and the whole outside of the house seemed to be covered with great chimney stacks. A perfect forest of chimneys began to rise up against the sky; little pillars of every kind and shape, many of them built of specially made bricks, moulded to give the most elaborate patterns. At last people were beginning to live in proper houses; the Middle Ages, with all their discomforts, had gone for ever.

People who like the old buildings of the Middle Ages are always complaining about the great damage Henry VIII did when he brought the beautiful abbeys of England to ruin. But if it had not been for this, we might never have seen the fine mansions which cover the English countryside, and people might have gone on living in badly designed houses for far longer than they actually did. And those who complain of the money that Henry wasted upon great palaces should remember that it was not only these that he built. For some time past, the coasts of England had been undefended against attack, for such castles as existed were hopelessly out of date and the French might at any time have decided to invade us. So Henry got an architect to come over from the Continent to show us the latest fashion in castles, and with the stones of some of the ruined abbeys he built a number of these along the southern coasts of England. Each one simply had a ring of very low towers with enormously thick walls upon which to stand the new cannon. In the centre was a sturdy tower or keep; the whole fort was built of immensely thick masonry to stand the shock of cannon balls and was surrounded by a deep moat to keep away storming parties. They looked very low and humble compared with the great castles of the Middle Ages, but their immensely thick walls could stand any amount of battering from great guns and would not topple into ruin like the towering strongholds of other days.

CHAPTER X

THE YEOMEN OF ENGLAND

For every one of the fine buildings—castles, cathedrals, palaces and large houses—about which we have been talking so far, there were many scores of wretched hovels in which the poor people of England lived. We said something about these in the first chapter; how they were, roughly speaking, either round cone-shaped huts, or else square-shaped huts with a roof having its two sides meeting at a central 'ridge'. This last kind of hut was of course much better than the round hut, as it was much more roomy; the square shape made it easier for people to sleep in it and the long 'ridge' gave much more headroom than the pointed top of the round hut.

The difficulty about having a ridge-pole was, however, that you had to prop this up at both ends, in order that it might do its job of carrying the upper ends of the roof-rafters. One of the simplest ways of doing this was to have a pole with a forked top stuck in the ground at each end of the hut so that the ridge-pole could rest in the forks. But poles of this sort got in the way of entrance doorways and the whole arrangement was also inclined to be rather wobbly. A better way was to have two strong poles leaning against each other with their tops tied together, at either end of the hut; this arrangement was much stiffer and there was nothing to get in the way of an entrance doorway. So really good huts were beginning to be built by first making a framework of five poles: the two end pairs, and the ridge-pole joining the tops of these. The rafter-poles, which were needed to carry the thatch, were placed with their feet on the ground and their tops leaning against the ridge-pole; by this means it was possible to make a strong and roomy hut.

The pairs of poles at the ends of the hut came to be very important. As huts grew larger and more roomy, properly squared timbers were used instead of poles, and the builders joined them together more neatly where they met. Pairs of timbers leaning

against each other at the end of a building are known as
'crucks'; these came to be the most important part of the poor
man's house all through the Middle Ages. At first the timbers
were straight; this, however, made the hut a very awkward
shape as there was no headroom where the roof came down to
the ground. When we were talking about the Anglo-Saxons,
we told how the large posts of their more important buildings
were stiffened with wooden arches made by leaning two curved
timbers against each other: during most of the Middle Ages
the 'crucks' of small houses were made in this way, just like
'Gothic' arches.

The village carpenters of the south-east of England were so
skilful, and the oak trees of their forests so fine and straight,
that from the days of the Anglo-Saxons onward the timber
buildings of this part of England have always been very fine.
Although probably the poor man's house was built 'on crucks',
none of these queer timbers can be seen to-day in the houses of
the south-eastern part of England. In the midlands and north,
however, crucks were used for quite good houses until well
into the reign of Elizabeth. When the art of making properly
framed timber walls came to be understood, and houses began
to have walls of this sort to support the feet of their rafters so
as to give more headroom inside the house, the great timber
crucks came to be designed not with curved beams, but with
each beam bent to form an angle so that its two lines matched
the roof and wall of the house (25). But it was not until very
late in the Middle Ages that timber houses were built with
walls; and even long afterwards the peasant was still living in a
hut of poles covered with its thatch of heather, reeds, or perhaps
just turf.

In the last chapter we told of the terrible disasters that visited
England in 1349 when half the people died of the Black Death.
Many of the country squires died; those who were left were in
great difficulty as so many of their labourers had died too. The
crops rotted in the fields and the cattle strayed among the corn
without herdsmen to drive them off. Labourers who were left
began to want very high wages which the farming squires could
not afford to pay; when the farmers tried to force their labourers
to work the men refused and there was serious trouble. The result was that many of the country squires had to give up trying
to grow corn. But as they had to do something with their land,

they followed the example of the Cistercian monks and began to breed sheep; it took far fewer men to watch the flocks of sheep than it did to plough the land and harvest the crops. In the end, the country squires became very rich through selling wool.

This change-over from growing corn to breeding sheep made a great deal of difference to the life of the English countryside. It was an expensive business to grow corn—anybody, however, could look after a few sheep. So not only could the owners of large estates start their flocks and begin to make money out of wool, but men with quite small farms could copy them and make money too. It was not necessary to have good land, such as was needed for growing corn or even pasturing cattle; sheep could be grazed on rough land which, being of little use for corn-growing or cattle-raising, had so far not been taken over by the squire.

So we find that during the Wars of the Roses scores of humble sheep-farmers were beginning to start flocks in various parts of England. While the great feudal lords were wasting their wealth and energies in fighting up and down the land with their private armies, these farmers were quietly becoming rich on the profits of their wool. All through the Middle Ages a class of merchants and tradespeople had been growing up in the towns; by the Tudor period the same kind of thing was happening all over the countryside with the small sheep-farmers.

These farmers—or 'yeomen' as they were called—would of course have been wanting to build rather better houses than the hovels of the poor labourers or the herdsmen. Although their only idea of a house would still be something that the village carpenter could build, they wanted it to be much more like the great house of the squire. So the village carpenters set to work and began to design small copies of the squire's house to suit the taste of the yeomen.

We have already said that great houses of the Middle Ages had two parts, the hall and the two-storied private house at the end of it. The yeoman's hall would be rather like a large hut; it may have at first been built 'on crucks'. It would of course be a very different thing from the 'great hall' of the squire; the yeoman's hall would simply be a farmhouse kitchen, in which he and his family and his few herdsmen would take their meals round the central fire. The house at the end would have on its ground floor a 'parlour', that is to say a private room for the farmer and his family to use when they required it. On the floor above would be their bedchamber.

All such houses would have been built entirely of timber. First of all, the lower story of the house would be framed to-gether with small wooden 'studs' or posts fixed between beams at the top and the bottom. When all four walls had been framed up in this way, the 'floor-joists'—upon which the floorboards were to be fixed—would next be laid across the tops of the tim-ber walls. The upper story would then be framed-up with wooden walls just the same as those of the lower story. The walls of the upper story would rest on the ends of the floor-joists, which themselves were resting on the walls of the lower story.

Now, in the Middle Ages, floor-joists were not fixed on their edges as they are to-day, but were laid flat on their sides. This was done because the builders were afraid if they were laid on their edges they might topple over. If you jump about on a floor which is carried by floor-joists which have been laid on their sides, the floor will spring up and down every time you jump. As the wooden walls of the upper story of the house were rest-ing on the ends of the floor-joists, you will see that if anyone jumped about on the floor, the whole upper story of the house might jump about also. The carpenters found, however, that if they made the floor-joists longer than they need be, so that the ends stuck out over the walls of the story below, they could then build the walls of the upper story on the ends of these floor-joists. Then the weight of the upper part of the house would balance the weight of people moving about inside. During the Tudor period, all two-storied wooden houses were built in this way, with the floor-joists jutting out over the lower story; this made the upper part of the house wider than the lower (26). The parts of the floor which overhang the walls below are called 'jetties'.

By the reign of Henry VIII, the yeoman's house of the south-eastern parts of England had become a beautifully framed-up wooden building having a great hall with wooden walls and a fine roof. The house at the end—which had usually by this time been fitted-in neatly with the timbering of the hall—had a chamber supported on 'jettied' joists and reached by a ladder-

like stairway inside the hall. You will remember that many
great halls had two storerooms at their lower ends in which food
and drink were kept. Some of the yeomen's houses also had
'butteries' and 'pantries' at the lower ends of their halls; in
which case there was often another chamber over these, so that
the hall looked as if it had a house at each end. In some fine
wooden houses of the reign of Henry VIII, these two end parts
of the house were sometimes made to form small wings; sometimes there was even a dining parlour in place of the storerooms.
In many of the village streets of the south-east of England you
will find Tudor houses in which one of the two parlours forms
a shop; you can still see the doorway leading into this with a
little shop window beside it.

All these wooden houses of Henry VIII's reign and that of
Elizabeth were built in the old style of the village carpenters:
with upright posts or 'studs' set very closely together so that
the spaces between could be filled up with stones, wattling,
mud, or anything handy. In Elizabeth's reign, however, people
began to realize that all this building of large timber houses was
using up all the English forests, so that there would soon be
none left for building ships for the defence of the country. So
the government gave orders that carpenters were in the future
to find a way of framing-up their houses which would use less
wood.

In the north-west midlands, where there had never at any
time been enough good building timber, the carpenters had
already been trying out different ways of framing-up their
houses. They made their walls in square panels and used short
pieces of wood across the corners to stiffen everything up (27).
They became quite clever in making use of curved pieces of
wood; even cutting them into shapes like those in the windows
of churches. In the end, the carpenters of the whole of England
had to follow their example by framing-up their walls in large
square panels instead of the old-fashioned wasteful method they
had been using for so many centuries. The carpenters of Che-
shire, Shropshire, and that part of England generally, went on
to build quite large houses, such as the Old Hall at Moreton,
entirely of timber framing. They were even able to build fine
bay windows such as had until then been made of stone. The
spaces between the timbers were carefully plastered and white-
washed so that the pattern of the dark woodwork could be seen;

this black-and-white style of building is often known as 'magpie' architecture.

In the last chapter we mentioned that during the Tudor period bricks were beginning to reach the east of England in large numbers and that builders were fast learning how to use them. At this time, a bricklayer was more difficult to get than a mason, so that only the finest houses could be built of bricks. But before the end of the reign of Henry VIII, bricklayers were coming over from Flanders and showing the people of the eastern counties how to build houses with the new material. In Norfolk and Suffolk, especially, you may often see these houses built by the Flemings. The gable ends of the buildings are very often arranged in steps, giving a strange un-English appearance.

The great trouble with a yeoman's house was probably the fact that its hall was not really big enough to take a fire built in the middle of the floor. It must have been very uncomfortable for everybody to be cooped up in such a small space—which was at the same time always reeking with smoke. So the yeomen did their best to find bricklayers who would make for them brick copies of the stone fireplaces which the owners of the great houses were now having built for them in the walls of their halls. In an old timber house you will often find a brick fireplace, dating from perhaps the end of the reign of Henry VIII, with its very flat brick arch and its wide 'flue' reaching right up through the chimney stack to the beautifully carved brick chimney-pot at the top. What a blessing it must have been to the yeoman to be able to clear away the fire from the centre of his hall and build it in a fine new fireplace at the side. And the greatest boon was that he could now put a ceiling across the upper part of his hall and have attic bedrooms in the roof above. As soon as the builders had grasped the idea that there was no need to worry any more about fires built on the floor because they could get bricklayers to make fireplaces in the wall, the old high hall disappeared once and for all from the yeoman's house. This then became a complete two-storied building: having a low hall or kitchen in the middle, a parlour at either end, and three or four chambers on the floor above. The yeoman's house was beginning to look at last something like a house of to-day. There was, however, one strange thing about it: the upper story still hung out over the lower on 'jetties'.

The Yeomen of England

As the carpenters became more skilful in using their timber they found that they could so frame-up a house as to be able to build both the stories together. Instead of having four wooden walls for the lower story and four more wooden walls for the upper, they began to use tall posts, passing up *both* stories, at the corners of the building and in two or three places along its sides. Between these posts, they framed-up the walls of the house in panels, tying the sides of the building together with strong wooden beams passing through the house from side to side. The floor-joists were laid on the tops of these big beams or 'girders'; as the floor played no part in carrying the upper story of the house but was just a floor, the builders found they could leave out pieces of the floor where they liked without interfering with the strength of the house. This was very useful indeed, as it meant that they could actually build a big brick chimney stack *inside* the house; if they put it between the hall and the parlour they could arrange for a fireplace on each side—one for each room. This meant that the yeoman could have a fire in his parlour as well as in his hall; he could then sit in front of the parlour fire and get away from the smell of the cooking. The space between the side of the great chimney stack and the wall of the house was used for building a stair leading to the chambers above; by the time of Elizabeth these stairs were often wooden copies of the stone spiral staircases of the great houses, built round a wooden pole like the mast of a ship.

By about the year 1600, the English yeoman's house had become a two-storied building of one of two kinds. The larger of these had a hall with a parlour at each end. At the lower end of the hall was its entrance doorway; at the upper end was the great chimney stack having the hall fireplace on one side and the fireplace of the best parlour on the other. But a smaller kind of farmhouse was also being built which did not have a parlour at the lower end of the hall. The entrance to a house of this sort would be beside the big chimney stack, the space between the stack and the door making a little lobby. On one side of this lobby would be the door to the parlour and on the other side the door to the hall. So you see that at last the plan of the hall has changed so much from the Middle Ages that it now actually has its doorway in the upper end near the fire.

These comfortable new houses, well warmed by the roaring fires built inside their brick fireplaces, must have been greatly

123

admired by those yeomen who were still living in the old-fashioned jettied houses. The owners of these, too, would be wanting inside chimney stacks, but could not have them because if they had cut away their floor-joists to build a chimney stack, the top story of the house would have fallen down. But by this time both bricks and bricklayers were becoming much easier to find; so the answer was to build brick walls under the old jetties which would support the wooden walls of the upper story. The carpenters could then take away the old wooden walls below and cut as many holes in the floor as they liked. You may see many hundreds of old houses where this has been done.

It must have made a great difference to the streets of the old towns of the Middle Ages when the carpenters stopped building with jetties. The great difference between building in the country and building in towns is that you are so cramped in towns that you cannot spread your house out sideways; you have therefore to build it upwards like a skyscraper. Every time you added a story you had to make the floor-joists stick out as a jetty to support it; the taller your house, therefore, the more top-heavy it begins to look (27). In the narrow streets of the Middle Ages houses like this facing each other across the way must have made everything very dark and gloomy down below.

During the reign of Elizabeth, the English carpenters were having the time of their lives. The rich yeomen were all wanting houses, and the forest trees were falling in their hundreds, to be sawn up into posts and beams and dragged away to the carpenters' yards. The carpenters had all their plans ready for framing-up houses to the sizes required by the people who wanted them. Timbers were quickly laid out on the ground, marked and cut and joined together with their wooden tongues or 'tenons' fitted into the slots or 'mortices'. Holes were drilled through each joint to take the wooden pegs which secured it. When the walls of the house had been framed-up and were lying on the ground, each joint was marked with a number; this number was cut with a chisel on each of the timbers meeting at that joint. Roman numbers were used because they could be easily cut with a jab from the carpenter's chisel. (As a matter of fact the ordinary man of Elizabeth's reign did not understand the Arabic numbers we use to-day; if you see a date earlier than 1550 written on the wall of a house you can be pretty sure it is a fake.) When everything was ready the wooden pegs were knocked out, the timbers all dragged to the place where the house was to be built and then framed-up again on the ground. Then came the important matter of lifting the walls of the house up into position. The neighbours usually helped, pushing and hauling until the four walls were up and could be joined together and fastened with wooden pegs. If you look at the timbers of an old house to-day you will still see at every joint the numbers cut by the chisels of carpenters who worked perhaps four hundred years ago.

In the days of Queen Elizabeth, the raising up of a wooden house was a very important matter. Everybody who could do so joined in; when the ridge timber was finally fixed in position the owner of the house was probably expected to give all his helpers a party. Sometimes when a house is being built to-day you will see a Union Jack tied to the ridge timber or perhaps to a chimney-pot. This is a reminder of those old days; when the owner of the building sees it, he should make some kind of present to the men who have been working to build his house for him.

In the old days, if a villager misbehaved, his neighbour might well ask him to go away and live elsewhere. He might then take his house with him; this would be quite easy to do because the main framework of the house could be taken down by knocking out the wooden pegs and pulling the joints apart. The neighbours who had helped him to build his house would now help him to pull it down. You will notice that even to-day when we *knock* down with pickaxes and heavy hammers we still talk about '*pulling* down', as if it were a building of wood.

The village streets of England are still full of yeomen's farmhouses, some of them built as long ago as the days of Henry VIII, and many of them at least as old as Queen Elizabeth's reign. They may also be seen hiding away among the fields. But most of them are in villages; for, in those days, the farmers did not live on their own farms so much as they do nowadays, preferring to live together, especially as they often did not have separate farms but only a part of one large farm which belonged to the whole village.

Nowadays, most of these village farmhouses have been divided up into cottages, or even turned into village shops. But among the many doorways of all shapes and sizes, you can often find one which was the actual doorway of the farmhouse when it was built so many years ago. Sometimes there are modern shops, with the names of the tradespeople written in huge letters over the shop window; too often, the whole front of the old house is completely covered with notice boards and advertisements of all sorts. Yet if you will look above all this jumble, you will usually see what has never been altered much—the farmhouse roof. Its old thatch has probably long ago been taken away and tiles put in its place. But you can still see the long run of the roof of each house; perhaps it now covers three or four shops. People in the cottages, or in the bedrooms over the shops have spent the last two hundred years or so in building fireplaces in their rooms, with small chimney stacks which stick up through the roof in all sorts of places. Amongst all this jumble of brick stacks and chimney pots and cowls you will be able to see, every now and again, the great solid stack which warmed the yeoman's house when it was built, perhaps nearly four hundred years ago (39).

Inside these old houses, there are many things to be seen. When you have gone in through the doorway—which may either be a rough Gothic arch formed of two pieces of curved timber, or a finely carved doorway with a low pointed top like that of a church—you will find yourself in a world of greal beams. Many of the big posts supporting the walls have post sibly been covered up by plaster and wallpaper, but you wil probably still see the heavy 'girders', bent with age, which support the upper floor. Many of the beams may be decorated with patterns which were carved in the days of the Tudor kings.

You will find few old glass windows, except in very good houses or in the towns; glass was still too dear for the countryman to afford. Where it was used, however, it was set into windows just like those of a church, but flat-topped and made of course entirely of wood. The small pieces of glass were fixed together with strips of lead, and in some cases there were iron casements which would open and shut.

The cheaper houses and the unimportant rooms of all houses simply had windows with upright wooden bars fastened in them like the iron bars of a prison. These square wooden bars were fixed closely together so that burglars could not get in.

The pride of the yeoman's house—its great fireplace—can nowadays seldom be seen. We cannot get the wood to-day for making the mighty bonfires that warmed the yeomen's halls and cooked their food. Nor are we willing to put up with the clouds of smoke that the old fireplaces used to pour out into the rooms. So nowadays they are all bricked up and have small modern coal-burning grates built into the filling.

All through Elizabeth's reign, everyone who could afford it was building himself a house. This went on for the next hundred years or so, until much of the building timber came to be used up. By the time of the Great Civil War, people were finding that if they wanted houses they had to build them entirely of brick; there is, fortunately, plenty of good clay in England for making these, and brickyards were being opened all over the country.

The brick farmhouses were planned in much the same way as the old timber ones had been. Each had a large hall or kitchen with a parlour at one end; between the two was built the large chimney stack. Some of the larger farmhouses had another parlour at the other end of the kitchen, in which case the second parlour would generally be without a fire, though a chimney stack was sometimes built for it later. Towards the end of the seventeenth century people got so used to building parlour fireplaces in the gable walls that they began to give up the large double chimney stack which took up so much room in the middle of the house and build all three stacks separately. The way up to the bedchambers on the floor above was usually by a narrow winding stair fitted in against the thickness of the great chimney stack in the middle of the house; opposite it, in the case of the smaller houses, there was often a little lobby or inside porch. The larger farmhouses, with their entrance doorways at the other end of the kitchen, often had proper porches outside the house as in the old days (40).

The windows of these farmers' houses were quite small, and had heavy wooden frames built into the brickwork to carry the iron casements with their leaded glass panes. Each window was divided up into two or three 'lights' by a wooden 'mullion' or two; these, however, were quite plain and not ornamented with mouldings as they had been in the old days. Doors, too, were now no longer being hung on the wall with iron 'hooks and bands' but, like the casements, were being fixed into strong wooden frames built into the brickwork.

The old-fashioned building methods of the Middle Ages were fast disappearing; by the time of the Civil War houses were not very different from those in which we live to-day.

CHAPTER XI

GREAT HOUSES COVER THE LAND

In the days of the Tudors, England was a nation of rich folk anxious to spend money on houses. In the countryside, the squires and yeomen were making money by selling wool to the merchants in the wealthy cities. Many great lords had suddenly had their estates very much enlarged with land which had belonged to the old abbeys brought to ruin by Henry VIII, while there were also a number of people now owning abbey lands who had never been rich before but had now become enormously wealthy. Thus in city and countryside there were now large numbers of people who were wanting comfortable houses.

We saw in the last chapter how the middle class of yeomen persuaded their village carpenters to build houses for them. The wooden buildings which they made, many of which to-day would seem to us like cottages, were magnificent houses compared with the hovels in which the poor peasants of the countryside were still living in Tudor days. And yet that same Tudor period was one of enormous houses. For centuries, the nobles had been adding to their homes until many of these had become great rambling palaces, larger than almost anything which has been built since. In those days, anybody who had plenty of money and no huge house set to work and built himself one as soon as he possibly could, for there was no other way by which he could display his wealth to his neighbours.

We have explained how all the *old* houses had grown up from small beginnings. Now, however, people were having to set to work to build new great houses, complete in every detail, with nothing to start from.

Of course, what the rich man really needed was an architect to whom he could explain the kind of house he wanted. But in Tudor days there were no such architects in England. The buildings of the Middle Ages had been only very roughly designed by the men who wanted them built, the details being settled on the spot by the masons and carpenters who had to do the building work. There was nobody who could invent a complete building and draw plans of every part for the builder and his workmen to follow.

In the first chapter we talked about the great days of Ancient Greece and Rome. At about the time of Christ the architecture of Rome was of course magnificent, all the great buildings having been designed by men who spent all their lives in studying how to design and build. These men were architects; they drew out a plan of the building and all the various parts of it, telling the masons and carpenters exactly what they were to do. But during the Middle Ages all this magnificence had passed away, ancient Rome had become a city of ruins, and the ways of the old architects were forgotten.

About the time of the Wars of the Roses much the same sort of squabbling was going on in Italy; the great nobles in their walled cities were spending all their time besieging one another. The armies had with them skilled engineers who knew all about buildings, more particularly how to destroy them. (It is a strange thing that the army engineers of the Middle Ages, whose job it was to knock down buildings more than to build them, often seem to have become so interested in their work that in the end they made themselves skilled architects. One of the first English architects, you will remember, was Henry II's engineer Alnoth.) In the army of the Duke of Florence was an engineer called Brunelleschi who began to interest himself in the ruins of Ancient Rome. He made a careful study of the manner in which the Romans had designed their buildings, and tried to copy some of their designs to please his master and other noble families in Florence. Other would-be architects copied Brunelleschi's methods, all studying and copying the ancient glories of fifteen centuries before. Thus, in the city of Florence, a new architecture was born; it was called 'Renaissance', which means 're-born', because it was believed to be the old architecture of Rome born again.

The architects of the Italian Renaissance were a class of people whose like had not been seen for a great many centuries. They were not nobles or great churchmen who had many things to do and only now and again set to work to try to plan a building. The architects were men whose sole job it was to do this.

They spent their whole lives in studying great buildings of the past and in sketching them and measuring them, puzzling out the best ways of planning so that the rooms would be arranged in the most comfortable way while the house or whatever it was could still be built without too much difficulty. When they were actually preparing plans they did not just sketch these out roughly, as an abbot designing a new church might have done; the plans were all very carefully drawn with the lines ruled straight and everything properly measured. During the Middle Ages, when the plan had been laid out on the ground, nobody could be quite certain just how it was going to look when finished, because nobody knew what ideas the masons and the carpenters might have as the walls slowly rose. But the architects drew the whole building out first so as to make certain that everything would work. As well as the plan they drew the 'elevations' of all the walls. This meant they had to know their job thoroughly and also that they really had to be interested in what they were doing and take pains to get everything right. During the Middle Ages parts of a building often just 'happened'; the Renaissance architects saw to it that everything was properly designed before work was begun, so as to leave as little as possible to chance.

Anyone who is to become an architect must spend many years in studying buildings before trying to design one for himself. Some of the first English Renaissance architects were men who had been given the job of measuring up the abbeys after the monks had been turned out by Henry VIII, so that the king might know something about these buildings he was giving away to his various favourites. Some of these 'surveyors' became so interested that they took the trouble to go to Italy to see what was being done there by the Italian architects. Some Italians were invited by Henry VIII to come to this country to help in showing the English architects what the new style was like; a few brought books of designs with them for the English architects to study.

If you set out to try to draw the front of an imaginary house, you will almost certainly put the doorway in the middle of the wall, with the same number of windows on either side of it. This is the simplest way of designing a house: one end is balanced by the other, so that everything is bound to look tidy. This was the only method the Renaissance architects understood. The buildings they produced were rather dull to look at after the rambling old Gothic palaces with their oddly shaped halls and chambers, and their skylines broken by all kinds of towers and turrets. But such houses were not designed; they had just grown up through the centuries. When the first Renaissance architects set to work, they had to go by very simple rules of design; the first of these was that the fronts of buildings should be exactly balanced on either side of a central doorway.

We can imagine what difficulties the first real English architects came up against when they tried to plan a great house. Nothing would balance anything. The centre of the whole house was its great hall: this had a doorway at one end and the great bay window lighting the 'high table' at the other. No architect would have dared to suggest that the doorway of the great hall should be put in the middle of its wall; the whole idea of having a great hall would be ruined in an instant. So although they could make some attempt to balance the front of their house by making the wings at either end look as much as possible like each other, there still remained—in the middle of everything, where they wanted the chief effect—the great tall lopsided hall (24).

We have already explained the improvements which were made to the hall when it became no longer necessary to have the fire burning in the middle of the floor. Once the owners of great halls had taken to building proper fireplaces in the wall the whole hall could have a ceiling just like any other room. This was a great help to the architects. The old lofty hall had cut the house up into three parts; this made an awkward front because it was impossible to make a tidy 'elevation' if you had to have it looking like two houses separated by what seemed to be a piece of a church which had strayed into the design.

In the manor house of the Middle Ages, the great chamber had been reached by means of a stair at one end of the great hall; at first a straight wooden stair, it later became a stone one winding up inside a turret. If there happened to be another chamber at the lower end of the hall, this had to be reached by its own separate stair.

It was of course impossible for the architects to plan a house of this sort properly; for it was impossible to get from one bedchamber to another without going down a staircase, walking all along the hall, and then climbing another staircase. But once the hall had been lowered in height so that the first floor could be carried right across it, these difficulties vanished and the house began to look something like a house and not just a collection of odds and ends.

Now that at last only one stair was needed to reach the most important bedchambers, the architects of Elizabeth's reign decided to make this a really fine staircase. At this time it became the most important piece of woodwork in the house.

In an earlier chapter we said that the space in the attics of a house—that is to say up inside the roof—had often been used as a sleeping place; although perhaps it had sometimes been merely a matter of putting a few planks across the roof beams. In the days of Elizabeth, however, the attics began to be a complete story passing all over the house and having a proper floor just like the floor of the chambers below. In a small house it would have been quite easy to get enough light into the attics by just having a window in the gable at either end; but in the large Elizabethan houses the builders arranged a jumble of small gables along the sides of the house as well, so that they could have a window in each of these (40). Each little gable could have behind it a tiny bedroom. In very large houses there was often a long well-lit passage passing down the whole length of the building. This was the first time a passage of this sort had been planned as part of a house; up to now the rooms had always been entered one from another. These Elizabethan passages made it possible to reach the attic bedrooms without going through one to get to another; they were not, however, like the narrow passages that we have in a house to-day, but more like a long wide hall. The Elizabethans called this part of the house the 'long gallery' and, if the windows at the end were large enough for there to be plenty of light, pictures were sometimes hung there; this is how picture galleries first came to be used in this country.

The Elizabethans were not only interested, however, in making a comfortable and well-planned house; they wanted it to look well from the outside. In particular, they expected architects to see to it that the main front of the house was properly balanced, with the entrance doorway in the middle of the front and the walls and windows on either side of it matching one side with the other. They could only do this by making that part of the house which was at the lower end of the hall as long as the hall itself; so that the main doorway—which still had to be at the end of the hall—should be in the centre of the front. It was now easier to do this, as the hall was not the tall church-like room it used to be in the old days. Now it was just a large ground-floor room; quite easy to balance—as far as the front of the house was concerned—by several smaller rooms placed end to end until they equalled the length of the hall. Sometimes pantries, butteries, and other storerooms for food were provided in this part of the house so as to fill in this gap in the plan.

Another of the difficulties the architects met with in trying to tidy up the front of the house was how to match the beautiful bay window at the end of the hall. The Elizabethans would never have been willing to give up using this, the finest window in the whole house. So the only thing to do was to have another bay window to balance it; the architects did not mind if it only gave light to a pantry as long as they could put it in the right place on the front of the house.

Once they had started to use the bay window as an ornament on the front of houses the Elizabethans began to get very fond of these and used them in all sorts of places; sometimes making them go right up the whole side of the house so that there was a bay window on each floor (29). This is a very pleasant kind of window to have in a room as when you stand within it you can see much more than from an ordinary window; even to-day our smallest houses usually have a bay window if possible.

Now that there were, as a general rule, three stories (including the attics) in a large house the designers had to pay particular attention to the staircase. We have seen that only one would now be necessary; the architects thought they might just as well have one really fine staircase and make it an important part of the house. The difficulty was to know where to put it. It was going to be too big a thing to get inside a turret; sometimes, however, they built a square tower to take it. A favourite place for the main stair was at the back door of the hall, so that when you entered the front door of the house you only had to pass through the 'screens' passage and you could reach the staircase at once; this was now right in the middle of the house and led easily to all of its rooms. Up to this time, all buildings had been roofed very simply; the main idea being to keep them as narrow as possible, so that the roof would not have too wide a gap to cover. This had been necessary in the days when roofs were very steeply sloped; for a wide roof would have risen much too high, so that the building would have looked as though it were all roof. But now that lead was being used for house roofs, and these could be made much flatter, the builders could use a much wider roof without making it rise too high in the air.

During Elizabeth's reign, therefore, they began for the first time to arrange the main rooms of houses side by side, with one wide roof covering the two. It is not easy to explain this, but perhaps you can imagine that where before you would have been able to look right through a building from side to side (supposing its windows were opposite each other) the house was now much thicker from back to front and had a wall passing through the middle of it to divide it into a front and a back portion, both of which were under the same roof.

This brought about very big changes in the plans of houses. Up till the Elizabethan period, houses had straggled all over the place in long narrow wings, each with its own roof. Now they were getting bunched up together with one wide roof covering the whole building. In the Middle Ages, the builders liked steeply pointed roofs; they added to the height of the building and made it look more important. The Elizabethan houses, however, were already quite tall buildings, and did not need to be finished with a high roof like those of the old churches. The wide new roofs helped the architects to plan more comfortable houses. No longer was there any need to have ranges of lodgings straggling round the large courtyards; everything could now be packed inside the house. Great Elizabethan palaces still kept their courtyards, but these were so small compared with the great mass of the buildings surrounding them that it is quite a surprise to be told that there is one to be found behind the tall front of Burghley House (29) in Northamptonshire. But the smaller Elizabethan houses gave up these tremendous entrance fronts with their great gatehouses and opened up the courtyard with the main part of the house behind it for all the world to see.

The architects still kept, however, the two little wings at the ends of the house. They had been there for such a long time that everyone would doubtless have thought that a house looked unfinished without them. The entrance porch, of course, was also kept. Not only did it still help to keep draughts away from the hall; it was more than ever needed to make the entrance look as important as possible. And now the porch was in the very centre of the house front, with the whole design balanced about it; we generally find that Elizabethan house-porches are very ornamental.

The people who were ordering their architects to design houses for them would doubtless call every now and again to see how the plans were getting on. Somebody must soon have noticed that the ordinary house plan of the period, with its main block, two little wings, and central porch, looked just like a capital E. So the story got around that the architects were planning houses in this way to please Queen Elizabeth. This of course was not true, but it is a pleasant story, and makes it easy for us to remember what the plan of an Elizabethan house was like (31).

Now that the house had become one large block of apartments instead of a straggling group of buildings, the inside of this block had become quite a collection of rooms for all purposes. There were several parlours, both for sitting in and dining in. Some were sunny rooms for the winter time; others were cooler for use in summer. Above were two floors of bedchambers; on the first floor, the finest bedroom was still called the 'great chamber'. This, the bedroom of the owner of the whole magnificent house, was sometimes called the 'state chamber'—that is why cabins in ships are called 'staterooms'.

There was one room which was still left over from the Middle Ages. This was the great hall. No longer was it used as the chief room of the house; it was becoming rather bare and empty and taking up a lot of space. The main doorway of the house still led into it, but it had become really nothing more than a large entrance hall. It is interesting to remember that we still call the passage inside the front door of a small house the 'hall'—it is difficult to realize that the great banqueting halls of the days of the Wars of the Roses have been shrinking through the ages until nothing is left of them but the small space inside the front door.

Behind the entrance hall of an Elizabethan house was another small hall in which was the main staircase. The Elizabethan staircase was usually like a very large spiral staircase—generally made of wood—built inside a square tower instead of a round one. The stairs rose in straight flights up each side of the tower. These wooden staircases were becoming very much finer than they had been during the Middle Ages. They had proper handrails, fixed to sturdy posts wherever the stair changed direction. The central column of a winding staircase is called the 'newel'. Elizabethan houses often had wooden staircases of this sort. The larger stairs, built inside square towers, had four newels: square wooden posts into which the handrails were fixed. At first these newels ran right up the staircase from top to bottom as they had done in the case of the old winding stairs. Later on, the newels came to be used in short lengths only, where they were needed for fixing the handrails into. This is the kind of 'newel-post' that we still have in our staircases to-day.

During the last three hundred years or so, architects have invented all sorts of different ways of ornamenting the tops of newel posts; at the end of Queen Elizabeth's reign they were often being carved into little statues. Underneath the handrail and separating it from the stairs there were usually small moulded posts called 'balusters'. We shall have more to say about these later. The first balusters we used in this country were very heavy, clumsily made things. After the Elizabethan period they came to be properly turned on a lathe, like the balusters of to-day; but they were still very thick and sturdy.

Outside the Elizabethan house, the most important piece of architecture was its entrance doorway. House builders liked to have a really ornamental front door which would advertise the house as much as possible; very often, for example, there was a beautiful coat of arms over it. Some of the finest Elizabethan porches seem to be trying to remind you that it was not so very long since the entrance to a great house had been through a tall turreted gateway.

But the towers and turrets of the Middle Ages had gone for ever. Architects from Italy were travelling over here, bringing with them sketch books full of designs copied from the old Roman buildings; in this way the classical 'Orders' that we read about in Chapter I began to appear in England. At first these were not used actually for building, but as little copies fixed to the Elizabethan porches just for ornament. The Elizabethans seem to have liked the Corinthian columns with their pretty capitals; many porches of those days were ornamented with these.

By the reign of Elizabeth, the Gothic arch had gone out of

use in English architecture. Important openings such as doorways had half-round arches like those of the days of the Normans, but with such mouldings as the Romans used round the
edge of the opening. Windows were now always flat-topped.
During the Tudor period, each part—or 'light'—of the window had a flat-arched top to it; in Elizabeth's day the tops of all
lights were flat. Tall windows still had 'transoms' passing across
them so that the lower parts of some of the lights could be fitted
up with iron casements which could be made to open. Glass was
still in small pieces fixed together with strips of lead.

Inside the house the most important pieces of ornament were
the carved stone fireplaces. At last houses were becoming properly heated against the English winters; the Elizabethans
were very fond of sitting in front of their fine fireplaces. You
will often see the little Corinthian columns appearing there also.
But the architects from sunny Italy were not so good at designing fireplaces as were those from the colder parts of Europe. It
was the Germans and the Flemings who carved the elaborate
Elizabethan fireplaces in this country. Some of the designs are
very strange-looking, with columns which sometimes finish at
the top with the upper parts of the figures of men and women.
Outside the house, as in the days of the Tudor kings, you could
see how warm it was inside by the numbers of chimneys which
rose against the sky (29).

Now that the hall had become, like the rest of the house, one
story only in height, the high open roof disappeared for ever
from English house architecture. All rooms now had ceilings.
As was explained earlier, the first ceilings were merely the undersides of the floor above. These being all dark oak boards,
however, with heavy beams throwing deep shadows, made the
rooms rather gloomy, especially as the comfort-loving Elizabethans liked to have the walls of their rooms panelled with oak
also. But the Italian architects taught them how to make ceilings of plaster, such as we have to-day, by nailing thin strips of
wood called 'laths' across from beam to beam and covering
these with lime plaster. This is made, like mortar, of a mixture
of lime and sand, with bullocks' hair mixed with it so as to hold
it together and prevent it from falling to pieces. The Italian
plasterers were very clever at making patterns in the plaster;
the ceilings of the Elizabethan and Jacobean (James I) periods
are often very richly ornamented. A favourite ornament of this

137

period was 'strapwork', a design of curled straps which is not only found carved on stonework and ceilings but also used as fretwork in parapets and on gables. When you see strapwork used you can be sure that the house was built at some time not far from the year 1600.

The Elizabethan period was not a good one for church building, owing to the disagreements between Protestants and Roman Catholics. Some of the old churches, however, were made more comfortable by panelling; fine oak pulpits were in some cases put into the church for the Protestant preacher whose sermons were now becoming an important part of the church service.

The Elizabethans followed the example set by Henry VIII and founded grammar schools in many a town for the education of the sons of the townspeople. Even the smallest country towns began to build schoolrooms, each with its porch and, sometimes, a tiny two-roomed house for the master. In the Middle Ages, the old and sick people who had no one to look after them were cared for in the great halls of the hospitals built like those of the monasteries; from Tudor times onwards we find little rows of 'almshouses' each with a tiny kitchen and a bedchamber. Sometimes these are set round a courtyard like the quadrangle of a college; very often there is a chapel to make the whole thing perfect.

In the Middle Ages, nobody had travelled about the country much unless he was a merchant and had to do so. But the Elizabethans liked travelling. They liked to visit each other's fine houses and talk about the happenings in the world of which England now formed an important part. In some of the large towns, inns came to be built for travellers. These inns were built round small courtyards; this was always the arrangement for public buildings—such as colleges for example—in which numbers of people lived. As there were still no passages inside houses for getting from one room to another the rooms of the inn could only be reached by their outside doors, leading directly from the courtyard. As the bedchambers of the inn were on the first or second floor, there had to be galleries passing round the courtyard so that the guests could reach the doors of their rooms. It was in the inn courtyards that the plays of Shakespeare were first acted; the galleries of our theatres to-day should therefore remind us of the Elizabethan inn courtyards, and the travellers of those days coming out of the doorways of their bedchambers to look from the galleries at the play going on in the yard below.

There is another matter for which we have to thank the Elizabethans. Their architects were not satisfied simply with designing fine houses. They were not content to see these great buildings rising from a yard full of rubbish, or overgrown with weeds. So they surrounded each house with a properly laid out garden, with lawns, flower-beds and well-kept paths and hedges. There were special little gardens in which were grown the herbs which the Elizabethans used for medicines. Sometimes there were pools for fish, and little summerhouses like the temples of ancient Rome. Also there were orchards and gardens surrounded with walls of warm red brick, on which the peaches ripened.

CHAPTER XII

THE ARCHITECTS SET A NEW FASHION

At the beginning of the last chapter we talked about the great changes that were taking place in Italy, where the architects were beginning to bring back into use the old architecture of Rome. If you will turn back to Chapter I you will find that the Roman architects made great use of large stone columns and that these columns were designed generally in one or the other of two styles called 'Orders'. The most beautiful of these was the 'Corinthian Order' (47). There was also a much simpler Order called the 'Doric'. In the days of the Ancient Greeks, this Order was very rough and clumsy but the Romans altered it and made it more graceful; their Order is called the 'Roman Doric' (34). It was these two Orders—the Corinthian and the Roman Doric—that the architects of the Renaissance used. At first they did not use columns standing by themselves as in the porticoes of the old temples, but built them on to the face of the building as a kind of ornament; sometimes they were even built up in brickwork.

If you will look at the picture of the portico of Claremont (47) you will see that the stonework above the capitals of the columns is arranged in three layers. The lowermost of these—that is to say, the actual stone beam itself—generally has a moulding called an 'architrave' carved upon it. This moulding is a very important one; we shall soon be talking of it again. Above the architrave is a stone band called the 'frieze'; sometimes this is quite plain, but it is often carved with patterns of different kinds.

The upper most part of the stonework is finished with a large moulding called a 'cornice', which overhangs where the roof comes down on the walls, so as to make a sort of stone 'eaves'. The cornice is a very important part of a building; practically all Renaissance buildings are finished at the top with one.

The doorways of the old Roman buildings either had a

square top or 'lintel'; or, if the opening was too wide for one stone to reach across it, there was a round arch. These were the only two shapes of opening used by the Renaissance architects. The pointed arch disappeared absolutely; they thought that it was only fit for barbarians and Goths.

Whether the opening was flat or arched, it nearly always had an 'architrave' moulding carved round it. At first these mouldings were simple, like those of the old temples, but by the end of the seventeenth century in this country they had become bulgy and more ornamental. You will probably find that the doorway of the room which you are sitting in as you read this has an architrave moulding passing round it; if it is a modern house, however, the moulding will be quite plain—perhaps just a flat piece of wood.

So much for simple doorways. But a good architect would want to make more of his doorway than that. He might like to put a small column—either a Corinthian or a Doric one—on either side of his doorway with the three bands of ornament topped by a cornice joining the two columns at their tops. Doorways of this sort were very popular in Jacobean times— that is to say in the reign of James I who followed Queen Elizabeth to the throne.

An important part of the architecture of the Roman temple was its 'pediment'—the low pointed gable end with the cornice moulding passing all round it to form a triangle. Many Renaissance doorways had little copies of these pediments placed above them as ornament. Sometimes even the openings of the windows had pediments over them (35). Another strange piece of ornament is a sort of curly bracket—like a snail standing on its tail—which was placed beneath the ends of the cornice passing across a doorway as if it were helping to support it. Sometimes the columns, instead of being round, were square; such columns are called 'pilasters' (45).

It was in doorways like this that the architecture of the Italian Renaissance first came to this country. We have already talked about the people who used to make plans of the great houses of Tudor and Elizabethan days—'surveyors' they were called. Many of these people travelled abroad and picked up knowledge about the new style, so that when they came to make designs for new houses they could often include a doorway like this; there were also some Italian architects and masons who came over to England to show the English builders the new style.

You will remember that we explained how houses had by now ceased to be rambling collections of buildings and were being planned each as a solid block, all under one wide roof. This meant that the English architects had to set to work to plan the whole house 'on paper' before the work of building started, instead of letting it grow up anyhow. The most important drawing from which you build a house is the 'ground plan' showing how all the rooms are fitted together; there has to be, of course, a plan of each floor. The architect then has to draw each of the four 'elevations' of the house, showing how each will look when the outer walls have been built. The architects took great care to keep these four elevations neat and tidy; by keeping the house as a simple four-square block they were able to do this without too much difficulty. There were no wings now, nor was there any porch jutting out to break the front of the house; this made things even simpler.

The Jacobean architects generally planned their houses by dividing the ground floor into three main parts. The centre portion, which ran from the front of the house to the back, had in it the front entrance hall and the staircase hall behind. On either side of the central strip were placed the various parlours.

The 'elevations' were very simple but were nevertheless all carefully drawn out on the architect's drawing board. At the top of the building there was usually a stone cornice running round it; above this was a parapet hiding the roof. A new shape of roof was being used in these houses. In the long narrow buildings of the Middle Ages the roof used to run from one end of the building to the other, ending in 'gables'. The new square kind of house, however, had its roof running all round the sides of the square; the ridges where the sides of the roof met were called the 'hips' (45). Sometimes these wide-hipped roofs had a piece in the middle that was actually flat; it was, however, quite possible to make this watertight if the builders who laid the lead knew their job. Small houses which were not so thick from back to front might still have a 'ridge' running from end to end. In this case, however, there would be no gables; the ends of the roof would be 'hipped back'.

As we have already explained, lead roofs can be made practically flat; a roof covered with slates or tiles, however, must be steeply sloped or the rain and snow will blow in. In sunny Italy roofs can be much flatter; it was always possible to hide them behind the parapet of the building. As the architects of the Italian Renaissance did not allow their roofs to show, the English architects tried to hide theirs also. Where a roof was covered with lead, or with tight-fitting slates, it could usually be kept low enough for it to be hidden behind a parapet. But slates were difficult to get in the parts of England where most of the building was going on, and the builders had to be content with ordinary tiles; these are not very watertight and have to be laid on a steeply pointed roof or snow will blow under them. It was quite hopeless to try to hide roofs like this behind a parapet, so that architects had to let them jut out over the wall as 'eaves', just as they had always done in the history of ordinary simple English buildings. But as buildings of the Renaissance period had to have cornices to finish them off at the top, the architects designed beautiful ones, often in wood, and put them under the eaves (45).

The houses which were being built about the time of the Civil War were very plain. Except for their cornices, there was usually nothing to break the severe lines of the 'elevations'. The architect usually tried, however, to give his house a good entrance doorway, with pilasters, cornices, and perhaps a little pediment. We shall have more to say about these Renaissance doorways—often the only piece of ornament on the whole house front—in another chapter.

If you had been looking at a great house of Tudor days, what you would first have noticed would have been its great chimney stacks rising up everywhere from the walls. Renaissance architects could not possibly have put up with this sort of thing; their chimney stacks were all hidden away inside the building so that they only showed where they came up through the roof. With the new kind of planning—that is to say with everything well thought out beforehand and no tacking on of odd rooms here and there—it was easy for the architects to do this. Thus there was nothing at all to break up the 'elevations' of the building, so that they could design these as they pleased by arranging the windows where they looked most tidy.

All windows were now just square openings with a flat top covered either by a stone 'lintel' or by a cleverly built arch—called a 'flat arch'—in which the bricks or stones were all laid as if they had been an arch but with an underside which was quite flat. The windows still had the bars known as 'mullions' and 'transoms'; these were now changing, however, from stone to wood. During what is known as the 'Stuart' period, the usual arrangement was for each window to have one mullion and one transom, arranged to form a cross. Unlike the old windows, however, the two upper parts of the Stuart windows were smaller than the two lower (35). The opening parts were still iron casements, hinged to the woodwork and filled with the usual small glass panes fixed in strips of lead.

Now that brick was being used so much for building houses, it was found that the openings for doors and windows could be made much more easily and neatly. There was no need to have heavy, specially cut stones; bricks were small, light, and easy to handle. In the Middle Ages, the builders used to just leave an opening for a doorway and then hang the door to the stonework with iron 'hooks and bands'. In the seventeenth century, the door had a heavy wooden frame built into the brickwork specially to take it; this made a much more draught-proof job. The window frames were made in the same way, with stout wooden mullions upon which to hang the iron casements.

The reign of Charles I, which separates the Jacobean period from the Civil War, saw great changes in the pattern of English country houses. Not only were the house-fronts losing all their cosy-looking porches and bay windows, and the shapes of the ordinary windows becoming square and dull; the skylines of the buildings were losing all their pretty little turrets and twisted chimney pots. The new architects would only allow themselves plain square stacks finished at the top with a cornice.

The architects kept just one turret; right in the middle of the house where it would not upset the balance of things. It was usually designed as a sort of little copy of a round temple of Roman days; there were sometimes four or eight little wooden columns supporting a small lead-covered dome. While these turrets were really only put there for ornaments they often had a bell hanging in them. They continued to be used for a hundred years or more, often being placed at the top of church towers. When it became fashionable to have a large clock on the top of your house the little temple became a square clock turret; a hundred years ago the stables of a country house nearly always had one turret on the roof.

The Architects Set a New Fashion

The little temple-like turret which you may see in the middle of the roof of a seventeenth-century house may be a reminder of the turret which used to be perched on top of the roof of a great hall of the Middle Ages to enable the smoke from the fire burning on the floor to escape. Later on, when the grand stair came to be built in the middle of the house, the architects often found that it was difficult to get enough light to it, so they put a large turret over it, with windows in the sides to light the stair below. Many staircases are still lit like this to-day.

The grand stair was an important part of the great house of the seventeenth century. Placed in a fine large staircase hall, it swept round the walls of this in wide flights, with a moulded handrail, supported by turned balusters, dividing it from its 'well'. But a very large house had to have other staircases: some to reach those parts of the house too far away from the grand stair, and others for servants to use. Small houses which had no grand stair had to have some means of getting up to the first floor. About the time of the Civil War, the builders began to make simple staircases with two flights to each story, each pair of flights meeting between the floors at a 'half-landing'. They used to call these 'a pair of stairs'; nowadays we call them 'dog-leg' stairs, and most small houses have them.

By the Jacobean period the beautiful wooden ceiling had disappeared for good. Every room had a plaster ceiling and really fine rooms had their ceilings worked into elaborate patterns, sometimes in forms of panelling, and ornamented with all kinds of carved flowers, fruit and so forth. While the architects were busily plodding along with their drawing boards and their instruments—ruling out their rather dull plans and elevations—the English craftsmen, masons, carpenters, plasterers, and smiths, were still using the skill which their forefathers had handed down to them in making beautiful things of their own design.

Yet slowly but surely a change was coming over England. In the Middle Ages we had been farmers; either growing food, or rearing sheep for wool. By the Tudor period, many of our sheep-grazing districts, such as Somerset or Suffolk, had taken to making cloth from wool; in this way factory towns came into being. In Elizabeth's reign, coal was already being mined in the midlands, and the country squires were finding a new way of getting rich. This was the beginning of a new period in our history; England, once rich from the profits of wool, was now to become richer still from coal and iron.

The discovery of coal made a difference to the way in which the builders made their fireplaces. The fires of the Middle Ages had been great bonfires of logs, either piled on a hearth in the middle of the room, or else in a sort of cave-like fireplace built into the wall. Coal, however, was burnt in iron baskets—something like the brazier used by a road watchman—placed inside the fireplace, which could then be much smaller than it had been when the great logs were piled into it. The old fireplaces had just been stone or brick arches; the new ones could be much more daintily designed, for there were now no logs being thrown about in them. The ornament which the Elizabethans used round the fireplace opening had always been of stonework; with the new coal grates, however, which kept the fire away from the edges of the opening, the ornament could be in woodwork.

In the Middle Ages, the man who wanted a house built had to arrange everything himself. He had to find a mason and a carpenter, perhaps a smith and a plumber as well. He had to find and buy all the materials, and discuss where everything was to go with all the various people who were going to do the job. But at the time of the Civil War, some people began to set up as builders. They were willing to build a house without worrying the man who wanted it about the details. They would find all the workmen and materials, and see the whole job through. This was a great improvement on the old method; indeed, without some arrangement like this, the architects would never have been able to get all their designs built.

It was very much the day of great houses. Church building had been almost forgotten. England was becoming Puritan; nobody much wanted beautiful churches, which they believed were a sinful waste of money. The churches of the early days of the new architecture were therefore even plainer to look at than the great houses. They were just brick boxes with a low roof covered with lead or slates (37). When England became Puritan, people wanted to pull down the chancels of churches, saying that they were only fit for Popish worship. Although the old chancels were saved, new churches were built without chancels (38). The altar was an ordinary table, exactly the same as the dining-table used in a house; it stood up against the end

The Architects Set a New Fashion

wall of the church with a rail round three sides of it—like the 'banisters' of the staircases which were being made at this time —for people taking Holy Communion. The seats in the churches became plain wooden benches without any carving or ornament. A great many people, however, were wanting to worship inside these ugly Puritan churches. But most of them were as small as they were ugly, and there was not enough room for everyone. So, for the first time, we find galleries being built inside churches to provide extra seats. Even the old village churches became at this time cluttered up with wooden galleries, hiding the lovely old windows of the Middle Ages. Church pews ceased to stand in the open; being placed in box-like arrangements of panelled partitions, often with doors to them. They were just like little cubicles with seats inside. Above these boxes towered the pulpit, higher than anything else in the church; from its summit, the Puritan preacher thundered at his congregation below.

During the reign of Queen Elizabeth, England was being covered with great mansions, some of them almost palaces. Throughout the Stuart period the building of houses went on even faster than ever. But the Stuart houses were not so much for the nobleman as for the country squire, every one of whom was beginning to have his plain box-like house with its spreading cornice and its fine front door.

We saw in Chapter X how the house of the yeoman grew out of the manor house and how the little farmhouse of the seventeenth century was planned as a kitchen-living-room and a parlour with a great chimney stack between them and the entrance doorway near the middle of the front wall of the house with a small porch just inside it. The box-like houses of the country squires had their chimneys at the ends of the house so that the entrance porch could become a wide passage reaching right through the house from front to back. This passage was really the same as the old 'screens passage' of the Elizabethan manor-houses; but now the great hall had shrunk until it was just a living-room like that of the farmhouse. In the eighteenth century we shall see the farmhouse-builders doing away with their central stacks and building separate stacks at the ends of their houses so that these could have good straight staircases placed in them instead of the cramped old spirals.

The Architects Set a New Fashion

It was the bricks made from the clay of the lowlands which helped to spread the new style. But in the hill-country of the Cotswolds, where there was no brick earth, the builders kept to the old masonry style; lovely little stone farmhouses—and even squires' houses—were still being built there, complete with old-fashioned mullioned windows and many-gabled stone roofs all through the Stuart period.

Nor did the village carpenters cease from their labours. It is true that brick building was going on almost everywhere over the south and east of England. Bricks, however, took a long time to reach the more inland counties, which had, moreover, plenty of wood still left for building purposes. In the midlands, therefore, the carpenters went on building in the old-fashioned way, with half-timbered walls framed up in large panels and stiffened with short pieces of wood, some of them curved. Houses with overhanging 'jetties' had gone out of fashion for a long time past—James I forbade the building of them in towns, owing to the risk of fire spreading across the narrow streets—but the old half-timber style of building was still being used in country districts all through the Stuart period.

Farming was now flourishing and the farmer was now living in a well-built house and had money to spend on the buildings of his farm. Chief of these was his great barn; from 1600 onwards we find many a huge barn, cleverly framed together upon its huge posts (28) gathering in the produce of what had been the land of the country gentleman or the proud abbot.

When the Civil War came upon England, the countryside was still covered with the beautiful old houses of the Elizabethans—red brick and cosy mullioned windows with little forests of twisted chimney pots rising against the sky. Many of these stately homes had to stand siege by the armies of the Parliament. A great many were destroyed by the great guns of the Puritans. As the tall chimneys toppled and the old red bricks fell from the crumbling walls, it must have seemed as if all that was left of the Middle Ages was falling away with them.

CHAPTER XIII

ENGLISH RENAISSANCE ARCHITECTURE

When we were talking about the buildings of the Middle Ages, we explained how these were designed not by architects but by people calling themselves engineers who did not know very much about art, but were able to arrange for the planning of buildings so that they would not fall down. All the ornament was left to the masons and carpenters who actually built the church, house, castle, or whatever it might be. As in most cases several masons would be working on different parts of the building, these did not always match each other; so the building was not really designed but just grew up piece by piece, from a rough plan prepared by the engineer. In a later chapter we explained how, during the reign of Elizabeth, a number of people called 'surveyors' were measuring up the buildings left over from the days of the monks and making drawings of them. These surveyors were becoming very interested in the buildings they were measuring; they were beginning to study architecture and trying to design buildings for themselves. Some of them travelled abroad to France and Italy to see the new architecture which was growing up, and were able to bring back with them sketches and drawings of buildings which they had seen on the Continent. As a result of the studies which Elizabethan surveyors were making of the fine buildings which were beginning to appear throughout Italy, they found that they were able to design buildings of the kind themselves. They were teaching themselves, in fact, how to be architects.

You will remember that during the Middle Ages the king always had in his household a royal engineer who looked after his palaces for him. By the reign of Elizabeth this officer had become the 'surveyor-general'. In 1615 there was a surveyor-general named Inigo Jones who was a very clever architect and had spent many years studying the buildings of the Italian Renaissance. It was really to this man that the birth of our own Renaissance architecture is due.

One of the first important buildings that Inigo Jones designed was a house at Greenwich for the Queen; it is still standing. You will notice that Inigo Jones ornamented the outside of the house with columns—or, rather, square 'pilasters'—of the same sort that the Romans used round their temples. Columns like this, with their capitals and the big spreading cornices above, were a very important part of Renaissance architecture. You will remember that in the first chapter we learned that these were called 'Orders'; the Queen's House at Greenwich is ornamented with the Corinthian Order.

Only four years after Inigo Jones became surveyor-general the king's palace of Whitehall was burned down. Inigo drew out plans for an enormous new palace, of a size many times greater than had ever been seen before in this country. It was built round seven courtyards and was all designed in the new Renaissance style. Of this great scheme of Inigo Jones only one small block was actually built. It still stands to-day in the street known as Whitehall. This one small building—which is known to-day as the 'banqueting hall'—gives you some slight idea of the style of architecture which Inigo Jones brought into this country. You will see from the picture (36) that it has two main stories, each of which is ornamented with an Order of columns having its own cornices above it. This is the usual way of using Orders on a building; when very tall columns, two stories high, are used they are known as 'giant Orders'. You will see later that giant Orders came to be very popular for building fine columned porticoes such as the Ancient Greeks and Romans used to have before their buildings. The windows of the Whitehall building are not as Inigo Jones designed them; as we have explained, the Stuart type of window had a mullion and transom arranged to form a cross (35).

Inigo Jones's great schemes were all brought to an end by the Civil War, after which the King of England was beheaded outside one of the windows of the banqueting hall that his surveyor-general had built for him. Inigo himself fled to the great house of Basing in Hampshire where he spent several weary years —possibly designing fine houses which he knew he would never build—while the place was being besieged by the Roundheads.

At the end of another great civil war, Henry II began to lay the foundations of the England of the Middle Ages. The next civil war—that of the Roses—began to bring that period to an end, and lead the way for the coming of the new Age which we call the Renaissance. The Great Civil War of Charles I's reign swept away every trace which remained of the England of the Middle Ages. During the struggle many of the old-fashioned houses were burned down or destroyed by the great guns; the new houses that were built in their place were all designed in the style that Inigo Jones and his fellow surveyors were beginning to make popular.

We said something in the last chapter of the way in which the houses of the day were being designed. No longer were they being allowed to grow up piece by piece; they were all carefully drawn out on paper before the builders were allowed to begin their work. As a matter of fact these houses of the seventeenth century are not always very pretty to look at. The old houses of the Middle Ages, which had all grown up anyhow and were probably very uncomfortable to live in, must have looked much more cosy than the square boxes which were being built during the early days of the Renaissance in England. The surveyors were not as yet experienced architects. They did not really know how to plan a good house, nor were they anything like as skilful in the designing of ornament as were the masons and carpenters of the Middle Ages. But they did at least plan their house in a tidy fashion, without odd wings straggling off here and there, or windows, doorways and chimney stacks all turning up in inconvenient places. So, despite the plainness of most of the early Renaissance houses in this country, the tidy way in which they were planned made them look important by suggesting that the man who had designed them knew what he was about.

A great disaster came upon the greatest city of England when, in 1666, London was half destroyed by fire. Here was the chance for the surveyors who were teaching themselves to become architects to show what they could do. The assistant surveyor-general of the day was the man who was entrusted with the designing of the new city of London. Christopher Wren was more of an engineer than an architect; he probably had not the same knowledge of the Italian Renaissance as, for example, Inigo Jones; but he was a bold man and a good engineer who knew how to construct great stone buildings. England owes much to his skill and energy.

English Renaissance Architecture

Wren's first task was to rebuild the parish churches of the city. He also had to design an entirely new cathedral, for the beautiful old building had been entirely destroyed. This was indeed a problem for an English architect; no church of this size had been built in this country for hundreds of years. The only thing he could possibly do was to make some sort of copy of the great churches of the Italian Renaissance. That is what St. Paul's cathedral (41) really is. Amongst all the fine buildings of this country it stands quite alone, for neither Wren nor any of the architects who came after him ever had the opportunity of designing another church of this size. They built plenty of small ones, however, which we shall be talking about later on in this chapter.

As well as the burnt churches of London, the houses of the city had to be rebuilt as well. Wren and his fellow architects were soon building scores of plain little brick houses, with nothing in the way of ornament about them except their front doorways and the cornices which ran round the top of each building. In the country, however, there were still rich men who needed great houses as in the old days of the feudal lords. These huge country mansions of the English Renaissance were generally built in stone—which is after all the finest of all building materials. Even if they were built of brick, they were, more often than not, 'faced' with masonry so as to look as if they were stone built. The great palaces of the Italian Renaissance were all built of stone; the English Renaissance architects did not feel very happy about building large houses of common brick if it could be avoided.

However large the house was, all the most important rooms were always collected into one great block, covered by a wide roof. The main entrance to the house was usually marked by a wide columned portico, with a 'pediment' above it to make it look like the entrance front of an old Roman temple. In order to make the portico look even more important, it was usually placed at the top of a wide flight of steps. This meant that the entrance floor of the house had to be raised above the ground with a basement underneath it. So as to make these low basement stories look strong and sturdy and a good foundation for the fine house above, the stones of which it was built were often left rough like rock instead of being worked smooth as all masonry had been during the Middle Ages. This rough-looking stonework is known as 'rustication'; sometimes architects made the corners of their houses look strong by having all the corner stones 'rusticated' also.

Above the basement there would be two tall stories; the main entrance floor and the chamber floor over it. Whether or not columned 'Orders' were used to ornament the front of the house, the walls in any case would be finished at the top with a fine overhanging cornice. On top of the cornice there would be a parapet to hide the roof behind. We have explained before that Italian houses did not have steep roofs; so the English Renaissance architects always tried to hide their roofs behind a parapet (30).

In the finer houses, the parapets were not solid walls, but were made something like the 'balustrading' which was used to keep people from falling off the edges of staircases. You will remember that we explained how, from Elizabethan times onwards, the handrails of stairs were supported by turned wooden 'balusters'. The Renaissance architects used the same sort of thing in stonework to prevent people from falling off the tops of roofs and the edges of their wide staircases and terraces. A stone 'balustrade' made a very good parapet to a roof. The 'balusters' themselves were of course much fatter and stronger than the wooden ones on the stairs inside the house. (By the way, when we talk about the 'banisters', we really mean the 'balusters', or balustrading.)

Balustrading was entirely an invention of the Renaissance architects; it had never been used before. It made a very pleasant finish to the tops of the walls; something like the openwork parapets of Gothic days. There was not much to make the skyline of a Renaissance house look at all pretty. Although there would be chimney stacks to show that the house was well heated, there would be no forests of ornamental chimney pots. Each stack would be as plain and tidy as the house upon which it stood and, like it, would be finished at the top with a stone cornice.

The windows of the houses of the days of Christopher Wren were all quite plain and had a square top. At first they had the wooden 'mullion' and 'transom' forming a cross in each window with iron casements opening in the two lower portions. But when William of Orange came over to England to be our king he brought with him a number of Dutchmen who showed the English builders how to make the kind of window that was used in Holland. This is the window which slides up and down: to-day we call it a 'sash' window. Windows of this sort cannot be made in iron or they will stick instead of sliding up and down easily in their grooves. As the sliding 'sashes' had to be made in wood, therefore, the builders gave up using strips of lead to hold the panes of glass together and got the joiners to make strips of wood called 'glazing bars', which formed part of the 'sash' and separated the panes (45). At first, these bars were very thick and clumsy, but during the eighteenth century they became slimmer until in the end they hardly took away any light at all.

When you come to one of these great houses, climb up the wide flight of steps and pass between the columns of the portico and through the entrance doorway, you will find yourself in a large hall. This is really the same room as the great hall of a Tudor palace; instead of entering it at one end, however—which would have upset the balance of the architect's plan—you enter it in the middle of one wall. If you cross this entrance hall to, as it were, its 'back door', you then come to the staircase hall with the grand stair rising out of it to the chamber floor above. This was the same place that the stair had been built in during Elizabethan days; later on, however, the architects moved the stair to one side so that you could get a view right through the house from front to back and into the garden beyond.

In many fine houses columned Orders were used inside the rooms as well as on the outside of the building, so that the rooms had cornices inside them high up near the ceiling. In order to finish off the small piece of wall left between the top of the cornice and the underside of the ceiling, the Renaissance architects often designed a curved bit of ceiling called a 'cove' to round off the corner where the wall and ceiling met. The old beamed ceilings of the Tudor period had long ago been covered with laths and plastered. Plastering was becoming a great art; the plasterers were growing very skilful at making all sorts of designs such as used to be turned out only by the masons and carpenters. In the days of Christopher Wren and the architects who followed him, many of the plaster ceilings of fine houses were painted by well-known artists with gods and goddesses, cherubs, and other such fanciful folk.

English Renaissance Architecture

The main floor of a great house of this period had many fine rooms. Not all of these were, perhaps, actually needed by the owner of the house, but the architect had to keep his plan tidy and leave no corners unused. At the back of the entrance hall—where the staircase used to be—was often another large hall with tall windows overlooking the garden. This was called the 'salon', from which we get our word 'saloon'. Outside the windows of the salon there was usually a long terrace with a balustrading and steps leading to the garden (35).

Only the smaller houses had 'parlours'; the owners of fine mansions called them 'withdrawing rooms'. There were also, of course, the rooms in which meals were taken. There was sometimes more than one dining-room; as there were usually several rooms to spare on the main floor of these great houses, it was possible to have a sunny room for the winter and a cooler one for summer.

On the floor above were the bedchambers. Up to the time of Queen Anne these were still entered one from another; corridors with rooms entered off them had not yet been invented.

Although the main block of the house had no wings as in the days of the Elizabethans, there were often low ranges of buildings, one story high, joined on to it. The architects liked having these low ranges because they made the main house look larger; also it was possible to find room in them for the kitchens, sculleries, and storerooms necessary for feeding the people in the great house. Ranges of buildings like this were generally very carefully designed by the architects, often in wide sweeping curves. Sometimes they were ornamented with rows of columns or even had long porticoes or 'colonnades' passing along them like those of the old temples; covered porticoes like this made useful outside corridors, for joining the doors of the rooms together in the same way as the cloisters of the monasteries of the Middle Ages.

We have seen how Inigo Jones's huge design for the Palace of Whitehall, with its seven courtyards, was never carried out. Nor was anything so vast as this ever attempted again. At Henry VIII's old palace of Hampton Court, Christopher Wren built on a large addition which had a courtyard in the middle; but for ordinary houses, or even large mansions, the method of planning a house round a courtyard had quite gone out of fashion. The finest houses of the day were simply great blocks. But these huge houses had to have a great many servants to run them and it was necessary to provide buildings in which these could live and work. People were travelling about more than they used to; so each house had to have large stables to house a good supply of horses, both for riding and for drawing coaches. We have seen how the great houses had ranges of low one-storied buildings built for these purposes; sometimes they were arranged along the sides of a square courtyard placed beside the main block of the house. One of these courtyards might be the kitchen yard and another the stable yard. Up to fifty years ago, when the motor car began to come into use, even a small house would have its stable yard; the only thing left to remind us of the courtyards of the Middle Ages.

One of the greatest of our Renaissance architects was Sir John Vanbrugh, the designer of Blenheim Palace (30) and Castle Howard both of them begun just after 1700. In huge palaces of this sort we find the great hall still appearing in the plan; it is not a dining-hall, however, like that of the Middle Ages, but simply a huge entrance hall leading off the columned portico in the middle of the house-front. The great halls of the early eighteenth century palaces were magnificently designed and often covered with domes; in ordinary houses they just shrank into entrance lobbies such as we have in our houses to-day, halls in name only and nothing at all like the great banqueting halls of the Middle Ages.

Another great architect of those days was one of Sir Christopher Wren's pupils, Hawksmoor, who designed several London churches. In the last chapter we explained how, after the end of the Middle Ages, churches had come to be simple preaching houses with none of the many parts that the old churches used to have: not even a chancel. These box-like churches were just the thing for the new architects of the English Renaissance to try their skill at designing. Outside they were left quite plain; but with the entrance doorway at the west end standing on a wide flight of steps. These buildings looked so entirely different from the kind of church which had been built throughout England during the Middle Ages that it must have been very difficult to make them seem like churches at all. One thing the architects did, however, was to give the windows round tops instead of flat ones; this made them look slightly more like church windows and less like the ordinary ones of a house.

Another thing the architects could do was to give each church a tall tower for its bells. Some of these towers were perfectly plain, with just a cornice and a balustraded parapet round the top. But Christopher Wren, when he was planning the rebuilding of the London churches, thought he would try his hand at designing a church spire which would look well with a Renaissance building. He made a number of very clever attempts to do this, perching little round and square temples one on top of the other and finishing them off with a stone 'obelisk' such as the Romans used to use. The church of St. Mary le Strand, built just after Wren's day, shows the tall steeple (42) which became the Renaissance architects' answer to the spires of the Gothic churches of other days.

It was in Inigo Jones's day that the little bell-turrets of which we spoke in the last chapter came to be finished with small lead-covered domes. These domes were, of course, only for ornament and were never used as real roofs over large rooms. But Christopher Wren, who was a trained engineer, was able to build domes very much larger than had ever been used before in this country. As well as using them to ornament his towers and steeples he was actually able to roof some of his churches— even the great cathedral itself—with a dome. We have already spoken of the domes which, in the great palaces, took the place of the little turrets lighting staircase halls.

The great architects of the English Renaissance must have sometimes thought it was a pity that their churches were so very plain. They could not do much to improve the buildings, for they had designed all the ornament themselves instead of leaving it to the masons to carve stones here and there with their own designs, as they had done during the Middle Ages. The architects were not sculptors or carvers, but only draughtsmen; so the buildings had to be plain. But when it came to the furnishing of the inside of the church it was another matter. There were fine woodcarvers, such as Grinling Gibbons, who could be allowed to carve an altar piece, or a screen, or communion rails. The pulpit—a very important part of the church of those days —might be a very fine piece of furniture. Then there was the chance for the stone carvers, such as Nicholas Stone, to try their hand at making fonts—looking like old Roman vases (38) and not a bit like the fonts of the Middle Ages—out of beautifully finished marble. There was no room in these Renaissance churches of course for the great canopied tombs of the great days of the abbeys. But people still liked to have fine stone memorials to themselves and their families placed in the churches.

The more beautiful the insides of these churches became, the more people went to them. As they were all so small compared with the churches of the Middle Ages it became necessary to provide more seating room by filling up the inside of the building with wooden galleries.

The Civil War, which brought to an end the old rustic ways of the Middle Ages, helped to clear the way for the new England which was to come. We were finding other ways, besides selling wool, of getting rich. Mining for coal and iron was bringing work and wealth to parts of England which had not known them before and old villages, tucked away in the heart of the country, were becoming new towns.

Some old towns were growing up and clearing away their old-fashioned buildings. During the Middle Ages marketing had been done on the steps of the town cross. In the fifteenth century many old crosses were surrounded by shelters to cover the goods set out for sale on the steps; during the Renaissance period the cross itself disappeared but the shelter remained, some Georgian market crosses, as that at Bungay in Suffolk, being designed as little Roman temples having a lead-covered dome carried upon a ring of columns. But in large towns the townspeople built a proper market house supported by twelve or fifteen columns amongst which the market could be held while in the town hall over, the city fathers could sit in council (44). To-day most of these market houses have had their lower stories filled in with solid walling. Some towns—such as the Roman city of Chester—which had no market place made shelters for markets beside the main streets by carrying the upper stories of houses out over the road and propping them up by rows of columns.

People were travelling more and more. There were regular services of stage-coaches. The roads had to be kept up properly so that the coaches would not get stuck and arrive late. Bridges were rebuilt with fine wide arches; the old narrow ones of the Middle Ages blocked up the river too much, so that the water rose at times and swept the whole bridge away. The Renaissance bridges had, instead of plain parapets—or even wooden handrails—fine stone balustrading along their sides.

In the same way that the Elizabethans had surrounded their great houses with pleasant gardens, so did the architects of the English Renaissance think out carefully planned gardens to make the ground round the house look as tidy as the house itself. Everything was very neatly arranged, of course; nothing could be out of balance. There were long wide paths, running straight and well-kept between smooth lawns. There were terraces and flights of steps, and stone balustrades. Some of the fishpools were very long—called 'canals'. There were neatly clipped hedges, and, here and there, marble statues of gods and goddesses from the days of the old Greeks and Romans.

CHAPTER XIV

GEORGIAN ENGLAND

During the Middle Ages, houses were built by a number of different people each working at his own trade; there was nobody whose sole job it was to look after them and watch what they were doing. In the chapter before last, we noted that, towards the end of the reign of Queen Elizabeth, houses were being built by people whom we call to-day builders —men who would actually take upon themselves the task of building the house and finding the masons, bricklayers, carpenters, plumbers, and all the people needed to finish off the job. This was a very important step in English architecture, because it meant that it was very much less trouble for anybody to get a house built. Instead of having to hunt round himself and find all his various tradesmen, he could now employ somebody to do it for him.

The use of brick was making building very much easier; even as early as the reign of James I, that king was encouraging everyone to build in brick; this saved both timber and trouble. When William III came over from Holland, brick building started to go with a swing. In an earlier chapter, we spoke of the 'bonding' of bricks and how these were always laid so that every other 'course' showed the ends of the bricks with the courses between showing the sides. During the reign of William III, bricklayers began to use the Dutch way of laying bricks which was to have not one course of 'headers' and then one course of 'stretchers', but each course the same and with the bricks arranged as first a stretcher and then a header. This 'Flemish' bond, as it was called, was more ornamental than the old 'English' bond and if you used bricks with black ends these 'black headers' made a pattern on the wall.

All sorts of new building inventions appeared at this time. Hitherto we in this country had always built with timber from our great oak forests. This, however, was very tough and difficult to work, so carpenters began to look for softer wood which would make their work easier and quicker. The soft wood of the pine tree was brought in from the Continent; it was greatly admired when it first arrived and even fine woodwork—panelling and so forth—came to be made from it. But its chief use was for the ordinary building timbers of a house. About this time, the builders discovered that the best way to lay a floor-joist or a rafter was on its edge; this made it much stiffer than when laid flat on its side as in the old days, so that the floor was much less likely to 'spring' when people moved about heavily upon it.

In the Middle Ages, craftsmen had been taught their trades when they were very young by being set to work beside an older man who would show them how he worked. Each trade kept to itself; the man who wanted a house built had to find people from each trade to do the various jobs connected with the building. At the end of the seventeenth century all this was changing. The new builders wanted to know all about each trade themselves; they did not want to have to go looking for, say, a carpenter every time they wanted a worn-out door repaired. So that the builders could learn all about the various trades, books came to be published explaining what had been the secrets of each. During the reign of Queen Anne, when such difficult new pieces of joinery as sash windows, for example, were coming into use, books with carefully drawn illustrations were printed explaining how these were made.

So all the while the great architects of the English Renaissance were teaching themselves architecture and building their great mansions, the builders in the English country towns were teaching themselves how to build small houses. They did not have to be architects, because the style they were using was very plain and designing was quite easy. Houses were just brick boxes with a door in the middle of one side and the windows all neatly arranged in each of the four walls. If a house were big enough to be two rooms thick it would have its roof 'hipped' all round like those of the big houses; if it were a cottage, then gables at each end would do. The country builders could not afford lead and they often could not get slate, but they were able to make do with ordinary tiles provided that they kept the roofs steep enough.

The most important part of this kind of house was its roof,

which had to be designed so that it would look well but still keep the rain out. We have explained how the roofs of great houses were kept as low as possible, so that they could be hidden behind a parapet and would not show above the square top of the building. This meant, however, that the roof had to be covered with lead or slates and provided with a lead gutter behind the parapet to carry the water away through 'down pipes' to the ground. All this was likely to be too much trouble and expense to the Georgian builders, so that in small houses they left out the parapet and allowed the steep tiled roof to overhang the walls as it used to do during the Middle Ages. All the best houses, however, simply had to have a cornice round the tops of their walls; the builder made his cornice serve instead of eaves so that the roof came down and finished on top of it (45).

It is this kind of house which was being built during the reigns of the four Georges and for this reason we always speak of the architecture of these small country houses as Georgian. Georgian houses are usually quite plain, but they are so small that every little piece of them seems to help to make them look attractive. There are the brick walls with the tiled roof coming down over the wide cornice, and the white painted windows with their small panes of glass fixed in the wooden 'glazing bars' to make little patterns of black and white here and there on the front of the building. White paint was now in use to cover up and protect the woodwork of doors and windows, which now were being made of soft wood instead of the oak of the Middle Ages.

The only real piece of ornament on the front of the Georgian house was its entrance doorway. During the Middle Ages, the doorway was a doorway and nothing else. It often had to have a porch to keep out the draught, but architects paid little attention to it until the Italian craftsmen began to come over here in the days of Henry VIII. From then onwards, however, the most important part of the main front of the house came to be the entrance doorway. The Renaissance doorways which the Italian architects began to bring over here nearly always had a column or pilaster either side, with a cornice joining the tops of these over the opening itself. The simplest Georgian doorways were like this too but they nearly all had, wherever possible, the top finished off with that triangular piece of cornice which we call a 'pediment'.

Although pediments were at first always triangular, the Georgian architects made all sorts of experiments with the shape. They often used a curved or arched pediment instead of a triangular one. Then they tried putting some piece of ornament such as a shield or a head in the middle of the pediment. This, however, was apt to be rather cramped for room, so the next thing they did was to cut away the middle part of the pediment so that the shield, urn, bust—or whatever it was they wanted to put there—could rise up above the pediment; this is known as a 'broken pediment' (45).

Sometimes Georgian builders made a small copy of the porticoes of the great houses by putting two small free-standing columns on either side of the doorway and bringing forward the cornice to make a kind of porch; this was useful for keeping the rain from driving into the hall when the door was open. Another pleasant trick was to support the top of the porch not by two columns but by two large carved brackets. This is known as a 'door hood'; you must often have seen charming hoods like this over the front doors of the houses in many a village street.

We have explained that the pediment was the most important piece of ornament used by the Georgian architects. Not only did they use it over their doorways but sometimes over their windows as well. The tile-covered roofs of the small Georgian houses had to be much steeper than the lead- or slate-covered roofs of the large mansions. This made it possible to get plenty of attic bedrooms inside these roofs. In order to get light into these rooms it was necessary to make little windows, called 'dormer' windows, in the roof. These windows would be finished with a cornice, often raised to form a little pediment.

When we were talking of Elizabethan houses, we mentioned how fond they were at that time of bay windows jutting out from the rooms for people to stand in and see what was happening outside. The great architects of the English Renaissance would never allow the plain walls of their buildings to be broken by anything—except the front porch—which jutted out in front of them. The Georgian builders, however, were very fond of bay windows; they often placed one on either side of the front door, so that the house looked like a small copy of an Elizabethan mansion of a hundred and fifty years before.

In the last chapter, we spoke of the change that had come over the English fireplace when coal began to be burned instead of wood; how the large stone or brick arches of the old fireplace openings had come to be framed round with wooden mouldings. The wooden chimney pieces of the Georgian houses were something like the front doors of the houses themselves; they had 'architrave mouldings' running down the sides and passing across the top of the opening, which was usually finished with a wooden cornice, like that over the front door, to serve as a mantelshelf. When iron came to be used more and more in English architecture, one of the things it was used for was to make a sort of iron fireplace for putting inside the actual opening in the wall. These grates were made out of a sheet of cast iron—England was becoming a great iron-founding country—filling up the lower half of the fireplace opening. The iron sheet was decorated with all kinds of patterns cast into the metal and had the actual grate in which the coal was put fixed to it. You may often see Georgian firegrates still filling the painted wooden mantelpieces for which they were made.

The Georgian builders were very fond of using woodwork inside their houses. They liked to cover the walls of rooms with panelling instead of plastering them. Georgian panelled rooms are often beautifully designed with the chimney-piece all fitting in with the scheme of the panelling. Sometimes in important rooms the doorways are almost as much ornamented as the front doorway outside the house. In any case there would always be an architrave moulding passing round the opening, and very possibly a cornice over the top of the door as well. Georgian staircases are also fine pieces of woodwork, with their moulded handrails supported by gracefully turned balusters; the whole stair often fitting in, like everything else, with a well thought-out scheme of wall panelling.

We saw in the last chapter that even as late as the Georgian period our architects were still being called upon to build huge palaces. By the Regency period, however, which is the end of the eighteenth century and the beginning of the nineteenth, the day of palaces was at last over for good. Most of the great families lived in great houses which had been building since the Middle Ages; it was now the turn of the country squires to build fine houses. England is covered with these country houses of the Regency; they are usually quite plain looking except for the columned porticoes copied from the great Renaissance palaces.

Georgian England

We have explained how by the beginning of the eighteenth century books were being written to help people who wanted to learn about Renaissance architecture. In 1728 the architect James Gibbs, who designed St. Mary le Strand (42), published a *Book of Architecture* which was sent to America to help the architects there. Upon this book with its drawings of buildings was founded American architecture; by the end of the century they were building fine mansions in what is known as the 'Colonial' style, which is like our Regency but the buildings are framed up in wood and covered with boarding painted white to look like stone.

Georgian architecture was intended to be a copy of the style of Italy where most Renaissance buildings are of stone. No English architect was really happy to build a brick house. He would often cover it with plaster to make it look like stone, but plaster, which is made from lime, is not really waterproof and will not last long. During the second half of the eighteenth century the builders were trying to find how to make it waterproof by mixing other things, such as oil, with it; in the very last years of the century they found that by burning a special kind of stone found in south-east England instead of ordinary limestone they could make a plaster which was far harder and would last much longer. After this time most English buildings began to be covered with new 'cement plaster' or 'stucco'.

Up to the end of the Civil War, people had only built houses to live in themselves. But at the time when the old Tudor palaces and Elizabethan mansions were falling to ruin and being deserted, while the house builders were making more up-to-date homes for themselves, many large rambling old houses were being taken over by poor people who lived in the various rooms and made the whole place into a sort of small village. This made somebody think of the idea of building houses not for his own use but for other people to use, in return for paying him a rent. At about the time of the great fire of London there were builders who were making whole streets of houses, not with each house specially designed for somebody who wanted it, but for the builder to let off, house by house, to people who were looking for homes. These rows of houses, all touching each other and built to the same design, are called 'terrace houses' (49). Nothing of the sort had been seen in England before; everybody had built his own house in the way he wished it to be. These terrace houses were very tightly packed together to save valuable land, and they were usually several stories high, with the most important room, the drawing-room, on the first floor.

By the Georgian period these houses were being built in large numbers on the outer edges of our towns. New streets were laid out for them; not lanes like the old streets of a town of the Middle Ages but set out in orderly straight lines. This was the beginning of what we call 'town planning'.

Terrace houses are apt to be rather dark inside, as they only have front and back walls in which to make windows; the houses on either side make it impossible to have side windows. As soon as you enter the front door, you are in a narrow hall, with the staircase rising out of it. This hall might have been very dark, as the front door made it impossible to get a proper window in the wall there. What the Georgian builders did, however, was to make an arched top to the door and put a little half-round window there, over the door itself. They usually filled the little window with ornaments made out of iron, often shaped like an open fan; these windows are therefore called 'fanlights'.

When it became fashionable for the Georgian gentlemen and their families to go down to Bath and bathe in the waters there for the good of their health, houses had to be built for them to live in during their stay. This was the opportunity for the builders of Bath to lay out terrace after terrace of houses, in which the visitors from London could find lodgings. It so happened that Bath stood in the centre of a countryside which is full of stone quarries. Instead of the usual brick terraces therefore, those of Bath were all built of good stone. This pleased the Georgian architects very much, for they could build much finer-looking houses in stone. They even tried to pretend that each terrace was not just a collection of small houses joined together, but one big palace with columns and fine windows— just like the palaces of the Renaissance (50).

In the second half of the eighteenth century the most fashionable architects were the Adam brothers. Georgian architecture was becoming rather heavy, but they tried to make it a little more graceful, especially inside the rooms, which they covered with ceilings ornamented in a far daintier style than had ever been seen before. Adam porticoes, too (32), are far less clumsy than those of fifty years earlier.

Georgian England

In the Middle Ages the centre of every market town was the market place. This was at first just an open space in the middle —perhaps outside the west door of a great church or the entrance to a large castle—in which the stalls of the market were set up in alleys. The Georgian country architects began to clean up these untidy open spaces and turn them into proper 'market squares' like the fine ones that had been laid out in Italy. People began to like the look of these fine squares, which generally had houses arranged in 'terraces' along the sides; sometimes each terrace was designed to look like the front of a large palace. So 'squares' like them came to be built in London and the large cities, not as market squares, but just to look well.

During Georgian days it became fashionable for people to bathe, not only in the health-giving waters such as those of Bath, but also in sea water. In the same way that a new town had risen around the springs of Bath, so did the 'watering places' come to be built along the coasts of England. Chief of these watering places was, of course, Brighton. Terraces of houses began to be built all along the sea front. But in the south-eastern parts of England there is no building stone as there is at Bath; so the architects of the watering places covered their brick houses with thick coats of stucco to make them look like stone. The builders discovered how to make all kinds of stucco ornaments—even columns with their capitals and fine large cornices —doing their best to pretend that they were building stone palaces (51).

At the end of the eighteenth century, in that period which we call the Regency, brick had become most unfashionable. Everybody who could afford to do so had his brick house covered with stucco outside, to make it look white like stone. There were still quite a number of old half-timber houses left in the south-east of England; as it was always difficult to prevent the rain from coming through half-timbered walls, many of these had been covered over with roofing tiles in what is called 'tile-hanging'. During the Regency period many people took to covering their old timber houses with deal boards called 'weather-boarding' which they then painted white (46). Very probably they got the idea from the new land of America, where very large mansions were being built entirely of wood and then covered over with white painted boarding to make them look like stone.

Now that the windows of a house had to be placed, not just where they were wanted for lighting the rooms, but where they would look well on the outside of the building, it was sometimes difficult to make the tall narrow Georgian windows large enough to do their job. In the Regency period they were often widened by placing a narrow window on either side of an ordinary one so that the window had a wide middle part and two narrow side ones. Sometimes the middle part had an arched top like the fanlight of a doorway; windows like this were often used for lighting staircases.

We have already mentioned that the Georgians were very fond of bay windows and often used them in their houses. In the Regency period—which is really the end of Georgian days —they used a special kind of bay window called a 'bow' window. This was simply a curved window, not jutting out so far from the wall as the old bay window had done; the name comes from it being curved like a bent bow. When the Regency watering places were being built, many of the terraces were built with bow windows for people to sit in and watch the passers by. Sometimes the whole end wall of each house was bowed outwards so as to make it like one large bow window. It was at this period that the bowed shop window first appeared; thus was invented the 'shop-front' with its large windows for the display of wares (48).

In the days of the Regency, England was making a great many things of iron. Not only were iron machines being invented for making all sorts of things like clothes and so on; even parts of houses were actually being made of iron too. The balustrading of staircases was often made of iron; this was not the 'wrought' iron that the smith used to hammer into beautiful shapes when he was making a fine gate or railings for a gentleman's park, but iron 'cast' into patterns and framed up piece by piece.

In the days of the Regency it was very important to be in the fashion. Not only did you have to be in the fashion with your house; it was even more important to wear fashionable clothes and thus people liked to look from their houses upon the passers by to see what they were wearing. So you find that, as well as the bow windows, Regency houses often have balconies built out from them; with balustradings of cast iron and sometimes even little iron roofs over them so that people could sit on the balcony and watch what was going on without having to fear that a summer shower might drive them indoors. Possibly these little 'verandahs' were first used in India (52).

But it was in the staircases that the Regency builders made the best use of their ironwork. The older staircases had been built square, with the end arches fixed to newel posts at the corners where the 'landings' were; but ironwork could be bent much more easily than wood, so the stairs of the Regency period sweep in graceful curves from floor to floor. Very often the window which lights the staircase hall is the finest in the whole house; it may have a very large centre portion with an arched top and a narrower square-headed window on either side.

In the last chapter, we talked of the churches which were being built in the days of Christopher Wren; and how they were, after all, rather plain square boxes—very different from the beautiful churches of the Middle Ages. But the Georgians did their very best to make the insides of them as fine as possible with panelling and carving and often columns and cornices (34). There were nearly always galleries; hardly a village church was without its gallery in those days.

In the Middle Ages only very large churches had organs. In the Georgian period all town churches had them. They were nearly always placed, in finely carved 'cases', on the west gallery opposite the altar. In the village church, which had no organ, the west gallery was where the choir sat, and where musicians played on queer old-fashioned instruments during the church services.

All through the Georgian period the churches grew ever finer as the architects filled them with Corinthian columns and imitation plaster vaulting and sculptors and painters decorated their walls and ceilings. There were still many people who did not believe in so much ornamentation and liked to worship in simple little box-like buildings called 'meeting-houses'; the Georgian period can show many of these plain little chapels as well as fine parish churches.

We have talked of how the people of England were beginning to travel more and more about the country. New roads were being made and all important roads between towns were being properly kept up. The main roads were called 'turnpikes', in memory of the day when a man used to stop travellers by barring the way with his pike until they had paid a small sum of money for the upkeep of the piece of road he was guarding.

In Georgian days there was just a turnpike gate, beside which was the 'toll house' in which the gate-keeper lived. You can still see many hundreds of these little houses, most of them with just a single room; you can tell them by the way they are built right at the very edge of the road and usually have windows placed so that the gate-keeper could look both up and down the road without leaving his house. With better roads came more and better carriages and, at last, a regular service of public 'stage-coaches' between important towns.

Many of the village streets, and even those in towns, were too narrow for two big lumbering coaches to pass each other. During Georgian days, therefore, a great many streets were being widened and their sides lined with new houses of the kind we have been talking about. Often, in villages through which a main road passes, you may see this running through a fine, wide Georgian street; while at the backs of the houses on one side of this is still the old village street of the Middle Ages with its half-timbered houses.

The Georgians were great builders. People were taking a pride in their houses and liked to see them wearing a fashionable style. Many a man who lived in an old-fashioned timber house standing in a village street amongst new houses had a new front built to his own house, so as to bring it up to date. If he could not afford to have this done he would at least get a builder to make him a fine new front door in the Georgian style, perhaps with columns and a cornice, or even a pediment or a hood supported on curved brackets.

Even the tiniest cottages liked to have a doorway which looked something like the kind of thing which was being made for the finer houses. You will see hundreds of little cottage doorways with hoods, brackets, pediments—all the kinds of things you see on a fine doorway—just roughly made by the village carpenter out of pieces of board. For some time past the farmhouses which stood in the village streets had been deserted by the farmers, who had moved out on to their farms and built themselves houses there. The old farmhouses had then become divided up into cottages, village shops, or ale houses (or, as we call them to-day, 'public houses').

The real inns—that is to say, the houses in which travellers lodged for the night—were becoming very large and fashionable with plenty of bedrooms and a large dining-room with its kitchen and so forth all properly planned just like the houses of the period. There was a large yard with plenty of coach houses and stabling for horses for both riding and driving. The entrance to this yard was often by a very big archway in the middle of the front of the inn. The architects of the day were just as careful in designing an inn with its entrance front as they were when planning a great house. The inns of the big towns usually had fine porticoes like those of country mansions. Even lesser inns generally had a porch with two sturdy columns supporting the roof; the roof of the inn-porch was a favourite place for members of parliament to speak from.

People were taking much more interest in their public buildings. Besides the fine theatres which were being built in all the towns of England, most towns also had their 'assembly halls' where balls were held at which the fine Georgian gentlemen and their ladies could display their clothes. The assembly hall became the most important building in the town; the townspeople often met there to discuss politics, listen to speeches, or for various kinds of merry-making. It was, in fact, the town hall; and, as such, took the place of the old market hall as the most important public building in the town. Georgian town halls are often very fine, with their columned porticoes just like those of a church or great house; the town hall is generally the most noticeable building in the market square.

In the next chapter, we shall talk about a kind of building we have not mentioned before—the place in which people work at their trade. During the Middle Ages, almost every village had in it a mill for grinding flour from the corn grown in the fields. At first these mills had their stones turned by water. At the end of Henry II's reign, however, windmills came into use. At first these were just flimsy contraptions of wooden beams. By Georgian days, however, a little house of white painted weather-boarding had been built around the works of the mill, making it look like an old-fashioned smock worn by a countryman. These mills are called 'smock' mills. I expect you know that a mill has always to be turned by a horse so that its sails face into the wind, as otherwise they will not go round and drive the stones. Until the Regency period the whole mill with all the works and the little wooden house round them had to be turned every time the wind changed; by the nineteenth century, however, the Dutch had shown us how to build a brick tower with all the works of the mill in it and fix the sails of the mill to a dome-shaped roof which turned on top of the tower while the main building itself stood still. At the time when we were fighting Napoleon and were afraid that we might not have enough flour for bread, water mills became very popular again so that a number of very large ones came to be built over the south and east of England. They were hurriedly put together of timber framing covered with the white painted weather-boarding which had become so fashionable.

In the next chapter we shall talk of the 'factories' which came to be built in the busy towns of the midlands and the north. But the Georgian towns and villages had many tiny buildings of this sort where carpenters and other craftsmen worked at their trades and cloth was spun or woven. You can often see these workshops with their very large windows made up out of hundreds of small panes of glass separated by the usual white-painted 'glazing bars'.

The Middle Ages had been left very far behind. Even the peasant was now beginning to have a proper house with walls and a roof, instead of the hovel in which he had been living for thousands of years. Squires and farmers actually began to build cottages for their labourers to live in, as well as dividing up the older farmhouses for the same purpose. Pairs of cottages—like two taken from a terrace—were at this time built for farm servants. This was a cheap way of building, as it saved one wall; many of the houses in which we live to-day are of this 'semi-detached' plan.

CHAPTER XV

ONE THING AFTER ANOTHER

We have already spoken of the way in which the people of England had been moving, since the days of the Civil War, from the country to the town. In the Middle Ages we had lived on our own wheat and mutton and had grown rich by selling wool; then we had discovered coal and how it could be used, not only for warming houses, but also for smelting the iron ore of which we had fortunately so much in this country. Thus, by the end of the eighteenth century, England had become a country living, not on wool, but on iron.

We had so much iron that we were able to make plenty of machines; with these we could make all sorts of things—clothes, blankets, carpets—much more quickly and easily than before. England was thus becoming a 'manufacturing' country. This meant that there had to be buildings in which manufacturing could be carried on: that is to say, the buildings which we call to-day 'factories'.

A factory is a building in which you put machines; there might be row after row of these, all taking up a lot of room. There would also have to be plenty of space for storing the material upon which the machines were to work and still more space in which to store the finished articles; thus a factory is both workshop and storehouse. It is of course a good thing if you can have two or three floors to your factory; for then you can save having to spread the building over acres of ground. So we find that the first factories were usually large buildings with several floors in them.

The floors of a factory have to be very strong, so that they will stand the weight of the material stored upon them; in some cases there may even have been heavy machines on the upper floors of a building. Ordinary wooden beams, however large they may be, are bound to sag if you put weights of this sort on them; they must therefore be propped up underneath with posts of some sort. By the end of the eighteenth century, our ironmasters were so clever at making anything they wanted that they were actually casting iron columns and using them for building. This was a very important improvement; a slender iron column, a few inches thick, will support the same weight as a massive wooden post or wide brick pillar, and take up very much less room.

A difficulty with all large buildings is how to roof them. If you make the building too wide you cannot 'tie' the sides of your roof together and prevent it from collapsing. When we were talking of the great churches of the Middle Ages we saw how the carpenters were trying all sorts of schemes for tying in their roofs over wide buildings. Iron, however, altered all this; the heavy timbering of these old roofs could now be exchanged for light iron bars and rods, all bolted together. Very wide roofs could be made in this kind of ironwork, so that you could have much larger buildings than ever before to hold your rows of machines and your great stores of materials. Iron was even being used for making the large factory windows; the strong frame, and the smaller bars holding the panes of glass, all being made out of strips of iron.

The factory age of the last century saw many new towns rising in those coal and iron districts of the midlands which, during the Middle Ages, had been all cornfields and sheep pastures. Where once the highest building of the countryside had been the spire of the village church, it was now the tall chimneys of factories which stood, like forests of brickwork, against the sky. Each chimney poured its smoke into the air; at its foot was a furnace which heated a boiler and made the steam for turning the engines and working the machines.

People began to flock in their hundreds, from the fields in which they and their forefathers had worked for thousands of years, into the towns where the new factories were giving work to all, the whole year round. Houses had to be built, as quickly as possible, for all these people to live in. They were built in long rows like the 'terraces' which we spoke of in the last chapter; each house, however, was very tiny. The terraces were often built back to back without any gardens in between, so that the only windows the house had were in their front walls, towards the street. The factory owners had to get these houses built as quickly as they possibly could, so that people could move in and begin to work at the machines. Neither time nor money was wasted over building them; a kitchen on the ground floor and a bedchamber above was generally considered good enough for a worker and his family. Although these 'slum' houses seem terrible to us to-day it must be remembered that when they were built the country people who came to live in them had been living all their lives in shacks such as we have never seen, often built of sticks and mud and probably without a floor above the ground.

These factory towns of the midlands flourished; the factory owners became very wealthy and built fine houses for themselves to live in. They took a pride in their towns and generally saw that these had good public buildings, especially fine town halls. But in these new districts the architects and builders were not so plentiful as in the older towns of England and one does not find an architecture as beautiful as that which had been growing through the centuries, before factories had been thought of. But the public buildings of the factory towns were very large and fine and much money was spent on them.

Shops, too, had to be built for the people crowded together in the new towns. The old shop of the Middle Ages had merely been somebody's second-best parlour. Before this it had been a stall set up in the market place. In Georgian days it was a ground-floor room of a house in the main street, probably with a bow window glazed with small panes of glass fixed in slender bars of wood (48). But we had discovered a new way of making glass in very large pieces; so that windows, instead of being divided up into small panes, could be filled with much larger sheets of thick strong glass known as 'plate' glass. By the middle of the nineteenth century, therefore, shop windows had become much larger and more important in the streets of our towns. The invention of plate glass also entirely changed the appearance of the windows of ordinary houses; the old wooden 'glazing bars' of Georgian days disappeared and window 'sashes' were each filled with a single piece of plate glass.

As the people who made cast-iron became more and more skilful in using it they found that they could not only make iron roofs but could even cover the whole building with iron frames filled with glass. A fashion came in of having rooms called 'conservatories', made almost entirely of glass in iron frames, added on to the sides of houses so that you could walk about in them and almost imagine that you were in the open air. The greatest of all these conservatories was the enormous building known as the Crystal Palace, which was destroyed by fire only a few years ago.

In Georgian days, when much attention had been given to the tidiness of the town streets, upon the pavements of which the fashionable men and women of the day showed off their clothes, oil lamps had been fixed to the houses and on the railings so that the streets could be lit after dark for the safety of people who still wished to walk in them. Just before Queen Victoria came to the throne it was found that a gas could be made from coal and led through pipes to burners fixed where the old oil lamps used to be. In this way, gas lighting came to the streets of our big cities; the lamps being fixed at the tops of cast-iron columns planted at the edge of the pavements. By the middle of the century, many houses had gas lighting inside them instead of oil lamps. If you look at the ceiling of a large Victorian room, you may often see the plaster 'rose' through the middle of which the gas pipe used to drop to feed the 'chandelier' hanging below (to-day, we still call the small china cup, from which the electric wires hang, a 'rose'). Victorian rooms are usually very high, because of the fumes from the old gas burners.

In the Middle Ages, a house generally had its own well or pond; if not, somebody had to go each day with a bucket to the well or pump in the market square or village green. This sort of thing would not do, however, for the factories with their steam engines; water had to be taken in pipes to the boilers. By the end of the Victorian period, most city streets had water pipes laid along them, so that each street, and very often most of the houses, had a water tap.

In the Middle Ages goods had generally been carried from place to place by water. The rivers of the south-east of England helped very much with its trade. The important ports of those days were not the sea-ports but the great river-ports: such as Norwich, once the second greatest city in England. There were practically no roads along which carriages could move, so everything had to be taken on horseback down to the nearest river and then shipped by boat to the sea, along the coast, and up another river to reach the point at which it was required. About the time of the Civil War, roads had become sufficiently well

kept for large wheeled carts to move between the chief towns;
by Georgian days there was a fairly frequent service of waggons
carrying goods about the country. And then just at the time
when Queen Victoria was coming to the throne, the railways
were invented which enabled waggons to run on a road made
of iron bars and to be drawn, not by horses, but by the new
steam engines mounted upon wheels.

The trouble about these new railways was that the steam engines were not strong enough to pull the waggons up a hill
unless the slope was very gentle; the tracks had therefore to be
laid out with very great care to keep them as level as possible.
In many places it was found that the only way to get the railway
across a deep valley was to build a long high bridge, many
arches in length, called a 'viaduct'. Sometimes a tunnel had to
be pierced through a hill and lined with a strong skin of brickwork; very deep cuttings through soft soil had to have their
sides propped up with strong walls—called 'retaining walls'—
of thick brickwork.

The railway engineers became so clever at using iron for
their buildings that they were even able to make long iron
bridges which would carry the weight of a railway train over
valleys and rivers. In the great railway stations, they filled the
enormously wide roofs with glass from side to side, so as to
keep the platforms below as light as possible.

It was almost as if a new architecture were being invented:
an architecture not of stone, brick or wood, but of cast iron.
The new 'watering places', which were springing up all round
the coasts of England, were being provided with long 'piers'
supported upon strong cast-iron pillars rising from the bed of
the sea; the new steamships, with their big paddle-wheels,
made their journeys between the watering places from the end
of one pier to another.

The floors of the huge buildings of Victorian England were
supported by forests of cast-iron columns. Their walls were of
solid brickwork, sometimes several bricks thick. Up till then,
there had been very few buildings more than four stories or so
in height, but land in the manufacturing towns was becoming
so valuable that people were building as high as they dared so
as to get as large a building as possible without spreading sideways. Vast quantities of bricks were being made for these huge
buildings, and for the works of the railway engineers; a new

kind of very strong brick, called a 'blue' brick, came to be used for the engineering works.

At the beginning of the century England had a serious war with France. Such was the fear that Napoleon's armies would invade us that we began doing something which we had not done for many centuries: we began to fortify our coasts. It was not castles that the engineers of the day were building, but great forts of earthwork to protect the huge iron cannon that peered over the tops of the ramparts. In order that these forts should not be captured by an enemy they were surrounded by deeply cut ditches. These ditches, however, were not like those of the old Norman castles but were very wide and had their sides supported by walls of strongly built brickwork.

These forts were mostly built by French prisoners. This was the first time we had been forced to keep prisoners of war in this country. At first they were kept in floating prisons formed by the hulks of old ships, but in the end we had to build proper prisons to hold them. In other days people who had to be imprisoned were kept in the dungeons of castles; now, however, we had to build great brick prisons with hundreds of tiny rooms or 'cells'. They were several stories high and the cells were reached by iron galleries. Large brick barracks were also being built in many of the towns of England for our own soldiers to live in; the barrack-blocks did not have small cells in them like the prisons but had huge dormitories on their several floors, all reached by iron staircases and balconies.

The old hospitals of the Middle Ages had been large halls in which the beds of the patients were lined against the walls. In the nineteenth century we were beginning to build much larger hospitals with several stories of 'wards' planned in very much the same way as the barracks of the period.

From all this it is clear that the architecture of England at the time when Queen Victoria came to the throne was far from being beautiful. Once upon a time the largest buildings had been the great churches; later on there were the fine houses. The style in which both of these were built had been growing through the centuries, as has been explained. But now there were all these great factories, and the storehouses—or 'warehouses'—connected with the new manufactories of England. There was no known style in which these could be designed. They were just huge brick blocks with windows in them. Even

public buildings such as town halls or railway stations were being built in this dull brick factory-like architecture.

But with all the wealth which was coming into Victorian
England there came to be many people who could afford to
travel abroad and study beautiful things. Some went to Greece,
at that time struggling against the Turks. There was a great
friendship between England and Greece during the early years
of the nineteenth century when Byron was writing his poems.
Among the Georgian visitors to Athens there had been two
architects called Stuart and Revett; they made a study of the
ancient temples and brought back fine drawings of these which
they published in a book. Many English architects who came
across this book thought that it would be just the thing if they
could ornament their dull factory-like buildings with samples
of the architecture of ancient Greece. In particular they admired the fine columned porticoes of the ancient temples, and
so began to use them on the fronts of their buildings (53). All
this interest in Greek architecture was in full swing at the time
when the railways were being built; thus it is that the finest of all
these Greek porticoes is that at the entrance to Euston station.

This period, towards the middle of the nineteenth century, is
known as the 'Greek Revival'. Many public buildings were built
in the style; churches, town halls and London clubs are amongst
the buildings which were given much of the Greek ornament
collected by Stuart and Revett in their book. Even small houses
were built in the style; they came to be known by the name of
'villas', which was what the fine houses of Rome were called.

There was yet another style which was beginning to interest
people who had taken to studying the architecture of the past.
In the last chapter, we spoke of how fond the Georgians had
been of travelling and study. They also liked reading the new
novels which were being written; in particular, they liked tales
of the olden days when gallant knights rescued fair ladies who
lived in castles. As a result of this they began to admire the
architecture of the Middle Ages, and wish that it were back
again, until at last it even became fashionable for people to try
to design houses like those of the Middle Ages. Unfortunately,
there were no longer any masons who could design Gothic
buildings, nor was there anybody who could even build a Gothic
house if anyone had designed it for him.

But you may remember that the plasterers of Georgian days

had become very skilful at making almost any kind of ornament with their material. Anything which used to be carved in stone could now, in fact, be made in plaster. So, towards the end of the Georgian period, a curious style of plaster Gothic came into fashion. The leader of this fashion was Horace Walpole, who built himself a queer-looking house at Twickenham called 'Strawberry Hill'; the plaster Gothic style in which this house was built is sometimes known as 'Strawberry Hill Gothic' (54).

At the middle of the eighteenth century everyone was becoming Gothic crazy. Nobody understood the style properly and the architects of the day began to invent a queer world full of turrets, pinnacles, windows and arches of fanciful shapes—all of plaster. Not only were there real buildings such as houses and churches in this plaster world, but also odd parts of buildings and imitation ruins called 'follies'; these were often built upon hill-tops where they could be seen from the windows of the squire's house to remind him of the 'good old days' when his ancestors fought in shining armour beneath waving banners instead of merely riding round a farm and looking at the animals.

All this interest in Gothic architecture had rather died away in the excitement of the discoveries made by Stuart and Revett. But in the middle of the nineteenth century, people had become so tired of the factory-like Victorian architecture that they began to long to go back once more to the days of the beautiful buildings of the Middle Ages. They began to take a great interest in the ruins of the old buildings which still remained in this country, and to study them to see if they could build anything of the sort again. They understood, of course, that the old buildings had all been made by craftsmen who had been masters of their trades: masons, carpenters, smiths and so forth. The architects of the day tried to set these trades to work once more; they were bored with having everything made in factories and wanted to see hand-made things for a change. The leader of this new fashion was a man called William Morris. Gothic became quite a craze; even small houses such as villas all came to be built with high pointed roofs, 'mullioned' windows, pointed arches over doorways, and much carved ornament—most of this made in plaster.

The sash windows, so admired by the Georgians but not the right thing for Gothic buildings, gave place to the old hinged casements once more. These were often made, however, not of iron, as they had been during the Middle Ages, but of wood. Sometimes they had leaded panes fixed in them, sometimes wooden glazing bars like those of the sash windows; often they were just filled with large sheets of the new glass.

We have said how the style of the Greek Revival was being used for large new churches. When the new Gothic craze came in, people began to try to bring back the old churches of the Middle Ages with it; large copies of those lovely old buildings began to spring up all over England. Chancels, which had gone out of use at the Reformation, came back into use once more; in the old days they had been long empty halls leading towards the altar at the end, but the Victorians put seats in them and filled them with rows of choirboys to lead in the singing of hymns and help to brighten up the rather dull service which had come down from the time of the Puritans. There were even some monasteries built, and a few people became monks and lived in them. England was full of architects in these days of the 'Gothic Revival'. Not only were there hundreds of fine new churches being built, but all the old churches were having everything that was not Gothic taken out of them and everything that was Gothic 'restored'. A lot of damage was done to our old buildings at this time, because the architects were so keen on their work that they destroyed a great deal of beautiful work simply because it was not Gothic. They also destroyed much old work which really was Gothic because they did not like to see it looking so old and shabby; they tried to rebuild it all as they supposed it really ought to look.

The Gothic craze became at last absolutely absurd. The architects saw nothing ridiculous in building, for example, Gothic factories. St. Pancras is a 'Gothic' railway station complete with tower and spire. When the old royal palace of Westminster was destroyed by fire, a huge building—planned as Victorian parliament houses but covered all over with pieces of Gothic architecture—became the new seat of Government of the British Empire.

You will probably have noticed that all through this history we have been finding that any new architectural style was always first used for religious and public buildings and for the houses of wealthy people, and that ordinary folk went on for the time being in the same way as before. While the large Victorian

Gothic buildings were being designed by the architects, therefore, there were still the builders who were going on with their
rows of terrace houses in the 'Greek' style of the beginning of
the century, but all in brick covered with stucco instead of the
more expensive stone. These stucco terraces were now becoming very large and magnificent looking; most of the big squares
of the west end of London and other large cities are of this
'Mid-Victorian' period of Gothic Revival churches, town halls,
and railway stations.

Towards the end of the nineteenth century, some people
were beginning to get tired of all this romantic Gothic which
was so uncomfortable to live with. The architects began to study
other styles; you may even see factories and warehouses designed in styles such as the Italian Renaissance or even the
Byzantine. By this time, however, the ordinary man had taken
a fancy to the fairy-tale Gothic, and the suburbs of the big
cities began to spread into miles of streets of small houses with
bay windows, Gothic pillars with moulded capitals, steeply
pointed roofs with spiky tops to them, and all the little odds
and ends which seemed so English after the plain square fronts
of the Greek style.

By the end of the reign of Queen Victoria, everyone had had
enough of the Greeks and their architecture. Although the
architects had at last discovered that Gothic was unsuited to
modern times and that it was no good trying to pretend that
railway stations were built in the Middle Ages, everyone felt
that there was at least something English about the Gothic
style which no other could show. People began to hanker after
the warm red brick of Tudor days; it was so much cosier than
white plaster and did not show the dirt from factory smoke. As
the people of Holland have always been the best designers in
brick, some architects began to study the Dutch style and built
large town houses with curly gables of red brickwork, something like English Jacobean architecture.

This brought to mind the kind of house which so many of us
really like best of all—the house which seems like a part of the
countryside of England—the half-timbered house of the yeoman. A craze for this style of architecture spread all over the
country. Large mansions came to be built with ordinary boarding just stuck on to the brickwork to imitate the timberwork.
Even to-day we can still see the same sort of thing in the small

houses in our suburbs with their 'half-timbered' gables rising above bay windows, reminding us of the great halls of the Middle Ages.

If there is one part of the English house which will always be popular it is the bay window. Although it belongs to the banqueting halls of the Middle Ages it is still with us. The Georgians nearly always made it of wood; in the Regency it became bowed. The Victorians liked to make the whole end of the drawing-room, with its best bedroom over, stick out of the front of the house like a large bay window with one wide window in the front wall and a smaller one at each side. This idea seems to have been invented by the 'Gothic' architects of the Regency (54), but it was copied in most of the stucco 'Renaissance' houses of the early Victorians.

The reign of Queen Victoria began with very plain-looking buildings. As the wealth of the country increased and people once again began to advertise their riches by building, they tried to make their buildings look as expensive as possible. Even factories and warehouses were covered all over with ornament; an immense amount of money was spent on all this decoration, not because some architect really believed the building needed it, but simply to make the whole thing look as if its owner were a rich man. In the same way, the inside of the building came to be covered with ornament. Staircases, fireplaces, ceilings— everything became a mass of decoration of all sorts and styles. People bought books of designs so as to give them new ideas for ornament; none of it fitted in the least with the style the building was supposed to be in, but nobody minded this as long as there was plenty of it. This was the state of affairs at the end of the nineteenth century.

As people kept on steadily moving from the country into the towns, so that these grew ever bigger and bigger, all sorts of different kinds of houses came to be needed. In London, the great families owned fine mansions just like those in the country. Wealthy people lived in squares and terraces of great tall houses, first of stucco and then of warm red brick. For ordinary folk there were now many miles of suburbs, with streets of houses, some of them terraces and some in pairs or singly; these too grew in the same way out of stucco and into red brick (although some of the earlier ones were just plain yellow London brick to save expense). In the country towns, and the cities of the midlands and north, where land was not so expensive and there was more room to spread, only the poorer people lived in terrace houses; everybody tried to have a house standing on its own if possible.

We have already explained how the factories brought with them arrangements for a proper supply of water. Houses which until then had merely drawn their water from wells began to have a supply of piped water laid on to iron tanks for storing it. People began to have taps inside their houses; 'sinks' cut out of great blocks of stone began to appear. By the middle of the nineteenth century most houses had their stone sinks. Some of the better houses were beginning to have proper baths fixed in bathrooms and joined not only to the water supply but to pipes leading to underground drains which carried the water away to the sewers. Water-closets began to appear in town houses.

What with all the business which was going on in England during the Victorian period, and all the travelling that business men had to do between one town and another, the old inns were becoming far too small and out of date. Huge hotels were now being built, complete with all the new inventions such as bathrooms and water-closets, so that business men could be as comfortable on their travels as they were in their homes.

As the towns grew larger and richer, the shops in which the people spent their money grew bigger too. Up to about the year 1900, each shop had sold only one kind of thing. The villages had their little stores in which you could buy almost anything you wanted, while in the towns each shopkeeper was just a butcher, baker, clothier, bootmaker, and did not go in for everything. In America, however, the idea of the village store was spreading to the towns, in which huge shops were beginning to appear. These were called 'Department Stores', because each trade had a department of its own inside the one building. At the end of the Victorian period, the same kind of shop was built in this country too.

A great deal of business was being carried on in Victorian England. Everyone was wanting an office in which to do business. People began to buy up the old houses in the centre of towns and turn the rooms into offices for their clerks to work in. At last somebody had the idea of planning a large building in which each room was an office for a business man to rent if he wished; such buildings are known as 'office blocks'.

One Thing After Another

With all this new building, the towns of nineteenth-century England were becoming terribly crowded. The old 'slums' of the early Victorian period were now much too small to hold all the workers and people were having to build tall blocks with houses on each floor, one above the other, reached by winding staircases. Land in the great cities was becoming so expensive to buy that people could not afford to put only one house upon a building plot; they had to pile them up one on top of the other (this is the reason for the skyscrapers of America). Even business people had to live, on top of each other, in buildings like this. There was a house on each floor called a 'flat'; buildings of this sort are, of course, 'blocks of flats'.

A very important part of business is the advertisement of goods. In Victorian England this was done by means of what was known as 'exhibitions'. Special buildings had to be made in which to hold these shows; they were usually just great halls with large windows and, very often, wide roofs of glass and iron like those of the railway stations. The most famous of all these exhibition buildings was the Crystal Palace.

So much interest had been taken in architecture during the nineteenth century that the country was now full of architects. Every now and again there was a fashion in one style or another; generally speaking, however, each man had his own particular fad. Architects were educated by being 'articled' to another architect who passed on his particular fad to his pupil. It was obviously high time that proper schools of architecture should be founded; towards the end of the Victorian period this at last came about. As well as the design of buildings, the students were taught how to plan streets and towns. At the end of the Victorian period they were becoming interested in planning large villages called 'garden cities', in which people could live who wished to get away from the noise and dirt of the great factory towns.

CHAPTER XVI

NOWADAYS

In the last chapter we explained how the most important building of the Victorian era was the factory in which the wealth of the country was made. These factories, at first very plain prison-like buildings, by the end of the century had become over-ornamented and were apt to try to disguise themselves as Gothic palaces and so forth.

Then there were the great 'commercial' houses. At first these were connected with money; the chief example of this is of course the bank with its branches at every street corner and its great banking halls in the centre of the city itself. The trading company which had taken the place of the old merchant guild of the Middle Ages also had its fine hall. There were insurance companies to which men paid money in case they should meet with a disaster of some sort, in which case the company would pay them and set them on their feet again. All these kinds of important companies needed large and magnificent buildings as a form of advertisement. We explained in the last chapter how there also had to be blocks of small offices which could be rented by business men needing them. At the beginning of this century the large department stores were appearing in all the big cities.

All these buildings—business houses, office blocks and multiple stores—formed a different kind of architecture from what we have seen before in this history. The nineteenth century—the Factory Age—was the period of the 'industrial' buildings in which wealth is made; our own century is one of 'commercial' buildings by which wealth is displayed and advertised.

Yet another kind of building was appearing in the English countryside. The old factories had been worked by steam engines placed in engine houses, each with its tall chimney to make the furnace 'draw' and carry its smoke high into the sky. The invention of electricity caused these engines to give place to electric motors, ranged in rows in 'power houses'. The electricity had to be made by means of steam engines; these, however, were not attached to the factories as they had been in Victorian days but were grouped together in huge buildings called 'generating stations' each an enormous block with several very tall chimneys beside it. These are the great buildings of the twentieth century; even the cathedrals of the Middle Ages look very small beside them.

In the last chapter we explained how during the Victorian period so much interest had been taken in architecture that it had been decided that schools of architecture must be founded so that people could be properly taught how to design buildings. The difficulty was that people could not agree as to what was the proper style to use. Some liked the Greek and Roman, some preferred the Renaissance; there were a few who still thought that the Gothic was the only proper style for Englishmen to use. But the schools very soon agreed that the day of Gothic, with its pointed arches, its mouldings, and its carvings, was over for ever. The only really large building you can build in the Gothic style is a cathedral. The people who liked Greek and Roman and those who liked the Renaissance were not really so far apart; for after all the Renaissance was only a different version of the Classical, and both of them were 'architects' styles.

What the architects of fifty years ago had to understand was that buildings were now going to be far larger than they had ever been before. This was not true of ordinary houses; in fact the day of the great mansion with its swarm of servants was over. But all these huge 'commercial' buildings, many stories high, belonged to no style of architecture which had ever been seen before. Churches, palaces, great houses, were things of the past; only Victorian factories were anything at all like the new buildings of the twentieth century. The factory, however, was a building containing great rooms full of machinery; the commercial building had great numbers of small rooms. Architects have always had some sort of idea how best to design a fine large room; it was another matter to know how to deal with a building which simply consisted of hundreds of tiny rooms. It would be very easy to have your block of offices looking very little better than a prison if you did not design it carefully.

At first the twentieth-century architects began to copy what had been done two hundred years before; designing the fronts of their buildings, and afterwards fitting in the rooms behind. Then they began to try to collect all the rooms into little groups and design each of these separately, but so that they could all be gathered together in one design for the whole building. But at last they discovered that there was no need to trouble about designing buildings in this way at all. They could give up using columns and cornices and all the old tricks that had been used during the centuries and do away with ornament altogether if only they could get the *shape* of the building to look right.

The architects of to-day have to be more clever than those of the Victorian period; there is a great deal more for them to do. They have to plan all their hundreds of little rooms, and the staircases and corridors which lead to them, so that everything will work properly, and still have windows in just the right places on the outside of the building; then it will look well designed without having to be covered all over with columns and ornament of all sorts. In the big buildings of to-day you will very seldom see any columns or carved ornament; there may be just a spot here and there where the architect has allowed himself a little decoration, but on the whole it is considered vulgar to display too much of this sort of thing nowadays.

Until the days of the Renaissance, architecture, as has been shown in the early chapters of this history, just grew. Later on, we saw how architects copied the 'styles' or architecture which had gone before, trying to make them fit the kind of building they were planning. But architects of to-day do not work like this, for the schools have taught them 'rules' by which buildings may be designed. They have to make sure they get the length and breadth of the building right. If it has several parts, they must see that the sizes of these are correct and that each is joined-on correctly to its neighbour. Doors and windows must be of just the right shape, and in just the right places.

There is no real need for any 'style' to be followed; if everything is correctly 'proportioned', the building should look all right. If the architect wants a little ornament, he either designs it himself or gets an artist to do it for him; again, there is no need for any 'style' to be followed. So nowadays it does not matter if a building has to be designed which is nothing like anything ever seen before; the architect can, by following the 'rules', make it look right. There is no need, for example, for buildings of to-day to be equally balanced about a central door-way like a great house of Elizabethan days; as long as the architect can get his 'proportions' right, the building will seem to be properly balanced after all.

Some architects of to-day still like to use the Renaissance style of architecture for the fronts of their buildings; they use it, however, in a much simpler form than in the days of Christopher Wren. In his time there were still craftsmen who could provide plenty of carved ornament with which to cover buildings; sometimes people call Wren's style of architecture 'Baroque', which means 'fanciful'. (In actual fact, we never saw the real Baroque in this country. The nearest thing to it is the gay style which came in with the restoration of Charles II (43); but this soon gave place to the serious style that our own architects were busily working out.) In these days we have to do without this sort of thing; our Renaissance-style buildings are therefore much plainer and simpler.

There are many architects who try to make up for this by inventing styles of their own by altering the shapes of the tops of windows, designing unusual kinds of columns, and so forth. In gay buildings like cinemas, for example, our architects do not hesitate to design all sorts of curious architectural features. There is no reason why they should not do so, for a cinema is a kind of building which has never been seen before in the history of architecture and may therefore certainly have a special style designed for it if the architect is ingenious enough to invent this. Many, however, prefer to keep the fronts of their buildings quite plain, using only simple shapes which can easily be built up in ordinary brickwork or cast in the new material—concrete.

In the last century, the floors of even the largest buildings had still been of wooden boards supported on timber or iron beams and propped up through each story by cast-iron columns. At the end of the century an important new material was beginning to be used for floors. At the beginning of this book we explained how mortar is made by mixing up lime and sand. Mortar is really used, of course, for laying stones or bricks so as to stick them together; but if you mix it with small stones and cast it in moulds you can make a kind of artificial stone known as 'concrete'. You can, if you like, lay your concrete while it is wet all over the ground on which the building stands so that when the mortar has dried out you have a concrete floor which is very hard and clean. Another use for concrete is to pour it into the trenches you dig for the foundations of your walls and columns so that you have a hard smooth surface from which to start your building.

Nowadays we do not use lime for making concrete but a much stronger substance called cement; made, not by burning limestone alone, but by burning limestone mixed with clay. Concrete is a very valuable building material but it is troublesome to use because it is almost liquid. Although you can lay it on the ground, once you try to use it above this you have to make some kind of a platform or mould of wooden boards to support it on until it is dry. You cannot of course make an upper floor of concrete by itself for it will not hold up of its own accord. But the late-Victorian builders found that if they made a floor of iron beams set very closely together, they could fill up the spaces between these with concrete and make a very good strong floor.

In this way there came to be invented, at the end of the last century, the very important building material which is called 'reinforced concrete'. The reinforcement—that is to say the strengthening—is not to-day made of cast-iron beams but of steel rods buried deeply in the concrete as it is being poured into its moulds.

We spoke of the iron beams which the Victorian builders used for their floors and for their great wide roofs. Cast iron, however, is not really very strong; you could not have your pillars very far apart, or design an iron beam which would carry the wall over a wide opening. But—also at the end of the last century—it was found that *steel* could be made into beams which were very much stronger than the iron ones, so that quite a light steel beam would carry a weight over an opening which would have needed an enormously heavy iron one. In the same way they found that very large steel beams, or several of these placed side by side, would carry across a far wider opening than would ever have been thought possible. This meant that many of the old cast-iron pillars which had cluttered up the Victorian buildings could be done away with.

We explained how the first factories were just like large storehouses, several stories in height. These buildings, however, were only used to house machines which made clothes, carpets, or something of this sort; in Victorian days, however, factories were being built in which machines were actually making other machines. This kind of work—called 'heavy' industry—is carried out in factories which use much heavier machines than the older kind, so that it was not possible to have these on upper stories for fear that the floor would not be strong enough. So the Victorian 'engineering' factory had become a large rambling single-story building, generally with a glass roof which gave the machinists plenty of light by which to work. Nowadays, the rounded cast-iron roofs of the last century have given place to triangular roofs supported on light steel framing. Only the short slope nearest the north (to avoid the glare of the sun itself) has glass in it; such roofs are called 'north-light' roofs.

As builders learned more and more about how to use steel beams it occurred to them that they might try to use them in the same way as the village carpenters of the Tudor period had used their great beams. They tried to frame-up a building in steel beams instead of in wood. Instead of using round iron pillars they used square steel ones so that the pillars or 'stanchions' could all be bolted together with the beams. This made building both cheaper and easier. For if you try to build a very high brick wall it has to be very thick at the bottom and takes up a lot of room; now that the brick walls only rose from beam to beam, however, no wall was higher than the height of one story. The great commercial blocks, therefore, came to be built as a steel frame with all the panels filled in with brickwork and the floors laid in concrete strongly 'reinforced' with steel rods. Concrete was also used to cover the steel frame and make it stronger and easier to build up to with brickwork.

Reinforced concrete is an interesting building material, for you can make it do all sorts of strange things. You can make it stick out in all sorts of curious ways that nothing except timber beams could have done before. You can also cast it into unusual shapes. You do not *build* with reinforced concrete so much as *mould* your building out of it. You may have seen some modern buildings, such as for example grandstands at racecourses or football fields, where a tremendously wide roof is all standing up apparently without any proper support; this was probably cast in reinforced concrete.

Another use for reinforced concrete is in the making of flat roofs. Concrete is not itself waterproof but it can be made so by covering it with a layer of asphalt—a sort of tar-like sub-

191

stance which is excellent for keeping out water. One of the troubles with all buildings is that water is likely to rise up from the ground through the lower parts of the walls; from the beginning of this century all buildings have had a waterproof layer built into them a few inches above the ground, called a 'damp course'.

Not only were the great commercial buildings of the early twentieth century becoming far plainer to look at than they had been in the Victorian period but houses too were losing all their decoration. The architectural schools had decided that the proper style in which to build a house was that which we all know and admire—the Georgian. The day of the great house, with its very tall rooms, was passing away. In Victorian days, the poisonous fumes of the flickering gas lighting had caused the builders to make the rooms of even small houses as high as possible; with the new electric lighting, however, rooms could be much lower.

After the Great War of 1914-18, when everyone was needing houses, nearly every town and village had a carefully planned 'housing scheme' of small, simple houses. In these cheap houses the builders could not afford the expensive sash windows of Georgian houses and used instead a new kind of window made out of steel, something like the old steel casements of the Middle Ages, but with steel 'glazing bars' instead of lead.

Between the two wars numbers of private builders started housing schemes also. The houses that they built were made, not to rent to people who would only live in them for a short time, but for people to *buy*. So the builders were very careful to build, not what the architectural schools said was correct, but what they thought people really liked. So the houses of these private housing schemes are nearly always built with bay windows and 'half-timber work' and little porches and all the things which we have liked since the days of the Elizabethans.

At this time there was a serious shortage of wood for the joists of floors and the rafters of roofs. Some builders tried to get over this shortage by using reinforced concrete, especially for the roofs. So a new style of flat-roofed concrete house began to appear in this country. The new steel windows could be made in almost any shape you fancied; the architects, therefore, began to experiment with different designs of window. One of the things they did was to leave out all the upright glazing bars and keep only those which went from side to side. As they were now using reinforced concrete 'lintels' over their windows, instead of brick arches or wooden beams, they could make their windows very much wider; so the old upright Georgian windows began to give place to long low windows called 'landscape windows'. At the present time there is a fashion for very large windows to let in as much sunlight as possible. Our ancestors did not like windows; when they went into a house they liked it to be cosy and did not wish to be reminded of the wind and the rain outside.

The craze for sunlight inside houses is causing many of these to be planned so that as many windows as possible face the south. This was not so in the Middle Ages when men believed that the plague came on the south wind and would never have a window to the south if they could help it. But now we are so keen on sunlight that modern hospitals and schools are all built wherever possible in what is called 'suntrap' architecture with as many large windows facing the south as possible.

In the last chapter we spoke about how all buildings were being given a proper water supply with sinks, water-closets, and bathrooms. Nowadays there is another system of piping which is becoming more and more a part of large buildings and houses : the heating of rooms by means of hot water carried in pipes to radiators. The architect of a great building today has a tremendous number of problems to cope with. Not only does he have to plan all his rooms and corridors and staircases so that the building will be convenient to use or live in; he also has to think of miles of water pipes, drain pipes, and electric cables passing up and across his building. He may also have to arrange for air to be pumped into parts of the building by machinery if it is too vast to be ventilated by the old-fashioned method of leaving the windows open.

The invention of steel as a building material has made it possible for us to have buildings practically as large as we wish. Up to about 1950, some of the largest buildings to be built were our cinemas. Next time you go to a cinema look at the gallery which goes right across the back of the building without there being any sign of how it is supported; all this is done by using huge beams of steel. In the 1960s and 1970s we have been raising great buildings in our towns and cities on an unprecedented scale. We have also been seeing plenty of comfortable houses going up everywhere for us to live in.

We all prefer to see our house being built in the old-fashioned way. We like to watch the site being cleared and made level, and the trenches being dug and filled with concrete for the foundations. Then we can see the bricklayers building their walls—hollow nowadays so as to keep the weather out more completely than in the past—and building-in the doors and the windows as they go. Wood is used for the floor joists and the rafters of the pointed roofs, and the tilers come along and hang their tiles on the 'battens' which the carpenters have fixed to the rafters to take them. When the roof is on, the plumbers begin fixing their pipes and the electricians their wires and cables. Then come the plasterers to make the walls and ceilings smooth and clean, and, lastly, when the glass has been put in the windows, the painters come along and decorate our home in pleasing colours.

Well planned all these buildings must be, for, as we have seen in these pages, the first duty of an architect is to make sure that his building will do the job for which it is required. Nor will its beauty be of any lasting use to us unless it be well and firmly built, so that it may live down the centuries to take its place in the history of English architecture.

INDEX

Index

Index

Index

Index